GW00708240

TH
WEDDING
Cake

E Z Thompson

The Wedding Cake

Spiderwize
Remus House
Coltsfoot Drive
Woodston
Peterborough
PE2 9BF

www.spiderwize.com

A CIP catalogue record for this book is available from the British Library.
The views expressed in this work are solely those of the author and do not
necessarily reflect the views of the publisher, and the publisher hereby
disclaims any responsibility for them.

All characters in this publication are fictitious and any resemblances to real
people either living or dead are purely coincidental.

ISBN: 978-1-912694-58-7

THE WEDDING CAKE

ELISABETH C THOMPSON

SPIDERWIZE
Peterborough UK
2018

For Julie Ann,
the bravest of
the brave

One's destination is never a place,
but a new way of seeing things

Henry Miller

CHAPTER 1

Barque House stood on the edge of town, double-fronted, three storeys high, roof blemished with moss and a chimney stack attached to the west wall topped with burnt umber pots; she had been told that it lacked a ghostly presence, but this had not prevented her from pondering the possibility of some sort of supernatural activity in the house. She reckoned that at the very least, such an old house must harbour the 'presence' of secrets. Whatever might have occurred between those four walls she had a sense that Barque House would reveal nothing; it was like an old family retainer, solid, safe, respectable and trusted to keep its secrets.

Once the shelter for four lives, it had been reduced to sheltering one, that of her great-aunt Blanche. She had not had much to do with the old lady until the recent daily visits; it was then that she had discovered Blanche held firm views on most things. During the time they spent together she had been encouraged to debate topics ranging from politics to personal trainers, even the health benefits of honey, but never, she had to admit, ghosts.

Naomi Henry was perched on a bar stool in her mother's kitchen watching her dash off urgent emails; she asked herself what sort of a relationship her mother had enjoyed with Blanche when she was younger, what intimate chats they had shared or not, at the same time asking herself why she had not posed this question before.

Helena Henry, conscious of her daughter's scrutiny sat back to finish her coffee. "All done," she said. "I will never understand how people can be awake enough in the middle of the night to be sending emails." She removed her glasses to flick back a lock of dark hair, evidence of their Spanish heritage. She liked to think this set them apart from others; strong genes, strong profiles, strong women like Blanche, although for the moment Helena did not feel strong.

Her aunt's death had brought her whole life/work balance into question. It had forced her to re-evaluate every facet of her life. Work had become like a cuckoo in her nest, kicking out quality time with her daughter and hindering her search for a partner. A death in the family focused the mind for sure, but it brought with it no easy answers.

"Caffeine freaks," Naomi said.

"You're probably right."

"I wish you didn't have to work so hard, Mum."

"I'm used to it."

"I feel really guilty. If only I had a job …"

"Don't worry about it, Nims. You'll get another job soon. Your CV is really good."

"Not good enough, apparently," Naomi said.

"Perhaps you need to spread the net wider."

"Maybe, anyway, I thought I'd go over to Barque House this afternoon."

"Are you sure, do you want me to come with you?"

They both knew this was a fatuous offer. Her mother had not set foot in Barque House since the funeral. Neither of them had. "You've got work. I don't mind going on my own," she said.

"I really have to decide what to do with the house now Blanche has gone."

"You don't have to make a decision straight away."

"I want to do what's right for all of us," she said.

Naomi smoothed the end of the single plait resting over her shoulder. "I know," she said. In all her thirty years, she had never witnessed her mother doing anything else. Coming home after years of an independent life could have been difficult, instead it had been an easy transition thanks to her flexible attitude. She might be fussy about men, but where her daughter was concerned, she was prepared to compromise. "I am going to miss her."

"Me too … you spent a lot of time together. Did I ever thank you for that?"

Naomi smiled. "Only about a million times. It was good. It's made me think about what I want to do in the future. I might take up caring full-time."

Helena recoiled. "Really? I can't think of anything worse."

"Old people are fascinating; walking, talking history books. Some of her stories were pretty cool," Naomi said. "She told me loads about her parents, not so much about herself. Don't you think that's odd?"

"Blanche was a very private person."

"Not that she lived in the past. She was up to date with all the news; she loved a good debate."

"Oh yes, I remember that."

"From what she told me the garden must have been lovely when her parents were alive."

"It was," Helena said elbows resting on the table, chin cupped in her hands. "Maud loved her flowers. Harold was never happier than when he was pottering in the greenhouse. He spent hours in there when he retired, cross-pollinating goodness knows what. When they died, Blanche seemed to lose heart, didn't have the same dedication to keeping it going."

"Maybe it had all been too much."

"She was a funny woman."

"I loved her," Naomi said.

"I loved her too, but we never had much in common. She spent a lot of time with her father, reading up on things, doing experiments, shutting herself away to examine specimens under the microscope."

"I don't remember much about her when I was little. What was she like when you were little?"

"I can't honestly say what she was like … a bit strange, reclusive; she didn't know how to talk to children. She wasn't like her sister. Nana loved children, anyone's children. She spoiled Martyn and me. She adored you. From a child's point of view, I guess she was a non-person, but Nana wouldn't hear a word against her. It was better after I grew up."

"She left you her house. She must have liked you," Naomi said.

"I'm being mean, aren't I?"

"You're only saying what you think."

"It's always the same when someone dies. You trawl through everything, remember how things were, question who did what to whom and why. It doesn't solve my problem, though. What am I going to do?"

Naomi gave her mother a hug. "Whatever you decide is fine by me," she said. "I'm happy with the desk."

"God knows what she squirrelled away in there."

"I'm looking forward to finding out."

"Make sure you have a black bag to hand; a whole roll would be better."

"Shock horror," Naomi said. "Blanche would be turning in her grave if she thought I was going to bin everything."

Helena shut the laptop with a snap, stood up and tucked the fine linen blouse into her skirt until the garish embroidery decorating the hem was hidden from sight. She had known when she bought the blouse that the pattern was too fussy, but the scoop neckline and three-quarter-length sleeves were perfect for her. Once hidden away, she reckoned the embroidery could be forgiven and forgotten. "Well, much as I'd like to, I can't sit here chatting. I need to open the shop," she said picking up her bag.

"I'll clear the breakfast things. Oh, by the way, what do you know about Mr. Minns, Mum?"

"Alf Minns ... not much, why?"

"I just wondered. He often visited Blanche, brought her flowers from his allotment."

"They were old friends," she said.

"Are you sure it wasn't something more, undying love, a hidden romance ... an affair?" Naomi said full of anticipation at discovering the first secret.

"Unlikely. Blanche wasn't interested in men and Alf was devoted to his wife."

"Oh well, perhaps I'll discover some other dark secret in the desk," Naomi said.

"All you'll find in there are the things anyone else would have chucked away years ago."

"Where's your imagination?"

"It left home when I realised the only person you can rely on is yourself," Helena said. "I need to go."

"Erm, Mum, are you sure there aren't any ghosts at Barque House?"

"Quite sure. Whatever gave you that idea?"

"I don't know," Naomi said. "I just thought, well, it's such an old house."

"And because it's an old house it's full of things that need to be re-cycled. You know Blanche liked to keep everything. Goodness knows how long it will take us."

"You might end up with new stock for the shop."

"No *might* about it; you know the sort of things that sell."

"Sure, don't worry about it."

"I'll be better when everything's sorted out. It feels all wrong that she's not here," Helena said. She brushed her daughter's cheek with hers. "See you later, love, oh, I might be late back. I've an appointment with the solicitor."

"Guy Hampson?"

"Yes, he said in his letter that he'd found something I needed to see, a codicil I think."

Naomi pulled a face. "That sounds like fun," she said. "I'll start dinner for you. What are we having?"

"Whatever you can find in the fridge," Helena said. "Failing that, fish and chips. I haven't had time to think about food."

"Will Isla be back?"

"No. The conference doesn't finish until Friday."

"Oh yes. I knew that," Naomi said suddenly remembering her cousin's promise to be back by the weekend. "Good luck with Mr. Hampson."

"I'm sure it's nothing to worry about. She probably forgot to leave Grandpa Harold's notebooks to posterity."

"Hey, what if there are some long-forgotten seeds stashed away in a vault, triple-frilled delphiniums or something; something so rare gardeners everywhere will be clamouring to get their hands on them. We could end up millionaires."

Helena laughed at her daughter's optimism. "I can't see that happening any time soon; see you later."

She walked the short distance from home to the charity shop mulling over the hundred and one things she had to do that day. She was only functioning on half a brain after the funeral and trying to come to terms with her aunt's death. As she had explained to Naomi, they had not been close, but it was the loss of what she represented that upset her. Blanche had been the last link with her mother. It made it hard to concentrate, left her with mixed feelings. Blanche's death had signalled the end of an era, the end of all childish things; her childhood was long past, but

6

strands lingered in her mind. There was no-one more senior in the family now, except for her brother to whom she had never been close. He had moved to Italy and they seldom had contact.

She was touched that the house had been left to her but also bewildered that it had. She did not understand why. She had never expected to inherit, had always surmised it would be sold and the money donated to some medical charity or other. She seemed to remember that her mother had thought so, too. She was grateful to Naomi for helping her sort things out. She would have found it much more stressful without her daughter's help.

Barque House was too big for one person. She had asked herself many times why her aunt had wanted to stay there for so long on her own, but then, Blanche had never done things like other people; she had never done anything she had not wanted to do. If only she could be more like her, more single-minded.

She did not want to be on her own like Blanche, of that she was certain. She had been alone for too long. Long enough to know that was not how she wanted to spend the rest of her life. She needed someone to love and to cherish; someone to cherish her. She acknowledged that she was difficult to please. Was that so wrong? She could not respect a partner who did not match up to her high standards. She had made that mistake once and she was not about to do it again. Naomi was the only good thing that had come out of her marriage to Kevin Henry. She appreciated their closeness, loved having her back at home but she knew her daughter would eventually find another partner, would want to live her own life, start her own family; maybe move away from East Knoll. It was a depressing thought, but she comforted herself with the knowledge that it wouldn't be happening for a while, at least not until Naomi found another job.

Her mind drifted on to Guy Hampson. What was this codicil he had mentioned? Would it lead to more problems? She did not relish that thought. It was difficult enough to decide whether to move into Barque House or stay where she was. Would the girls want to move with her? They could have a floor each. Independence with a certain amount of inter-dependence, the best of both worlds. Surely that would work? It would not matter if she left the decision for a few weeks, but she wanted it settled in her mind. Like a trip to the dentist, it was not something she could avoid for ever.

Work was equally unavoidable and even more stressful. Management meetings, advertising campaigns, sourcing good quality clothes, staffing problems; she was tired of having to make decisions for everyone, even for herself. Retirement, which had once been dreaded, considered diminishing, the end of everything stimulating or exciting and the start of knee-highs, failing health and shopping trolleys, now seemed beguiling; it could not come soon enough. She fished her keys from her bag and opened the door, scooping up the post as she did so, hoping the codicil Guy Hampson needed to show her would turn out to be something and nothing.

CHAPTER 2

It was past two o'clock when Naomi arrived at Barque House. She looked up at the imposing building, at the stately windows shrouded in net except for the one over the front door. On that window the net had been parted to reveal the model of a brigantine mounted on a wooden plinth.

The door at the top of the steps was substantial, Georgian green with a brass knocker and boss. A bell push let into bricks at the side of the door invited visitors to PRESS and a brass plate screwed to the wall above, still bore witness to the original owner and his standing in the community, Harold Black, MB BS, her great grandfather.

As she slotted her key in the lock she imagined unwanted callers having been given every opportunity to admire the boss at length while patients and invitees would only have had time for a quick glance before they were ushered in.

It had been three weeks since her last visit and she wondered how different it would feel now Blanche was no longer there. It had always seemed like stepping into the past once she had crossed the threshold; there was an amicable tranquillity about the place, a refinement borrowed from an earlier time. She replaced the key in her pocket and found herself listening for Blanche's voice. All she could hear was the muffled rumble of machinery demolishing a nearby building in preparation for the construction of a new block of flats. Life moved on.

Her eyes were drawn to the brass stair rods gleaming in the afternoon sun. The window at the turn of the stairs depicting a cottage garden in full bloom, daisies, delphiniums, dahlias intertwined with rosebuds and ivy, glowed, projecting rainbow hues onto the walls like a magic lantern show. "The garden was as colourful as that window when I was a child," she recalled Blanche saying. "Mother loved flowers, but she wasn't a gardener; she left all the planting and picking to my father. When his legs gave him trouble and then his back, he gave up. Gardening's not my thing. We had to employ a gardener. That was when he took to model-making. You've seen the ship in the landing window? He was very proud of that one."

Whilst the garden had not been allowed to become a wilderness, it was not the explosion of colour it had once been. The lawn had given way to decking except for a small strip under the trees; the greenhouse had been demolished, replaced by a summerhouse floating on the decking like a houseboat on a canal.

In Spring the garden was charming. Snowdrops and lesser celandine appeared under the sycamores lining the back wall and daffodils and narcissi huddled together in the broad flower beds cosying up to the cyclamen and winter-weary lavender. It was then that she could imagine how the garden might have looked in Harold and Maud's time.

She made her way across the crimson carpeted hall to the breakfast room at the back of the house. The will had been clear. The house had been left to her mother and all the furniture apart from the walnut desk, to her cousin, Isla. The walnut desk was hers; she had memorised the bequest. *To Naomi Charlotte Henry, I leave my walnut desk in recognition of the time she has devoted to me over the past few months. I trust her to do what is right with the contents.*

She presumed that meant she should share anything she found with other family members or donate what she could to charity. Blanche had hated waste. There were many beautiful artefacts in the house; pictures, furniture, books and they all had a purpose. There was nothing that was neither beautiful nor useful in Barque House. Naomi was determined to follow her lead. She would dispose of the contents of the desk appropriately, find a home for everything she could and only discard the useless or the broken.

Everything on the desk told a story or at least she liked to think so. Sadly, she had no idea what those stories might be. There was a silver-framed photograph of a baby in a sun hat next to an original oil painting of a pansy with the initials 'C.F.' printed in the bottom right-hand corner. Those initials meant nothing to her. She had no idea who the artist might be but he, or she, obviously had talent. The flower had been captured in detail. The cushion-like petals were deep purple with a sun-burst yellow centre and such a realistic sheen, she felt moved to touch them. She was almost surprised when her fingertips detected cold hard paint and not the velveteen she had imagined. Pansies were modest, under-rated flowers, overlooked in a garden full of more showy blooms and yet someone had thought this pansy worthy of being captured for posterity, but who, and did it harbour a romantic message. Was the artist significant? She doubted it. Blanche had probably bought the picture at a church bazaar intending to use the frame for something else. That was a more likely explanation from what she knew of her great-aunt.

A pile of books covering a range of topics from Napoleon to Queen Victoria and an ornate brass frame hosting a family portrait of Blanche's mother and father with the two children, took up most of the rest of the space. In the picture, Blanche was sitting on a sheepskin rug beside her sister, Betsy, Naomi's grandmother. There were various other family snapshots, which needed no explanation; the picture that intrigued her was the one of the baby in the silver frame.

She picked it up to take a closer look. The photograph was as clear as if it had been taken that day, the baby smiling out from under the hood of a large pram. It was an old-fashioned pram. The sort of pram, Naomi thought, that anyone back in the day would have recognised instantly, nothing like modern day versions of the same thing. A true baby carriage, not a deckchair on wheels.

She could not ask Blanche the identity of the baby. She could not have asked her before; the desk had always been concealed under a paisley shawl with an edging of knotted silk. It wasn't until after her death that the shawl had been lifted to reveal its treasures. On reflection she thought her mother might know the identity of the silver baby; when things settled down she would ask her.

Sitting on the tapestry seat slotted into the space between the drawers of the kidney-shaped desk, she pondered what she might do with Blanche's other bits and pieces; she wondered what had been squirreled away in the drawers and as she had no intention of opening them that day, she had no way of knowing. Her eyes were drawn to the baby once more. She dismissed the possibility of it having been Blanche's baby. Blanche had never married, plus she knew the arrival of an illegitimate child in those days would have been hushed up. There would have been no pictures of the child displayed in a silver frame for all to see. Naomi had not heard a whisper of scandal in Blanche's life. This baby must have belonged to someone else.

It had surprised her how much she had enjoyed spending time with the old lady. Her mother had not expected it. She had not expected it. "Tell me if it gets too much for you, I'll have a word," her mother had said offering her a way out.

"It's fine, Mum. I can manage," she had replied.

"You don't have to stay long. Pop in, ask how she is, see if she needs any shopping or if you need to do a load of washing for her and check she's had something to eat. She could afford to go into a home, you know."

"She doesn't want to."

"I expect she thinks it would be a waste of money."

"That's exactly what she thinks. Anyway, she's got me. I really don't mind, I've nothing else to do."

"You'll get a new job soon."

"Maybe."

"I'm sure you will. When you are ready, something will turn up."

"I'm happy looking after Blanche. That's more important just now."

Naomi liked to think that she and Blanche had developed a special bond over the hours they had spent in one another's company and when Guy Hampson told her of the bequest, she realised she had been right. She would certainly make use of the desk. She did not have much furniture to take with her when she could finally afford a flat of her own and there was no point looking for one until she found a job. She stroked the silky wood and tried to look forward to the forthcoming task, but it was too soon. There was no hurry to delve into Blanche's past and dispose of everything just yet. Her mother had not made up her mind what to do with the house and so the desk would be safe where it was until she had.

She reflected that the family, which had once been a core of four women, Blanche, Helena, Isla and Naomi, now comprised only three. Men had drifted in and out of their lives, none of them staying for long. Harold and Maud had been the exception. Theirs had been a love match and a bond for life. So much so that within twenty-four hours of Harold's death, Maud too, had died peacefully, mid prelude. "I left her playing Chopin while I made tea," Blanche had explained. "By the time I returned the

13

music had stopped, like mother's heart. She had gone just like that…" she had said, clicking her fingers in the air "… sitting at the piano, hands still on the keys."

Naomi had been touched by the poignancy of that story, but Blanche had merely added in a matter of fact fashion that it had been the perfect death for her mother; music had been so much a part of her life.

As far as Kevin Henry was concerned, Naomi had never been able to work out what had gone wrong in her parents' marriage. Was it unreasonable for her mother to have expected him to fund the occasional school trip, to help with homework, or share the spoils of his advertising career with his wife and daughter?

He had been away on business so much that neither of them missed him when the final break came. She had no idea where he was now. She seldom thought of him, he had no part in her life and she had none in his. She saw him as a fake father, a biological anomaly, nothing more.

Her uncle Martyn and his wife, Alice, had decided that Italy was the place to be in retirement which is why Isla had moved in with them until she found a place of her own. Tuscany was good for holidays, but Isla seldom took advantage of this. As a busy GP, she was dedicated to her patients and the minor surgery facility she had set up in the practice in Linchester. Naomi admired her drive and self-knowledge. She reckoned it must feel good to be doing work that meant something, instead of being in a job that was merely a means to an end.

Isla wasn't looking for love. She had told Naomi so. "Now I've spent all that money getting qualified I want to make sure I don't waste it," she had said, in an echo of her great aunt's philosophy. "Life's too short to spend the rest of it polishing some man's ego. Men just complicate things."

Naomi did not agree with her cousin. She had been happy

with Luke for years, but their relationship had not lived up to expectations. They had grown up together, spent hours on the beach in the holidays walking, swimming, or just lying on their backs in the sand dunes listening to the high rolling notes of skylarks chirruping in the clouds. They had been best friends at school and happy together until university split them up and they began to drift apart. There had been no drama at the beginning of their relationship and none at the end; it had grown slowly and ended in the same way leaving nothing more than the spent casing of acquaintanceship.

She was not happy to have lost her best friend but they had both moved on. To revert to 'just friends' had proved too difficult. Luke had found someone else and they had agreed a clean break would be best for everyone.

She was not ready to start again with someone else, but she had not ruled it out for the future. Her only non-negotiable was that any new partner should be taller than her above average five feet ten. She automatically checked the height of every man she met. It was hard to get out of the habit when she looked down on a large proportion of them. There was no way she wanted to look down on her husband for the rest of her life.

She was aware of her mother's search for another partner; she had been looking for years but Naomi did not hold out much hope of her finding a soul-mate any time soon, not while she was being so picky. If it wasn't the shape of his nose or the length of his hair, it would be his style of dress or his job that would deny all hope to a putative suitor. He had no chance at all if there was a hint of football in his life.

Naomi remembered that one hopeful had been discarded when he had sent a birthday card to her mother misspelling his flowery description of her as, 'the most *buotiful* woman' he had ever met. She wanted her mother to be happy; she figured that if she didn't get real and relax her expectations a little she would end up like Holly's mum ... alone with a fridge full of ready meals, a stash of Prosecco and an empty diary, waiting for the phone to ring.

CHAPTER 3

Alf Minns tossed potato peelings into the recycling container and scraped his plate into the bin. He missed Blanche, but it hadn't put him off his food. Steak and chips was one of his favourites. Home-made, of course and accompanied by cherry tomatoes and courgettes from the greenhouse on his allotment. He prided himself on eating well despite being on his own. His mother had told him that was the way to a healthy life and not having had a day's illness in his life, he reckoned she must have been right. "Fred …" he remembered her saying; she had always called him Fred, he mused, despite everyone else referring to him as, Alf "… never skimp on food. Your body needs fuel to keep it going. You can't go wrong if you eat three decent meals a day."

Tall and upright despite his eighty plus years, he prided himself on his strong heart and lungs, full head of hair, albeit white, and his fine military moustache. He had been a widower for several years now. Sarah had faded away after a long battle with cancer and, at the end, he had been glad to see her go. It had been difficult to watch her suffer, sitting at her side as he had for endless hours, watching her flesh waste away and her skin stretch ever tighter over her bones until she had become no more than a living skeleton. The Macmillan nurses had given him some respite, but he had only managed a patchwork of sleep in the last few weeks. A couple of hours at night and brief periods during the day when Sarah slipped into a restless doze.

Blanche's death had been a gentler release and not unexpected. If he was honest, he missed her more than he missed his wife. He had loved Blanche, but not in the same way. They could never have married. They had discussed science, politics, current affairs, all subjects Sarah had found boring; however, he had always felt there was something missing with Blanche, a certain coolness in her character, a detachment from others, an ability to stand alone, to keep her private affairs private. She hadn't needed the physical closeness he and Sarah had enjoyed.

Sarah had been a real people person. She had loved chatting with the customers who came into their shop. He couldn't imagine Blanche doing that. He smiled as he remembered how she would never use two words when one would do and how she would chide him for rattling on, as she called it.

He had told Sarah that she was their biggest asset in customer relations and he believed it to be true. Customers would soon go elsewhere if they were not treated to a friendly smile at the counter and an enquiry after their children, their health or a discussion about the weather. She'd had a talent for remembering their faces and names; a talent for making each one feel valued and special.

He recalled her fondness for the Royal Family. She had been a major fan; so much so, they had bought a new television with a much bigger screen in order that she might get a closer look at the guests attending the wedding of Prince Charles and Lady Diana Spencer. She had persuaded him to buy in some royal memorabilia for the shop and, much to his surprise, it had sold out. He had ordered more and now all that was left were three souvenir tea-towels in the kitchen drawer. He smiled as he remembered the way she had crowed over her success. She had been devastated when the marriage failed. He was glad she had lived long enough to see Prince William marry Kate Middleton. "They're just right for each other," she had told him when their engagement had been announced.

"How can you tell?" he had asked.

"You just have to look at them," she had replied. "I'll die

happy if I can see them married. Look at the way she smiles at him. They'll have lovely children."

He would never have had that conversation with Blanche. No, Blanche could not have been described as a 'people person'. She had not suffered fools gladly. She liked to keep her own counsel. She had enjoyed her own company. Even in the last few months with her eyesight failing and her energy levels sapped, the life force had been strong within her, her brain needle-sharp. He was still of the opinion that had her body not aged, her mind would have gone on and on. It wasn't until the last few days that he knew she wouldn't be there much longer and she had known it too.

Even so, her passing had been a shock. She had always been there, at the end of the road where the roundabout led to all points north, south and west. His shop was at the other end, nearer the town. He reckoned it was lucky his parents had bought the property when they had. Prices had been rocketing ever since. Now he was sitting on a little gold mine and he had no intention of selling. Dr. Black had brought him into the world in the flat above the shop and he intended to stay there until it was his turn to go.

How times had changed, he thought as he polished his dinner plate on one of the queen's corgis. In the old days, the Minns had little to do with the Blacks unless they were ill. They had lived in different worlds, moved in different circles. Dr. Black had a newspaper delivered daily, a medical magazine monthly and seed catalogues as and when. He remembered his weekly trek to Barque House with Mrs. Black's copy of her favourite magazine.

It had been common knowledge that the old doc was as interested in propagating new varieties of plants as he was in trying experimental medicine. It was Dr. Black who had persuaded his mother to have her sons vaccinated against polio, even though they were young adults by then; it had saved them from the iron lung. He shuddered as he thought of the iron lung; it had seemed like an instrument of torture then, but it had been a life saver for those infected with that terrible disease.

He recalled his mother telling them how Renee Bryan had ignored the doctor's advice. Jim had not taken the vaccine on a lump of sugar as they had. He had been one of the unlucky ones, suffering with his breathing and weak legs for the rest of his life, poor chap.

The past had not been a bed of roses. A bed of roses, he mused; why was that considered a good place to be when roses had sharp thorns? It was as silly as his father's favourite expression when describing chancers as *'flying by the seat of their pants'*; that had never made sense to him either, but he could not spend more time on idle thoughts. He had some serious thinking to do. Time was running out. Now Sarah and Blanche had gone, the responsibility had been left to him. "To tell or not to tell," he muttered, his expression grim. Blanche had wanted him to tell, he knew that, but she had left the final decision up to him. He wished she hadn't. He had no idea how he would go about it. He was concerned that the telling might not be well received. It might cause more harm than good. Whichever way it went he would have to give the whole matter some careful thought before he did anything.

CHAPTER 4

Hampson Tailor and Palmer's offices were a ten-minute walk from the charity shop. Nowhere in the town was more than a ten-minute walk away from anywhere else. For Helena, the compact nature of East Knoll was one of its many charms. It was a sleepy place, the sort of seaside town frequented by Victorian holiday-makers who had not been bold enough to sample the excitements of Bognor.

The solicitors' offices, hidden behind the station in a purpose-built block, were on the far side of a cobbled quadrangle scattered with olive trees. As she made her way through the fake olive grove, Helena considered Guy Hampson's assets. He was not conventionally handsome; tall, gaunt with drooping shoulders and heavy-lidded eyes. His once blonde hair was now white and sparse at the crown, but his sombre demeanour hid a wicked sense of humour, which she had always found attractive in a prospective partner, although she had never thought of Guy Hampson in that way. They exchanged pleasantries when they met, chatted if brought together by a supermarket queue, smiled if they passed each other in the street. He had handled her divorce and now their paths had crossed again due to her aunt's death. Their relationship could be categorised as friendship, but only in the loosest possible terms.

He was single. His wife had died when their son was a toddler and he had never re-married although, she reminded herself, it hadn't been for the want of trying. He had been engaged at least twice in the last two decades. The second time he had nearly made it to the altar. He would have done if, only weeks before the ceremony with the venue booked and the invitations sent out, his fiancée had not raced off to America on business and had never returned.

She admired the way he had carried on without sinking into a decline or letting himself go. Unlike her, he filled his time with more than just work. Tennis was his thing, and walking. She recalled that at their last meeting he told her he had just returned from completing the coast to coast walk with his son; two hundred miles of blister-inducing endurance from Cumbria to Yorkshire taking whatever the weather had to throw at them, stopping at various hostels along the way and she thought he looked very well on it.

She was glad he was sorting out Blanche's affairs and not Derek Palmer. She would not have felt comfortable with Derek Palmer handling things. Whenever they met, he seemed to have an eye on her cleavage and a hand venturing towards her knees. He had an over-large ego and teeth to match. She had never liked him. Guy, on the other hand, she did like. He was a very likeable man and he had always been the perfect gentleman.

She had no idea what might be in the codicil. She understood it had somehow become detached from the will and had only been handed to him in the last few days. He had written to her as soon as he found out about it. She wasn't expecting their meeting to be a long one and she wasn't dreading it; it was, however, one added complication she could have done without.

Guy Hampson sauntered down the passageway to the small kitchen sandwiched between two offices and the photo-copier, to make himself a cup of tea. He ran a relaxed regime. He didn't expect to be waited on by a junior member of staff. He preferred to make his own tea.

He was looking forward to his meeting with Helena. Their relationship was an easy one, they had known each other for years. He admired her resilience and striking good looks. In contrast to Emma who had been a blue-eyed blonde, Helena was raven-haired with inky dark eyes, reminiscent of her aunt Blanche.

Sorting out the estate of Blanche Black was turning out to be complicated. He had uncovered a package of investments passed on from her father, which she had not touched since his death. Unravelling those would be a headache. The codicil was not straightforward either, there was no address for the beneficiary. He was hoping Helena would be able to help there, which is why he had written to her. He could have telephoned but he hadn't wanted to put her on the spot.

They had not seen each other since the funeral, when she had seemed incapable of stringing two words together. It had been a sad funeral, only five mourners to send Blanche on her way, but done according to her wishes. He had been joined by Helena, Helena's daughter and her niece, plus Alf Minns from the corner shop. He did not count the vicar or the staff from the undertakers. Grief was a funny thing, he reflected, affecting people in different ways.

The codicil had been a good excuse to get Helena to call into the office so that he could check she was all right. He was aware that she had no partner for support. She had her daughter, of course, but he had no idea how close they were. If she was anything like his son, unloading would not be easy. He felt a momentary pang of sorrow and then guilt. Emma had been taken too soon. He was unsuited to playing both father and mother. She had been so good at all the emotional stuff, he found it hard to share his feelings and he accepted that Jake had probably suffered because of it.

As the kettle boiled, it crossed his mind that he must have drunk millions of cups of tea in his time; strong breakfast,

Darjeeling, Earl Grey. He didn't claim to be a connoisseur, but in his opinion, green tea lacked flavour and strength. He reckoned tea needed flavour and strength to be effective. It was what saw him through some of the most hair-raising interviews. It could encourage convivial conversation, soothe sad hearts, settle disputes and at the very least bring a halt to proceedings for a few minutes to allow time for sensible reflection and tempers to cool.

From what he knew of Helena, she would be unlikely to dissolve into a fit of hysterics when she learnt about the terms of the codicil. He had to admit that the terms were slightly unusual. Blanche had not explained why she had insisted on them. If he had not been on holiday when she decided to amend her will, he would have asked. It was too late for that now. He was hoping Helena would be intrigued by the terms rather than annoyed or upset by them.

There were voices in reception as he made his way back to his room. He checked his watch. Two minutes to five, she was punctual. He liked that. He did not sit down when he reached his desk but hovered, sipping tea, waiting for the official announcement of her arrival.

The only person in the reception area when Helena arrived was the young woman sitting behind the desk. *Elsa March Receptionist,* it stated in black lettering on the wooden block placed at an angle to the computer. With hair cut shorter than short, large eyes and puck-like ears, Helena thought she had a strong resemblance to a kinkajou, but this was a solicitor's office in East Knoll not a rainforest in Brazil... Brazil, where had she dreamed that up? It was not like her to have such fanciful notions. Naomi had commented on her lack of imagination only that morning. She reckoned she must be more stressed than she had thought. Enquiring eyes were raised to hers. "Can I help you?"

"Mrs. Henry to see Mr. Hampson," she said in a business-like fashion.

"Take a seat." Elsa picked up the handset on her desk and pressed buttons. "Your five o'clock, Mr. Hampson," she said in a robotic monotone before replacing it and without waiting for his response or giving Helena another glance, but Helena had noticed the tears glistening in her eyes. Had she fallen out with her boy-friend she mused, had a tiff with a girlfriend, maybe. Should she say something? No. Elsa might be embarrassed her tears had been noted. Remembering that time in her own life, she knew that when immaturity tipped into maturity there was a mismatch between stoicism and emotion. She was glad to have left those years behind. Teenagers had energy and optimism, they were idealistic and principled without the insight to question their principles; sensible judgment came later. She reckoned there would be more texting and then the spat would be over. Her intervention was unnecessary and anyway, she figured Elsa would be uncomfortable opening-up to a stranger.

As she did not need to make small-talk, Helena sank into the padded upholstery clinging to the walls like cliffs round a coastline, wondering if she should get her laptop out of her bag. She decided against it. Guy wouldn't keep her waiting, it wasn't his style. Just as that thought had been discarded, he appeared in the waiting area; her critical analysis of his appearance was positive. He was dressed formally in a navy suit, striped shirt and red tie with a matching silk handkerchief peeping from the top pocket of the jacket. She gathered her bag and stood up, asking herself why she had not been aware of his athletic frame before. Most men of a similar age carried excess pounds around the waist but he still had the physique of a much younger man.

"Helena, welcome," he said. She detected a whiff of after-shave as he moved towards her and took hold of her hands. It was a pleasant scent, fresh, lemony, his hands strong and cool. They held hers for what she considered slightly longer than was necessary, but she did not object. "Come on through."

He relaxed his hold and led the way down the corridor to his office. The door was open. It was a square room lined with books and filing cabinets. The light was on and the blind pulled down on the window even though there was still a shimmer of light in the evening sky. As well as his mug of tea, there was a telephone on his desk, an industrial-sized stapler, several pens in a tray and a file bulging with papers. He raised the mug in front of her. "Tea?" he said as she sat down.

"I'm fine, thanks."

"How are things?"

"Better … it's taking me a while to get used to her not being here. Blanche had been at Barque House for ever."

"Death is a miserable business," he said. "It's my job to make it more palatable."

She felt him watching her as she studied her knees and then raised her eyes to his. "Yes, miserable," she paused "You have something to show me?"

"I have," he said opening the file and turning over papers until he found the one he wanted. "Ah … this is it, the codicil to Blanche's will." She took her glasses from her bag and balanced them on the end of her nose to scan the document. "As you can see, she has named another beneficiary, Mary Rose Glebe. Do you know her?" Helena looked blank. "You don't. Her name means nothing to you?"

She pushed her glasses up into her hair Alice band-style and eased herself back into the chair. "No."

"She hasn't given an address. I was hoping you might be able to point us in the right direction."

"There might be a clue at Barque House. We haven't started to tackle that yet. Can't you find her?"

"The costs will mount up if we start searching."

"Ok. I'll get onto it, see what we can find."

"Perfect, um, there is something else."

"Oh dear, what now?"

"Blanche has stipulated that for you to receive your inheritance and for Mary Glebe to receive hers, you two must meet."

"How do you mean?"

"She wants you to have tea together at the Roman Reach Country Club. It's for me to arrange everything and be present to ensure that you have both complied with her wishes."

"But I don't know this, Mary Glebe and Roman Reach is half way to Linchester. Couldn't we meet at the Crab Apple on the Quay instead?"

"I think it was intended to be neutral territory."

"So, she doesn't live in East Knoll."

"We wouldn't be having this conversation if I knew that."

"I don't understand. This doesn't sound like Blanche at all. She was always down-to-earth, not willing to waste money on going out to tea. I've got a lot on at the moment. Taking tea with someone I don't know from Eve is not my idea of fun. Why did she attach such a strange condition to the will?"

"I only know what I've told you. There's no getting away from it I'm afraid, unless you don't want Barque House and I'm sure that's not the case."

Her stomach lurched. The thought of losing the old place made her uneasy. It had been in the Black family for years, why would she not want it to be hers? "I do want it," she said. She was surprised at the strength of her emotions. She had not expected to feel like this, but it seemed she had a need to own the house, whether she lived in it or not. It was part of the family history and she craved that continuity, at least for now. Perhaps Blanche had sensed that. Perhaps she was helping her make up her mind. "I am going to keep it," she said firmly "So, you had better arrange the tea-party."

"I will, as soon as we find Mary Glebe."

"Oh yes. I'll get Naomi to search for Blanche's address book."

"You haven't found it yet?"

"Not yet. How long will it take to get the estate settled?"

"A few months if there are no other hiccups, no outstanding debts ..."

"There won't be any debts."

"No, I didn't think so. I'll let you know when there's something for you to sign."

"Is that it, then?"

"For the moment," he said as he returned the paper to the others and closed the file. "How's your brother, these days? I was surprised not to see him at the funeral."

"Living in Italy, miffed Blanche only left him a thousand pounds."

"It's funny how people think they're entitled to someone else's money after they die. You can leave your money as you choose. I expect she thought he didn't need it."

"He doesn't and she hadn't seen him in years."

"She knew what she was doing, sharp as a pin to the end. She would have had her reasons," he said.

"I don't think he would have felt so bad if Isla hadn't inherited most of the furniture."

"Ah well, I can help you there. Blanche was impressed that Isla stuck to her studies and became a GP like your grandfather. She wanted her to have what had been his."

"That makes sense. I'll tell him."

"And how about you?"

"Me?" Helena said.

"Yes … apart from being sad about Blanche I mean, how are you?"

"Busy, stressed, wondering about the right thing to do, not having enough hours in the day, much as normal, really."

"You need to relax more. Treat yourself to some *me* time."

"The chance would be a fine thing."

"Look, you're my last client. I'm finished for the day, why don't we have a drink at Herman's wine bar?"

Helena wondered if she had misunderstood. She fingered her glasses and then removed them from her head, letting a screen of hair fall across her face for a moment as she put them away in her bag and thought through his suggestion. She looked up again, tossing the hair from her eyes. "You mean, you and me?"

"Well, there's no-one else here. It will do you good. Just one glass of their red?"

Helena asked herself if this would be a wise move and then she tried to think of a good reason why it might not be. She reckoned she had just as much right to a social life as the next person. She liked him, surely one drink could do no harm? Naomi wouldn't be expecting her yet, she had warned her she might be late; she felt her cheeks warm at her bold thoughts.

"We haven't had a proper chat in years," he went on. "We can mull over the pros and cons of selling your house, renting out Barque House or the other way about."

"Free advice from a lawyer?" she said.

He laughed. "Only for the select few."

As a chuckle escaped her lips she suddenly felt ridiculously young, daring; as if she might be bunking off school, which was odd, because she never had. "How could I refuse?"

Naomi had guesstimated the time of her mother's return and had prepared an omelette with what was left in the fridge. She was slicing the last two tomatoes as a garnish when she heard the front door open and close. "Just on time," she called. "How did it go?"

Helena deposited her laptop on the end of the table and slipped her feet from her shoes. After the wine and the walk, she felt warm, energised. Guy had been right. More *me* time was the correct prescription. "I'll tell you in a minute. I want to change into something more comfortable," she said as she picked up her shoes and headed for the stairs. She returned a short time later in leggings and an over-large sweatshirt and sat down at the table opposite her daughter. "This looks good."

"Thanks, so, what did Mr. Hampson say?"

"Blanche has named another beneficiary, Mary Glebe, but there's no record of her address. Have you noticed her name in any of Blanche's things?"

"I haven't had a proper look yet."

"I thought you went to Barque House this afternoon."

"I did, but I didn't do much. It still feels strange to be there without her. I couldn't bring myself to poke about in her things. It didn't feel right."

"Well, next time you go, see if you can find this woman's address."

"What did she leave her?"

"Premium bonds."

"How many?"

"All of them," she said.

"How much are they worth?"

"I didn't like to ask."

"See, you're as bad as me," Naomi said with a grin.

"Maybe we both need to get over it, now."

"Are you still thinking of selling?"

"What gave you that idea?"

"I don't know. If it was me, I'd move in there, do something with the garden. It's a shame it's been left to fade away."

"You don't know anything about gardening."

"I could learn."

"Well, I *am* keeping it," Helena said.

"Cool. It's very handy for town."

"I don't know if I'll live there. I might rent it out or I might sell this and move in, or I might rent this out. I have to admit the thought of packing up and moving out does not appeal, not one bit."

"I'll help."

"I know you will. I guess it's more psychological than physical. I'm still a bit emotional, you know, wobbly about everything. I need to know your plans and Isla's; whether you intend to carry on living with me or to get places of your own."

"Family summit time," Naomi said.

"As soon as she gets back. I've had an idea I want to run past you. We can talk about everything later. Oh, Guy said ..."

"Guy, is it?"

Helena lowered her eyes to examine the contents of the omelette. "You've put carrots and potatoes in here, unusual in a cheese omelette, but tasty. What do you mean, *Guy*? I've always called him Guy," she said.

"Just joshing, so, what did he say?"

"Blanche has stipulated that to get our inheritances, he must arrange for us to have tea together at Roman Reach Country Club."

"What, you and Guy?"

"No, Mary and me, but Guy must be there to verify all the terms have been complied with."

"That's mad. You don't even know her."

"Well, we have to do it or it's bye-bye Barque House."

"Can I come?"

"I'll ask. It would be nice if you could."

"Get Guy round here for a meal and we'll work on him."

"I don't know. It might give him the wrong idea. A glass of wine is ok, but…"

"Are you saying you went out for drink with him, Mum?"

"What's wrong with that?" Helena said. "We're old friends."

"Old friends with benefits, maybe?"

"Now you're talking nonsense," she said the pink glow suffusing her cheeks not entirely due to the wine she had consumed earlier.

"I don't know why you didn't think of him before," Naomi said giving her mother an impish grin. "He's single, his nose is fine; he's clever. I bet he can spell. What's not to like?"

Helena shuffled her feet about under the table and crossed her arms. "I'm more interested in finding out about this Mary Glebe."

"She could be an old friend. It can't be the cleaner, her name's something funny like Mrs. Sphinx."

"Irina Spinks. Blanche left her the painting of Salisbury Cathedral."

"Oh yes. I don't know, then."

"Neither do I. Mary Glebe is a complete mystery," Helena said.

"Not for much longer."

"The sooner you do your detective work, the better."

"Okay."

"Do you want help?"

"No, it's fine, Mum. I will do it. It's just, well, all her personal things. It seems a bit rude."

"She wanted you to do it," Helena said. "She gave you permission in her will."

"You're right. I'm being silly. I'll start…"

"Tomorrow?"

"I don't know, maybe; soon, I promise."

CHAPTER 5

The following day, despite more urging from her mother, Naomi decided to give Barque House a miss. The sun was shining, it was unseasonably mild for October and she hadn't been down to the beach in weeks. After lunch, she changed her jersey dress and thick tights for jeans and a hoody and set off at a jog.

The road curved gently down to the sea. It had no distinguishing features. The houses were set well back from the road, hidden behind Victorian brick walls. Unlike most of the adjoining roads, all the trees had been felled years before, victims of Dutch Elm Disease. None of the pavements had grass verges or paving slabs to break the monotony of the asphalt. She remembered there had once been a red telephone box at the crossroads leading into town or to the station, but that too, had gone. All she could see as she ran was tarmac and sky until she was nearly upon the sand dunes and then her pace slowed to a walk.

She could hear the sea, now; see ferries coming in and out of the bay, smell the seaweed she knew would be lacing the tide- line, along with plastic debris, drift wood and the frayed ends of salty rope. As she followed the path winding between sandy hillocks to emerge through a gap where the marram grass had failed to naturalise, she stopped to take stock of her surroundings.

Miles of empty beach stretched ahead of her. The tide was going out. She picked up her pace again and, glancing around to check there was no-one watching, she ran full pelt along the damp sand. When her lungs ran out of air and her ribs ached she flopped down on a rock embedded in the sand like a basking seal, propping herself up with her hands as she stretched her legs in front of her and caught her breath. She gazed at the grey-green waves rolling in over the hard-packed shore and then sliding back like crocodiles slinking back to the swamp.

She hadn't noticed anyone else nearby and jumped up in surprise when she heard the voice. "Nice day for a run."

She spun round, plait flailing like a shot-putter's arm. How could she not have noticed him? He was crouched on the ground in the shelter of a natural windbreak watching her, his blond hair blowing in the breeze; a pile of driftwood lay beside his empty rucksack. "You gave me a fright," she said.

"Sorry. I thought you'd seen me."

She reckoned they must be about the same age or perhaps he was a little older; donkey jacket, faded jeans, creased shirt and shabby trainers. Nothing much to recommend him except for those eyes. They were something else; piercing, blue, hypnotic. If they were the window to his soul, she thought, she would be scared to look inside.

He straightened his back and stood up at which point she realised they were about the same height. "I wasn't expecting to meet anyone down here in October," she said.

"I'm often down here," he said turning from her to stare towards the horizon. "It's a great place for drift wood. There's a spit out there. The tide deposits whatever it's carrying on this little corner of the beach."

"Why are you collecting drift wood?"

"For my models, I'm a sculptor … animals mainly."

"That sounds like fun."

"It's how I earn my living."

"Oh," she said feeling uncomfortable that she should have presumed it was just a hobby.

"My father's always telling me it's not a proper job," he said as if reading her mind.

"Do you still live at home?"

"No, I have my own place. How about you?"

"Out of a job and back at home," she said edging a bit nearer to examine what he had gleaned from the sea. "I can't imagine any of that turning into a sculpture."

"You'll have to come and see my work," he said.

"Is it on display somewhere?"

"No, just in my studio, well, workshop," he gave her a sheepish grin and she warmed to him. "Ok, in my dad's garage."

She laughed. "Where does he live?"

"Lincoln road, the house with the round window at the front. Do you know it?"

Naomi felt their rapport wither. Her eyes narrowed. "You're Jake Hampson."

"I am. Who are you?"

"Naomi Henry."

"Ah."

She bristled at his tone. "What does that mean?" she said.

"It means I've heard of you," he said starting to fill his rucksack with the wood.

"I've heard of you, too," she said. He was not as she remembered him. His hair was longer, his face fuller ... but to be honest she had only ever caught glimpses of him before.

The sun was going down, turning the sky to pink and the sea to treacle. It was time she left. She had promised to organise dinner again and she still had shopping to do, apart from which she did not want to be alone on the beach in the pitch black with Jake Hampson. "I'd better get home," she said flipping her plait over her shoulder in a dismissive fashion.

"See you around," he said.

"*Not if I see you first*," she thought as she set off at a jog the way she had come, wishing she had decided to go to Barque House after all.

She remembered the long hot summer when Jake Hampson had been everywhere, no party had been a party without him; several of the girls she knew had fallen for his charms. He had seemed like a celebrity living in a big house, rationing his appearances to the school holidays when he was home from his expensive private school, driving around in the mini he had been given for his seventeenth birthday.

The local girls had followed him slavishly wherever he went. The fact that he had strung them along seemed to add to his charisma. He had never been short of a girlfriend. Nothing had tarnished his image in the eyes of his adoring fans until Nicola. Nicola had been his nemesis.

The gossip had been rife; passed behind hands, whispered in queues, imparted in noisy bars, becoming increasingly lurid with each telling until there wasn't anyone under twenty in East Knoll who did not know, or thought they knew, what Jake Hampson had done and who with.

When Jake Hampson had been swanning round East Knoll as if he owned the place, she and Luke had become close; it was the summer their friendship had blossomed into something more … their summer of love. They had spent all their spare time together, shunning parties for quiet nights in or moonlit walks, barefoot along the shore. Jake Hampson and his peccadillos had passed them by and she counted herself lucky that she had escaped his clutches.

What was he doing back in East Knoll? She was there because she had nowhere else to go and no-one to be with; there were worse places and besides, she loved the sea. What was his excuse? She would never know, she told herself, because she had no intention of finding out.

As she put more and more distance between them she was relieved she had not been one of Jake's coterie, had never spoken to him before, could not claim to know him personally, only by reputation, which is why she had not recognised him straight away. At that time Luke had occupied all her spare moments. Her pace slowed as she thought of Luke. She was not looking for love again but she hoped love would find her at some stage.

She had done university. She was glad she had, especially as she did not have a substantial debt to pay back thanks to her generous grandmother. Her Biology degree had led to a job in marketing at Greenbank Pharmaceuticals and when they could no longer afford her services, she had not been unhappy to leave. Her mother had been disappointed for her but she had never wanted an office job or a career in marketing. Working in an office nine to five, day in and day out, had stifled her. She had been ready for a move, apart from which she had wanted to get away from Luke and reminders of their life together.

She thought of her future. To become an official carer; to grow vegetables, keep chickens and have a house full of children. Luke had not wanted children. Deep-down she had known this mis-match would drive them apart at some stage. She wanted children with the right person ... not with him and not with Jake Hampson for sure. She shivered at the thought.

She had kept well away from Jake Hampson and his friends in the past and she intended to keep well away from him now; she would make sure she avoided his part of the beach in future and then a most unwelcome thought entered her head. She went cold as she remembered how she had teased her mother about Jake's father. Her footsteps faltered. How could she have forgotten that Guy had a son, who that son was; what he had done? Guy Hampson's part in the affair had not been blameless. Jake must have learned his bad habits from somewhere. Like father, like son. She could not let her mother, vulnerable after Blanche's death, be taken in by such a man. She reckoned it was up to her to protect her from his advances now her defences were down. She would get Isla on side.

That stupid codicil would complicate matters, but she had to do her best to prevent their friendship from developing into something more intimate. Guy Hampson could not, would not, be allowed to winkle his way into their lives.

CHAPTER 6

Alf flicked through the pages of his stamp album, eyes drifting across the many designs, the different shapes, colours and styles; he lingered over the exotic flowers depicted on the stamps of far off countries he had never visited and now never would, Tanzania, Nicaragua, Ceylon, the Soloman Islands, countries that had changed their names or boundaries, countries that no longer existed; his album noted them all. He flipped the pages back to stamps of the British Isles. To him, these were the most attractive. He liked to study the kings and queens' heads. He liked the variety and colour; he liked the one-off specials … great masters' paintings, old houses, the Christmas stamps, but particularly the ones celebrating the International Botanical Congress. There were flowers on all the threepenny, sixpenny and ninepenny stamps; old money, proper money, not the Mickey Mouse stuff they called money nowadays. He sucked in his teeth as he thought of the plastic notes that were now in circulation and mourned the inevitable decline of stamps as more and more communications were made by email or text.

Closing the album, he recalled those summers years ago when the Blacks had opened their garden to the public, charging sixpence for people to parade around the flower beds and partake of tea with the ladies of the house. All these sixpences went to a medical charity dedicated to pushing the boundaries of science, how could it have been otherwise? The old doc had been keen to move medicine into the next century.

Betsy and Blanche had served tea and scones at the open day and his mother had never turned down the opportunity to take her place with the visiting public. She had been impressed by the fine china cups in which the tea was served and the lace doilies on the cake plates; she had gone on about them for days. His older brothers had not been interested in flowers, china cups, or doilies, but being the youngest and his mother's favourite, he had hung on to her every word. He chuckled to himself as he remembered the ribbing they had given him. He felt momentary melancholy as he remembered Jimmy and Norman. They had been lost in the War. Neville had emigrated to Australia on a ten-pound ticket and had lived and died there. He had stayed at home, helped his father in the shop and when his father died, he had carried on alone. By then he had married Sarah and after years of trying and many disappointments, Minty had arrived. Dear little Minty. She had been a good baby, a happy child and had turned into a beautiful woman, the spit of her mother. Now she ran the shop for him. He still sorted out the newspaper orders but only helped behind the counter as and when required, which suited him nicely.

He reckoned he'd had a good life with Sarah, bless her. Forty years of marriage which had come to a nasty end but through it all, in the back of his mind, he had taken comfort from the fact that Blanche was still there over at the big house and now she had gone he felt rudder-less, more alone than he had expected but not lonely. He had plenty to keep him busy.

He filled his days as he always had. Up early to sort out the newspapers and then pottering up and down the shelves tidying tins, replenishing stock, or over at the allotments followed by early to bed so that he would be up the next morning to start all over again. He was content with his life. He had thought of retirement but had done nothing about it. Now he was past eighty he reckoned he should think about it again. Minty had made a great success of managing his little empire. He recalled with pride how well she had done at school; how she had become head girl and had gone on to gain a business degree before deciding to work with him. Thanks to her, they now had a large property portfolio as well as the shop. She had persuaded him to agree to a re-fit and with modern shelving, new lighting and new lines, the profits were up. Even the organic vegetable section which he helped to fill with produce from his allotment, had gone down well with the customers.

He was considering leaving the newspapers to Minty. These days starting work on a winter's morning when his arthritis was playing up, had become agonising; like someone was hammering nails into his fingers. His father had often muttered about 'screws' in his joints and he had laughed at his complaints. He was not laughing now.

Selling the business was not an option. It would be a bad decision as it was doing so well and besides, he did not want to live anywhere else. He wanted, had always wanted, despite Minty trying to persuade him to move into a more comfortable and convenient flat, to end his days where he had started them; that seemed to him a neat way of completing the circle of his life. He took satisfaction from the fact that he had been born and would die without moving away from the town where he had lived and loved all his life and then it would be for Minty to decide the future of his business empire.

He guessed she would retire, sell up and move somewhere warm with that idle husband of hers who was neither use nor ornament. He only came to life when they planned their annual two weeks in the sun. He couldn't get away fast enough. Why his daughter had chosen such a wastrel for her life partner, he did not know; but love him she did, of that there was no doubt. He had never been sure if Ty's heart was so steadfast but while Minty was happy he would hold his tongue about the teacher who haunted the bread counter longer and longer each week and let Ty pack her bag. He had seen the way she looked at him. He had seen the way he looked at her. He had noticed how their hands touched as he handed over her bag. He might be old but he was not stupid and if he saw any sign that Minty was upset. He *would* say something.

There was no doubt in his mind that developers would snap up the plot. They would demolish the shop to make way for houses no bigger than rabbit hutches for which they would charge too much money. He shook his head at that thought. It was the way of the world. He thanked the lord that he would not be there to see it.

He and Blanche had grown up in a different world. A world where a man's word was his bond and a woman's too. Their bond had demanded silence. They had both been sworn to secrecy. He had not shared their secret with anyone apart from Sarah, but now Blanche had gone, it was time to tell the truth before he too disappeared from this world into the next. Blanche had left it to him to decide when and how it should be done but he was still having trouble with that decision. He was doubting the wisdom of stirring up other people's lives on a whim, when they had kept quiet for all these years

He would discuss it with old Sol without giving too much away. Sol wouldn't tell anyone and even if he did, no-one would understand a word he was saying now most of his teeth had gone and he refused to wear the false ones his daughter-in-law had tried to foist on him. Why did the youngsters always think they knew best? "They know nothing about our lives ..." he muttered to himself "... what's important to us, the meaning of loyalty. No-one can be bothered to do things properly now."

He reckoned Blanche had been right when she had told him that they lived in a throw-away society. "If it doesn't work get rid of it, that's what people do now," she had said scornfully.

"I know," he had replied. "No-one bothers to mend things

these days, but you won't hear me complain. It's good for business. If people didn't buy new, our profits would be down. I can remember my old dad buying replacement handles for the garden tools."

"No-one does that now."

"No and they don't unravel jumpers to re-use the wool," he had said.

"They don't have woollen jumpers from what I've seen. It's all these fleecy things."

"I remember mother sitting me on a wooden stool in our kitchen," he went on "Arms stuck out in front of me like joe soap as she hung the washed hanks over my hands and wound the wool into balls. Round and round she went until I thought my thumbs would drop off."

"We'll end up smothered under our own rubbish if we don't re-cycle more. Dinners in cartons, plastic egg boxes, people walking round with coffee cups, don't get me started on all that," she had said.

"I agree, we should take more care of the environment. I'm always picking up rubbish from outside the shop. All these takeaways don't help …"

"… and there's too much methane about."

"You're not suggesting we should get rid of all the cows."

"Think of the ozone layer."

"You can't have too much beef."

"You've forgotten the mad cow fiasco."

"Scare mongering," he had said. "It won't happen again."

"Don't you believe it. Nature has ways of re-dressing the balance. It's only a matter of time before society realises we need to stop eating so much meat. Cows will be kept as biological curiosities, nothing more."

"I can't see that happening."

"You won't, but Minty might and that's another thing, they'd do away with us oldies if they could," she had said. "They think we're an inconvenience, don't understand what makes us tick."

"You're right there," he had agreed.

"Society wants to tidy us away; lock us up in one of those homes and throw away the key."

"They wanted to take my Sarah."

"You did well to keep her with you to the end."

"It was what she wanted."

"I'm staying put," she had said decisively.

"Good for you," he had replied.

It was these exchanges he missed the most. He had always admired her single-mindedness, her ability to make decisions, her clear thought. "This is my place," he said to himself. "Where I was born and where I'm staying."

He left the album and went to fetch his coat from the stand in the hall, ready to head off to the pub and his heart to heart with Sol. He needed to talk everything through, get it straight in his head and then he reckoned he would be able to make up his mind when, how or even if, the truth should be told.

CHAPTER 7

It was Friday before Naomi went back to Barque House. When she got there, she was surprised to find Alf Minns waiting on the doorstep, a large book under his arm. "Hello," she said. "Did you want to see me?"

"I wasn't sure if you were coming today. I've brought you this," he said offering her the book. "Blanche lent it to me. It was the old doc's."

Naomi flipped through the first few pages. "It's all about roses," she said.

"Yes."

"Don't you want to keep it?

"Well …"

"I'm sure Mum won't mind. Blanche would have wanted you to keep it if it's useful to you. Did she ask you to return it?"

"No," he said.

"Well then, you're welcome to it," she said handing it back. "Keep it to remember her by. Are you coming in? I always have a cuppa when I arrive, um, what I mean is, I did when she was still here."

"Takes some getting used to, doesn't it?"

"Why don't you join me?"

"Never say no to a cuppa," he said as he followed her into the kitchen. She plugged in the kettle and produced mugs and milk. "I haven't started clearing her desk yet but when I do I expect to find all sorts, old diaries, stamps, Christmas cards from years ago, letters and goodness knows what else and then there's her clothes."

"She didn't like throwing things away."

"Before I began to call on her each day, she had been recycling the same teabag for days," she said popping one teabag into each mug.

He gave a bark of laughter. "That doesn't surprise me."

"The house seems strange without her."

"It does."

"Shall we take our mugs into the lounge?"

The lounge was Naomi's favourite room. It had deep-moulded cornices skirting the high ceiling, an impressive six-branch chandelier topped with a brass-mounted eagle dangling from a heavy chain at the central point. Despite its Victorian pedigree and solid-looking furniture ... a three-piece suite, nest of tables, mahogany side board and the grand piano she knew Blanche could not play ... the room was filled with light.

The open fireplace had a black grate inset with tiles, those either side decorated with hand-painted irises. The mantelpiece was marble, cream shot through with fine grey lines, the curtains, ruby red with a matching pelmet above. An aspidistra sat in a cache-pot on a stand against the wall shaded by the rich velvet drapes. She had no idea of the age of the plant. It could have been fifty or sixty years old, maybe more, but it seemed settled in its shadowy corner, the multitude of leaves a glossy green, tough, ribbed, obviously able to withstand neglect. It had not been watered for weeks; she was pleased, no relieved, it was still flourishing in the chinoiserie pot, it would have been her fault if it had shrivelled and died. She intended to water it before she left that afternoon.

The whole ambience of the room was formal but relaxed. She wondered if it was the parquet floor and light rugs that made it so, or it could have been the cream walls and south-facing window. Whatever the reason, it was not a gloomy room. She felt comfortable as she sat in Blanche's armchair which had been placed near enough the fireplace for the old lady to rest her slippered feet on the fender.

Alf took the settee. "It's been a while now," he said.

"You must miss your games of Scrabble."

"I miss a lot of things. We'd been friends a long time."

"Have you always lived on Ransome Street?"

"I was born here."

"In the shop?"

"Above the shop, in our flat. I used to deliver the old doc's papers when I was a nipper."

"What was it like, then?"

"What … our shop?"

"Yes."

"It wasn't anything like it is now. We had wooden counters and a beast of a till, a big heavy thing, it was. The shelves went up to the ceiling; most of the stock was in jars; tobacco, cigars, cigarettes, boiled sweets … and there were the newspapers of course. We kept everything from dustpans to drinking chocolate."

He grinned at her and she laughed. "I guess you worked long hours."

He nodded. "Still do. We were open from seven till eleven every day except Christmas day. We all went to church on Christmas Day. My mum and dad were hard workers, never took a holiday, they had to work long hours to make ends meet but we didn't mind hard work in those days. My son-in law's idea of hard work is to stand behind the counter and drink coffee," he said eyebrows knitted in a disapproving frown.

"I've never seen him in the shop. Danny usually serves me."

"Now, he *is* a hard worker. I'd swap Danny for Ty any day."

"I think Minty might have something to say about that."

"That's the only thing in his favour. They seem happy together."

"That's good. I've just split up with my boyfriend. My parents divorced years ago."

"That's another change from the old days. Couples stayed close then, come what may. These days people have no staying power. They give up at the first hurdle."

"They weren't happy," she said.

"It's sad when that happens. Sarah and me, we were happy. We stuck together through thick and thin."

"Have you ever thought of finding another partner?"

"Another partner … no. I'm not lonely. I'd never find another woman like Sarah."

"Mum's looking for someone else."

"How do you feel about that?"

"I don't mind. It's her life. I wish I could find someone like Sarah, a guy, I mean. Someone who would be perfect for me. Someone I could rely on. Someone who wanted to stay for ever. Have I left it too late? What if that someone never finds me, or I don't find him. Sorry, I'm going on a bit, aren't I?"

She hardly knew him and yet there was something about him, something that made opening her heart to him easy, natural, normal. She was telling him things she had admitted only to herself and that realisation made her cheeks burn with embarrassment. She put up her hands to hide the tell-tale flush. He wasn't looking at her, thank goodness. He was staring into the empty grate.

"Blanche said I was a good listener," he said.

"She was a good story-teller."

"Stories … yes," he said reflectively. "I'd better get on. I want to catch the library before it closes." He downed the last dregs from his mug and rose to his feet. She joined him, noting with surprise that he was a few inches taller than her. "Call in at the shop if you need a good listener," he went on. "I'm there most days when I'm not at the allotments."

She could see why he and Blanche had been friends. He didn't go on about himself and he was willing to listen. He was empathetic, kind, thoughtful and he knew not to outstay his welcome. "Thanks, I will." She saw him to the door and made her way back to the lounge.

The October sun was streaming through the net curtains, filling the room with dappled light, casting bright shadows on the furniture and threatening to bleach out the delicate shades in the watercolours on the wall opposite. She drew the curtains to protect them as her great-aunt would have done and sat down in the semi-darkness knowing she was not going to tackle the desk that day. She kicked off her trainers and rested her feet on the fender Blanche-style, while she finished her tea.

She felt bad for not making a start, but she had decided to return early the next morning and tackle the desk then. She might even be able to persuade Isla to go with her and maybe her mother. It would be more fun with them there and it would feel less like nosing around in things she shouldn't.

The difficult part, despite her mother's assertion that she had permission, was persuading herself that Blanche would not mind her searching the desk. She knew it was idiotic to feel that way, but she had the uneasy notion that her great-aunt's presence had not quite left Barque House. It seemed to waft through the rooms like the scent of lavender, echoes of their conversations still fixed in her mind. She imagined Blanche suddenly appearing and asking what on earth she thought she was doing, prying into things that didn't concern her.

If only they had the address book. If they knew where that was there would be no problem. She would not have to turn out the desk as a matter of urgency; they would know exactly how to contact Mary Glebe and the desk could be left until she felt more at ease with everything.

CHAPTER 8

Isla Ford trundled her case into the house. "I'm back," she called. The television was mumbling away in the front room. She waited to see if anyone had heard her.

Right on cue, Naomi burst into the hall to offer a welcoming hug. "Here you are at last. We've been waiting for you to get back."

"That's nice. Did you miss me?"

"I wouldn't go that far," she said a mischievous glint in her eye. "But now you're here we can get on with the family meeting."

"Family meeting …"

"All will be revealed. Do you want a drink, have you eaten?"

"I had a meal on the train. A glass of something cold and alcoholic would be good. I haven't drunk much all week, I couldn't risk Bollinger Brain, there was too much to take in."

"Bollinger … weren't you the lucky one."

"Ok, Prosecco. It was flowing like water. You'd think the medical profession would know better."

"I'll get the wine. Mum's in the lounge, she'll explain everything."

Helena was sitting on the settee, her legs tucked neatly to one side. She noticed straight away that despite the tinted glasses, there were shadows under her niece's eyes. She took in the travel-rumpled dress and thick hair, unruly as ever. "You've had a long day. Come and sit down. How did the conference go?"

"Very well," Isla said as she flopped into an armchair. "I didn't feel out of place. Lots of the delegates were on their own like me; marital break-ups or because they'd never been able to hold on to a relationship, any sort of relationship."

"If they all work as hard as you, I'm not surprised."

"I'm glad I live here and not in Linchester. At least I can switch off at the end of a day and not be tempted back to the surgery to do more work."

"And it's unlikely you'll meet your patients in town."

"There is that."

"It wouldn't be good for your stress levels or your private life."

"What private life? I don't have one," Isla said. "To be honest, I've never wanted one."

"You're so like Blanche. Medicine was the love of her life."

"I wouldn't put it quite like that, but I want to make the most of my training. I often wonder how doctors managed back in the day when they lived and worked amongst their patients and made home visits all the time."

"That was how Grandpa Harold worked. He knew all his patients really well."

"I have so many patients I can't even remember their faces."

"Do you think it was better then?" Helena said.

"No way. Doctors might have been able to make more complete assessments, treating the whole family and understanding their backgrounds, children didn't move far from home, but ..."

"But they didn't have computers," Helena said.

"No and there weren't so many treatments available. Surgery was barbaric."

"Maybe there weren't so many ailments."

"There weren't so many patients, that's for sure; people are living longer now, surgical miracles are being performed every day."

"No fast food, back then; no lack of exercise, not much obesity. Stress hadn't been invented."

"But there was tuberculosis, don't forget that was a killer and malnutrition and rickets. Patients now have more complex needs, multiple needs; diabetes, dementia, high blood pressure, but I wouldn't want to go back in time."

"From what I heard this week, gene therapy is well on the way. I'm sure Grandpa Harold would have approved."

"Yes, anyway, it was excellent but full on. I did some catching up and made some interesting contacts, learned a lot but I drank far too much coffee and nibbled more biscuits than was good for me."

"Once in a while won't hurt."

"So, what's been going on here? Naomi says we're having a family meeting."

"I wanted to talk to you about Barque House."

"Have you decided what you want to do?"

"I want to keep it."

"Ok, so you'll be selling this place. You want me to move out."

"That's what I need to discuss with you and there's something else. Do you know a Mary Glebe?"

Naomi returned to the room just then, armed with an open bottle of wine and three glasses. "Ah the mysterious Mary Rose Glebe. Wine, anyone?"

"Yes, please," Isla said. Helena held out her hand for the next glass. Isla took a sip from hers and straightened her glasses. "The name doesn't ring a bell. Who is she?"

"I wish we knew," Helena said.

"Blanche named her in the will. Mum has to have tea with her at the Roman Reach Country Club."

"Really, why?"

"If I don't, I won't get Barque House," Helena said.

"How come?"

"Well, Blanche left a codicil to the will stating that Mary Glebe should inherit the premium bonds, but that she can't claim her inheritance, and neither can I, unless we take tea together at Roman Reach."

Isla blinked at her aunt in a myopic fashion and ran a hand through her hair. "That's a bit odd."

"It's insane," Naomi said. "Mum doesn't know Mary Glebe and Blanche didn't give her address in the codicil."

"I'm sure it must be in her address book or something. Naomi was going to look for it, weren't you Nims?"

"I was hoping you two might come with me tomorrow to start the search."

"Were you, now," Helena said.

"Oh, go on, Mum. It will be quicker with three pairs of eyes."

"I've lots of other things I need to do."

"I was going to call in at the surgery, check my emails," Isla said "But I don't have to. I'll come and help. I haven't been to Barque House in ages. It'll give me a chance to look over my inheritance."

"Thanks, Isla. We can take lunch with us if you want."

"Let's go out, make it a proper outing ... Pizza Express?"

"Perfect, um Mum, I've just realised who Mary Glebe could be," Naomi said.

"Go on, then."

"Well, you said Blanche didn't like men, so ..."

"... so, you mean they might have been ..."

"... together, yes."

Helena shook her head. "We would have known. There would have been clues. You never noticed anything when you were there."

"No, but ..."

"But nothing. Blanche wouldn't have been able to keep their relationship hidden. You said she didn't have visitors."

"She didn't, just Alf, but I wasn't there twenty-four seven."

"Nana would have said something. No," she shook her head in a definitive fashion. "No, I don't think so. It doesn't fit the pattern. What do you think, Isla?"

"It seems unlikely."

"I agree. Now we can discuss my idea. Have you two decided whether you're moving out, or not?"

"I've *thought* about it," Isla said. "I just haven't found anywhere. But I'm happy to go if you want me to."

"Naomi?"

"I haven't thought about it at all. I haven't got a job. I'm not in any position to get my own place right now so I'm afraid you're stuck with me until I can scrape a deposit together."

"That's what I thought. How would it be if we carried on living together but at Barque House instead, take a floor each? I thought it would be a way of making us all independent but still together, families staying together like we said before." Isla and Naomi looked at each other. "Well, don't all shout at once."

"It's a great idea. I definitely want to do it," Naomi said.

"Yes, I do, too," Isla said. "At least for the time being. I'll have more room to display my glass. Pippa Chisholm called me last week to say there was a big batch of Orrefors coming into the auction rooms next month. I might buy myself something to remember Blanche by. What will you do with this house?"

"I haven't decided, yet. I've considered renting it out furnished, or sending most of the furniture to the auction and selling it empty. Barque House is already furnished. It's all yours, Isla ..."

"Apart from the desk," Naomi said.

"Yes, we know about the desk but apart from that, do you mind us using it, until you find somewhere else?"

"Not at all."

"So, those are my choices," Helena said.

"If you rent it out it would be extra income for you," Isla said.

"And more hassle," Naomi said. "You'd have to arrange to have it all decorated. You might have problem tenants. I say sell it."

"You could invest the money or buy a holiday flat somewhere else," Isla said.

"I could. I hadn't considered that. So, we reckon sell is the best option and move into Barque House together?"

"Yes," Naomi said.

"Definitely."

"We'll have to see if it would work before we make a final decision. If we want to go ahead perhaps we could ask Pippa to come over and value anything we don't need. We may as well try and sell it."

"I'll ask her for you. Now we just need to find Mary Glebe," Isla said.

Naomi topped up the glasses. "It's only a matter of time," she said.

"I could do without the hassle," Helena said. "I hope it doesn't take too long."

"It won't," Naomi said with a confidence her mother could not share.

"How do you know? For a start we don't know where she is; we don't know who she is; she might not want us to meet. If she won't co-operate, we could be back to square one."

"You don't think she'd turn down thousands of pounds?" Isla said.

"We don't know it is thousands and anyway, not everyone wants a shed-load of money. It's a big responsibility," Helena said.

"She could give it away if she doesn't want it," Naomi said.

"Surely she wouldn't want to stop you getting Barque House; why would she?"

"I don't know and until we actually meet I'm not likely to know."

"It might only be fifty pounds," Naomi said.

"There could be some winnings to claim," Isla said.

"On second thoughts, I will come with you tomorrow," Helena said. "It will be a chance for us to do a proper viewing and give me a better idea of what bits and pieces I want to keep from this house. Let's forget about Mary Glebe."

"We can't forget about her, Mum. We need to know why Blanche wanted you two to meet," Naomi said.

"You'll find out eventually," Isla said.

"I hope it's not a long wait. It's all so mysterious."

"Blanche wasn't mysterious," Helena said.

"You can't know everything about a person. I'm sure everyone has secrets."

"I haven't," Helena said.

"Nor me," Isla said.

Naomi gave them both a disbelieving stare. "I'd hate to think I was that boring," she said.

"So, what don't we know about you?" Helena said.

Naomi laughed. "That would be telling."

"She thinks there are ghosts at Barque House," she said.

"I don't believe in ghosts," Isla said.

"Neither do I," Helena said. "And Blanche wouldn't have had anything to do with ghosts. She was all about facts and figures, not mystery and imagination."

"I guess you're right," Naomi said. "But I'll be disappointed if there isn't something really spooky in the desk."

CHAPTER 9

Jake Hampson was plugged into Eric Clapton. Music usually took his mind away from the mundane, helped him concentrate, but not that day; that day he was having trouble getting the antelope's horns straight and his patience was wearing thin. He did not hear his father walk into the garage. Guy patted his son's back to attract his attention. He pulled out the earphones and looked up. "Very impressive," Guy said. "You've got the tilt of the head just right."

Jake got off his haunches and straightened up. He stepped back to take a critical look at his handiwork. "You think? This one's taken me days to complete. I need to leave it now and get more done for the craft fair."

"Did you finish that commission for Linchester High School?"

"I delivered it yesterday."

"Did they like it?"

"Well, they paid me, so I guess they did."

"To have one of your sculptures right outside the entrance is quite a coup, good advertising."

"I left a few of my cards in reception in case anyone asks who made it; I don't know if that was a good idea or not."

"Was *The Recorder* there?"

"Oh yes and the head teacher, all the sixth form who'd done most of the fund-raising and Jill Carmichael, of course."

"She gets everywhere."

"She said some nice things about my work."

"I should hope so. Local councillors need to show an interest, especially in local talent. It's good for you. There'll be a big splash in the paper. It's a slow business but you'll get there in the end. I know it hasn't been easy."

"I should never have come back. I've been thinking about that a lot recently, starting again somewhere else."

"You couldn't afford to be anywhere else."

"I'm sure I'd do much better where people didn't know me."

"You can't constantly harp on about the past, Jake. What's done is done. Move on. It's the only way."

"I wish other people would move on."

"How do you mean?"

"I met Naomi Henry down on the beach the other day. She made it plain she didn't want to know me, couldn't get away fast enough."

"She was never one of your bunch."

"Some of her friends were."

"People will always be judgmental, Jake. Mud sticks, I'm afraid. It's up to you to prove they're wrong, that you've grown up. You're not who they think you are."

"And how do I do that?"

"Be nice, play fair, get rid of the scowl."

"You make it sound so easy."

"It is easy. As soon as your work gets out there, you'll be known for your art and nothing else.

"I hope you're right. I'm doing ok on eBay."

"Just keep plugging away. I came to ask you to lock up when you leave. I'm off out tonight ... tennis club committee meeting."

"I'll be here a while, yet."

"Tell you what, give me some of your cards; I'll take them with me, see if I can drum up some work for you. The new head teacher from Parkside Primary will be there, he nearly made the Olympic tennis team a few years ago."

"You'll have to up your game."

"I'm working on it. He might like a few willow sculptures

for the playground or a willow bower." Jake made no comment. "Hey, you'll never guess what his name is."

Jake grimaced. "Djokavitch?"

"Close, Murray Andrews. I'm told he has a wicked serve." If he had hoped to raise a smile, he was unlucky. Jake's expression remained the same; sullen, brooding, grim. He had seen that expression before, when as a child Jake had been told there would be no pudding until he had eaten his dinner, or to stop gaming and go to bed. It made him feel inadequate, always having to play bad cop. Emma would have handled the situation better, he knew she would. The child in Jake had not yet come to terms with his loss and that bitterness needed to be addressed. He wanted to make things better for his son, but he did not know how; or maybe he did know how. He just couldn't face up to it. Jake's eyes were once more on the antelope. "You could come down to the club with me sometime, knock a few balls about. You used to enjoy your tennis."

"When I was a teenager; I haven't played for years. You know that."

"It's like riding a bike. Once you get on the court it will come back to you. How about the weekend?"

"I can't, Dad. I've told you. I need to make more stock for the craft fair."

"All work and no play …"

"I haven't done enough work to play," Jake replied tartly.

"Well, the offer's there when you're ready," he hesitated as if, Jake thought, he was about to say more.

His mood had lifted in anticipation of hearing the words he needed to hear and then spiralled down again as his father searched in vain for those words; a comment his mother might have made, what she might have thought of her son's work, that she would have been proud of him. He plugged his earphones back in. "Thanks," he said. "Have a good meeting."

Guy left him to it. Talking to his son had always been difficult. There was an invisible barrier between them and although it was never mentioned, they both knew it. He also knew that it was up to him to instigate the long overdue conversation, but the time never seemed right; he just wasn't ready and the longer he left it, the less ready he felt.

In the beginning he had not wanted to talk about Emma. It had been too painful. It had been hard enough to function day to day without her. Prolonging the agony by continually reminding himself of his loss in conversations about her with his son, had been too much.

Each time he found a new partner he told himself things would be different, that he was strong enough to tell Jake what he needed to hear. He would answer his questions about the past, set things straight and their relationship would be repaired. He had hoped for happiness for them all, but it was not to be. None of his new relationships had flourished and his memories remained shut away. He felt as if he had failed as a father, as a husband, as Emma's last connection with her son.

Would Jake forgive him for being a rubbish parent? Emma knew he would have trouble explaining life and death to their son … her life and death; explaining relationships, attachment, enduring love. She had understood his need to keep his feelings deep, exclusive, safe from harm. She had urged him to talk to the boy, to help him grieve. He had promised to try, however difficult he found it, to delve into his innermost feelings and reveal them to Jake so that he could come to terms with his own grief but so far, he had not fulfilled that promise.

He had let Jake down and by doing so, he had let *her down* and now Jake wanted to move away. He did not want him to go. If he didn't keep his promise to Emma there would be no closure for either of them. He had no choice, he had to make it right before it was too late; time was running out and without closure he knew the wound left by her absence would never heal and he would feel guilty for the rest of his life.

CHAPTER 10

The next morning as they sat in his car at the fuel station waiting to be rescued, Isobel and Adrian Flynn were not on the best of terms. "I'm worried about you," she said.

"It was a silly mistake. Anyone could have done it. You could have done it."

"I couldn't. I know my car runs on petrol," she said. "You should know yours runs on diesel. You've had it long enough."

"If only we could all be as perfect as you."

"It was an expensive mistake, Adrian. Two hundred pounds' worth of expensive," she said.

"It was a momentary lapse," he said with a grumpy shake of his head. "If you hadn't been banging on about Donald Trump's hair I might have been able to concentrate on what I was doing."

"Don't blame me, it was a stupid thing to do. How long will we have to wait?"

"Pass."

Isobel sighed. "There's no way we'll have time to get to Worthing before we're due back at Pippa's."

"I know. Look, now we're out this way, we could pop into East Knoll instead ... pay Blanche Black a visit."

"I thought she died years ago."

"Not as far as I know." He paused. "Well, I suppose it's *possible,* but I haven't heard anything from my contacts. She was a pleasure to do business with. Very decisive lady."

"The gardens at Barque House are worth a visit, I suppose."

"In October?"

"Maybe not. How long is it since you've seen her?"

"Ooh ... let me see," he said drumming his fingers on the steering wheel. "Twenty years?"

"She might not remember you."

"She will. Blanche never forgets anyone."

"Now I think about it, she can't have died. We still get Christmas cards," she said.

"There you are, then. Let's do it, Isobel. You know how much old ladies love visitors, especially when they can't get out."

"You don't know she can't get out."

"She's nearly ninety."

"Olivia de Havilland is a hundred and one. I saw a piece in the paper the other day about her wanting to sue some TV company for misrepresenting her in a docudrama ... *she* can get out."

"Now you're being silly."

"Just making a point," she said. He gave her a hard stare. "Anyway, I want to go out tonight. After the petrol/diesel fiasco you're treating me to dinner at Roman Reach."

"I thought we were eating at Pippa's," he said.

"We were but she won't mind. We'll all go. I'll text her now."

It was misty in East Knoll, the sky an unremitting grey as Helena, Isla and Naomi strolled through the town on their way to Barque House. A weak sun was trying to penetrate the gloom but like light behind frosted glass it was too diffuse to have much effect; brittle leaves rustled as they passed under the maples lining the deserted road and then dropped in silent swirls. "Autumn's really here now," Isla said.

"I love autumn," Naomi said. "Hallowe'en, Bonfire Night and then it's Christmas."

"Do you think we'll have Christmas in Barque House?" Isla said.

"Only if we can find Mary Glebe," Helena said. She was the first to reach the stone steps leading up to the front door and the first to cross the threshold. "How shall we do this?" she said.

"We need to have a good look round, get a feel for the place, see if it would work and how much we'd have to clear out," Isla said.

"Let's start at the top and work our way down," Naomi said.

"Right, but then we must look in your desk," Helena said. "The sooner we find the address book the better."

"I haven't forgotten. If we take a drawer each it won't take long. I'll feel better with you helping."

"Better?" Isla said.

"She has a problem with prying in Blanche's desk," Helena said. "I told her it was what she wanted. She said so in the will."

"I know what you mean, Naomi. I feel a bit weird about the furniture."

Helena laughed. "You two are funny. I've told you, the house isn't haunted," she said.

"You deal with other people's cast-offs all the time," Naomi said. "You're used to it. It's different for us."

"I keep expecting her to appear in a doorway somewhere," Isla said.

"In a white coat with a syringe in her hand?" Naomi asked, a ghoulish grin accompanying the question.

"That's ridiculous," Helena said. "She hadn't worn that coat in years. Right, come on, up we go."

The first flight of stairs was wide, the mahogany bannisters like a bob sleigh run. Naomi wondered if, as a child, her grandmother had slid down them from top to bottom; had Blanche? She tried to conjure up Blanche as a child. She imagined her with plaited hair and button boots and then smiled as a vision of Moaning Myrtle sprang to mind.

The carpeted landing curved to the left and the right. "This way," Helena said. They took the right turn which led them straight to the window in which the brigantine was on show.

Walking in single file up the next flight of stairs, much narrower than the first, they arrived at a bright landing. There were five doors on this landing, all of them closed. Light was flooding in from a lantern light in the roof.

Naomi held back waiting for her mother to make the first move. "I've never been up here before," she said.

Helena took the first door on the right and peered in. "Nothing to see in here except for the water tank," she said and moved on to the next one. Isla followed her.

Naomi found a bathroom with a free-standing bath, its feet like the paws of a lion. The taps were brass, each one with a tiny bead of water shimmering at the end ready to drop. A turquoise stain ran down the white enamel which she thought was a sure sign the taps had been dripping for years.

The floor was covered in lino, dusty, dull green, cracked where it had been worn through years of use. A couple of striped towels were folded over a wooden stand by the wash basin into which a spider had fallen and never escaped. Its desiccated corpse lay curled on top of the plug. There was a wooden cabinet on the wall above, the mirrored doors closed. She slid one of them open; the shelves were empty apart from a yellow shaving mug. There were no cut-throat razors, no pills or potions, no antique tooth powder to sell on eBay. She slid the doors shut again and walked across to the tiny window, which over-looked rooftops and back yards enclosed by high walls, washing lines strung across them like tight-ropes, empty except for a few stray pegs; she noticed a chocolate wrapper flapping behind a lamp-post like a fly caught in a web, a cat slinking along the top of one of the walls. She watched as it jumped down onto the pavement and padded on. Her eyes lingered on its stealthy steps until it disappeared around the corner. She turned to explore elsewhere and met Isla coming out of another room. "It's great up here," she said.

"This must have been the servants' quarters," Isla said.

"Blanche didn't have servants," Naomi said. "Only the cleaner."

"Harold and Maud will have done. A cook at least and a maid to do the cleaning, a housekeeper … maybe even a butler."

Helena emerged from the room opposite "Have you seen enough?" she asked.

"The beds will have to go," Isla said.

"Iron bedsteads aren't the most comfortable," Helena said.

"The springs looked evil," Isla said. "There's a good view out to sea from the one I've just been in and two wardrobes."

"There were two wardrobes in here, too," Helena said.

"The ones in there were full of mothballs and hangers, no clothes," Isla said.

"I love this bath," Naomi said. "Come and see."

They all trouped into the little bathroom. Isla ran a finger over the basin and frowned at the spider. "It could do with a clean-up."

"It's not an operating theatre," Naomi said. "It's got character. I love it. Can I have this floor? The ceilings are lower and the rooms smaller. I like the idea of being on top of the world," she said gazing across the rooftops again.

"You could certainly use the wardrobes," Helena said. "Most of your clothes are on the floor at home."

"With mothballs? I don't think so," Naomi said.

"We could sell them and buy new," Isla said. "We'll have to ditch a lot of the furniture."

"Let's not get ahead of ourselves," Helena said. "We haven't seen the rest of it, yet. Downstairs, girls."

The rooms on the first floor were large, high-ceilinged and as grand as the main staircase with their adjoining dressing rooms and ornate fireplaces. There were washbasins in all the rooms.

"I'm thinking en-suites," Helena said as they re-grouped on the landing. "The plumbing's already done."

"Could be lead piping," Isla said. "It will cost a lot to replace that."

"We'll have to check."

"The bathroom needs doing," Naomi said.

"We wouldn't have to make all the rooms en-suite," Isla said. "If we get the bathroom modernised that will do for a start. I'd be happy up here," she added. "There's so much space."

"Let's explore the ground floor, now," Naomi said as she galloped down the stairs in front of the others.

The kitchen was first. Unlike the rest of the house, it was ultra-modern with floor to ceiling stainless steel units. "When was this done?" Isla said. "It's amazing." She stroked the brushed steel of the fridge freezer as her gaze took in the rest of the room.

"A couple of years ago," Helena said. "The washing machine flooded and ruined the floor. The insurance paid out. Blanche decided she might as well have the whole room refurbished. It still had the original fittings in here; I don't know how she managed with it for so long. There were no worktops to speak of, just a wooden table, the old range cooker a couple of cupboards and a stone sink. I think she was ready for an easier life."

"She loved the dishwasher," Naomi said. "Even though she refused to use it more than once a week."

"I'll make the coffee," Helena said. "Get the milk, would you, Nims. You did pick it up as we left …"

"It's right here," Naomi said producing a small carton from her bag.

"She certainly liked her stainless steel," Isla said as they sat sipping from botanical mugs.

"It's quite clinical, that's probably why," Helena said. "I

think she would have been a doctor like Harold if she'd had the chance."

"Why didn't she do it?" Naomi said.

"I'm not sure. No-one ever commented on it, not while I was there, anyway. Perhaps she was expected to stay at home, look after her parents," Helena said. "She admired you, Isla. She was always saying how proud she was that you were a GP like her dad. That's why she wanted you to have the furniture."

"I should have visited more."

"She didn't hold that against you. She was happy with her own company."

"She told me some great stories," Naomi said. "But Mum's right. She did seem happy on her own. I felt guilty for only popping in for an hour or so each day, but she was insistent it was enough, all she needed."

"Apart from radio four and a good book," Helena said with a wistful smile. "She was always saying that."

"Are you sure she wasn't lonely?" Isla said.

"Absolutely, she knew you were busy with work," Helena said. "She didn't expect anyone to visit."

"I could have made the time."

"Blanche was content. You saw her at Christmas."

"I know, but …"

"She would have said 'but me no buts' come on, drink up. I want to do more exploring," Naomi said rinsing her mug under the tap and heading for the hall.

"You must have seen it all before," Helena said.

"I haven't. She didn't suggest I did the grand tour and I didn't ask."

"No, you tended not to ask Blanche for favours. Right, well, we all know the sitting room, so we can leave that for now; this way," Helena said opening a door that revealed a couple of stairs leading down to a passageway with a bell box still in situ high up on the wall. She opened the door on a windowless room and flicked on the light to reveal a butler's sink and wooden draining board surrounded by shelves of vases, earthenware pots and galvanised buckets. "The flower room," she said as they huddled in the doorway to take in the vast array on show.

"Awesome," Naomi said stepping nearer the pots to get a better look.

"There must be hundreds of vases in here," Isla said.

Helena flicked off the light and shepherded them out. "We haven't come to catalogue vases," she said moving on to throw open the next door. "This was the original scullery before Blanche had it turned into her study."

"It's quite small," Isla said.

"She had loads of books," Naomi said. "Do you think she read them all?"

"Probably," Isla said as she gravitated towards a microscope sitting on a side table surrounded by a muddle of papers. She crouched down to look through the eye-piece. "This must be at least a hundred years old."

"I wish I'd seen the house when they first moved in," Naomi said.

"Times have changed a lot since then," Helena said. She opened yet another door to reveal a downstairs toilet. "This is plenty big enough for a shower cubicle," she said and then pulled a face at the high cistern and quarry-tiled floor. "No carpet and that window doesn't fit properly. It was always draughty in here ... oh dear, there's such a lot to do."

"It doesn't all have to be done at once," Isla said.

She closed the door as Naomi opened the last one. "I've been in here before," she said walking across the coffee-coloured carpet to sit on the window seat over-looking the back garden.

The walls were covered in dated floral wallpaper which matched the curtains; there were two Ercol chairs by the fireplace, a small table laid with a white cloth and a silver cruet. Behind the door was the walnut desk.

"I like this room," Helena said. "It's bright and homely. Maud spent a lot of time reading by the window. I can see her now," she added. "As children, we were always brought in here. Children weren't allowed in the front room."

"Why not?" Naomi asked.

"It was the best room, kept for important visitors and grown-ups, not children with sticky fingers and clumsy feet. There were too many ornaments that might have been knocked over and the piano of course; that piano was Maud's pride and joy. No-one else was allowed near it. I was here once when the piano tuner called. She was on pins until he left."

"I never heard her play," Isla said.

"I did," Naomi said. "One Christmas, when I was very small."

"That was their last Christmas," Helena said. "It was as if the piano was part of her; the music flowed effortlessly."

"I'm surprised Blanche didn't learn to play," Isla said.

"She wasn't musical, neither was my mum. You two weren't interested either."

"I played the recorder," Naomi said.

"Dad wanted me to learn the violin," Isla said. "You should have heard me."

"We did," Naomi said. "You were awful."

Helena's eyes bored into her daughter's. "Naomi," she said.

"She's right, I was."

"Well, anyway, what do we think now we've seen everything, will it work as three separate floors?"

"We'll have to share the kitchen," Isla said.

"But we'll have our own bathrooms," Naomi said.

"We can still eat together like we do now, but we don't have to," Helena said.

"No, we can have our own breakfast bars, you know, like they do in hotels, a kettle, small fridge," Isla said.

"A mini bar?" Naomi said.

"Whatever, that's the charm of this place. There's room to do anything we like," Helena said.

"We do need to up-date the bathrooms," Isla said.

"I don't want mine changed," Naomi said. "I love that bath."

"*Your* bathroom?" Helena said. "It sounds like you've decided."

"I have," Naomi said.

"You both want to do this?"

"I do," Naomi said.

"Me, too," Isla said as they fist pumped.

"Good. It feels, I don't know, right, somehow. I'm sure we'll be happy here but now we need to find Mary Glebe."

Naomi moved across to the tapestry stool. "The desk's under here," she said removing the shawl which she had re-placed reverentially after her last visit. "I'll take the top drawer. You two help yourselves."

CHAPTER 11

Ivy Ellison creaked her way to the One-stop shop to fetch the paper as she did every morning, weather permitting. She stopped to catch her breath and sniffed the air. The days were getting shorter. Winter was on its way. She sighed and took a few more steps. As the air cooled, leaves would plummet in droves, she told herself, blocking drains and turning pavements into trip magnets; when frost marled the roof tops she would not want to be out and about so much, even with her stick. Still, she had been for her flu' jab a few weeks before and so she hoped she wouldn't have trouble with her chest this coming winter and that, she told herself, was one blessing at least. If she had a bad chest like her friend Judy, her life would be very different

She wondered how Edith was coping up in Cumbria, all alone. She would feel better when Isobel and Adrian went back to check on her. She knew Edith would not tell them if she didn't feel too clever. She did not want to be a burden. None of them wanted to be a burden. Old age was the burden.

She tutted impatiently as her stick caught a crack in the pavement and made her wobble, jarring her bad hip and knee; she winced, yanked it free and approached the little parade of shops thinking how difficult it must be for Isobel and Adrian with their children and granddaughter in Linchester and Edith at home in Cumbria. At least Judy had family nearby. She reckoned Isobel must be in a constant two and eight as to who needed her most, her mother or her daughter; no-one could blame them for wanting a break every now and then but was it really a break?

She stepped over the threshold of the shop and made her way to the newspapers. "Morning Mrs. Ellison."

Jericho Brown was the name above the shop door; Jerry she

called him, as did everyone else. She reckoned he was one of the good guys. He seemed genuinely pleased to see her each day, which she found flattering considering he must be at least forty years her junior and a handsome man with a muscular physique and smouldering eyes. He had, she thought, a definite look of Omar Sharif. When an Asian family had taken over the One-stop, eyebrows had been raised locally but she was pleased with the change. They had altered everything about the shop, from the opening hours to the wider range of products.

It wasn't just the re-decoration and re-organisation of the shelving system. There was now a photo-copier for the use of customers. They were happy to deliver small orders and Jerry was keen to chat, which set him poles apart from the monosyllabic Elias Strange who had managed the shop before him. Strange by name and strange by nature she had always said. Of all the managers she had known, Elias Strange was the oddest. No-one had become close to him. She had known he was not married and rumour had it he shared his home with seven cats, but that was about it. He gave away nothing, opened the shop at six every morning and shut it promptly at six every evening despite protestations from the customers. They complained about it no longer being a convenience store. They had been used to popping in at all hours to replenish cupboards or to buy cigarettes. It was no bad thing that Elias Strange had made this more difficult and it hadn't inconvenienced Ivy, however, she could see their point.

Jerry Brown was the exact opposite. She knew all about his family. She knew that Jerry's father had changed his name to Brown by deed poll when he met his Irish mother in Slough. She knew they had fallen in love and run away to get married and that Jerry had met his wife, Mina, when he was on holiday in Pakistan re-connecting with his estranged family. Theirs had been, according to what she had been told, an all singing, all dancing traditional wedding.

They had four children who were doing well at school … well, three of them were. The youngest was about to start the nursery class; if the others were anything to go by, she reckoned Ed would do well, too. He had the dark eyes and charisma of his father, destined to be a heartbreaker, she reckoned. Jerry worked all the hours God sent to make sure they had everything they needed. As before, the shop was open by six every morning, but now it stayed open until eleven at night. She often wondered when Jerry had time to sleep.

The oldest boy, Dev, worked behind the counter on a Saturday. Mina and the girls were not often in the shop, which was a shame because she loved to see Mina in her saris, the vibrant colours bringing sunshine into the shop and, she thought, a very elegant way to dress. She loved to see the little girls pirouetting around, blue-black ringlets tumbling down their backs, little brother in tow. They were so full of energy. She guessed he was still of an age when he was happy to let his sisters order him about, but she was certain it wouldn't be long before he started telling them what to do.

As well as being the backbone of the family, Mina managed the accounts and had master-minded the alterations. She was small, barely reaching Jerry's chest; a real little dynamo keeping everything running smoothly in the shop as well as at home. "Morning, how's Mina?" she said putting her paper on the counter.

"You've just missed her; she's fine, taken Ed to nursery."

"He's started already? Well, that's good. She'll be able to help you more in the shop."

"Indeed."

"Just the paper today, Jerry. No, what am I talking about?" she said turning away to search the shelves. "I was going to have peaches for my tea."

He put out a hand to stop her. "Let me get them for you," he said.

While he was gone, she took the opportunity to take the weight off her bad knee, which still ached after her wobble. He returned with the tin of peaches and rang up her shopping on the till. "Are you ok?" he said.

"Fit as a fiddle," she said trying to stand up straight. "I only have this stick because my daughter worries if I go out without it. It reminds me I'm not twenty-one, any more."

"We're all getting older, Mrs. Ellison, can't do much about that. It's the time of year for aches and pains and your daughter's right, there's nothing wrong with using a stick. It might prevent a bad fall. Mrs. Bailey had a bad fall, did you know? Her son told me when he came in to cancel her papers, said she'd be in hospital a while."

"Trina Bailey? I don't know how I missed that one. I must send a card. I won't be out so much when the cold weather kicks in. I haven't seen my friend Edith for ages, but what can you do? God didn't give me wings to fly over and visit her."

"I remember Edith. She lives up north somewhere."

She nodded. "Cumbria. She's on her own up there. Her daughter's down here visiting the family."

"Isobel … I met her yesterday. Phoebe came in with her to buy some milk."

"Phoebe is a darling."

"She knew what she wanted and how much to pay."

"She's only four but now she's at school I don't see her as much as I used to."

"Does she like it?"

"She loves it. It's that special school by the fire station. It's always a worry with special needs children. Pippa says they are really good with her."

"They're a nice family."

"The best and good neighbours. I've known Ian since he was a little boy."

"So, you know his brother, Mike."

"Oh yes."

"Mina thought we should ask him to quote for the new extension at the back."

"As far as I know he does a good job but he's not like Ian. Never has time for anything but work and those blessed fish. I always say Gaynor deserves a gold medal, living with him."

"Should I ask him for a quote?"

"He's fair, I'll give him that. His price will be reasonable."

"Ok, I'll get her to give him a call; do you need a bag?"

"No thanks," Ivy said flourishing a linen bag covered in a printed owl pattern. "It didn't take me long to get used to doing without plastic bags," she said as she packed her shopping away. "We always took bags when we did our shopping years ago. I don't know why we got out of the habit."

"Now we're saving the planet," he said with a grin.

"And a good thing too. See you tomorrow," she said and tapped her way out of the shop.

CHAPTER 12

"Go on then," Isla said. Naomi hesitated, eyeing up the desk as if it were a fractious child. She ran a finger over the wood, silky, nut brown, flawless.

"Just open it," Helena said.

She touched the simple brass handles, admired the chequered stringing on the front of the drawer and then slowly pulled it towards her. "Oh," she said with a disappointed sigh. "I didn't expect that."

"What is it?" Helena asked. "Something nasty?"

"More spiders," Isla said.

"No, it's just … well, look, there's hardly anything in here."

Helena and Isla peered over her shoulder. "Unbelievable," Helena said.

A few pencils rolled forwards as Naomi opened the drawer a little further, followed by a fountain pen and a wooden fan. She shut it again. "There's no address book."

Isla took one of the other drawers right out. "Nothing in this one," she said gazing at the empty drawer in her hands. "I thought it would have been stuffed full of all sorts."

"Nothing with Mary Glebe's name on it?" Helena said.

"Nothing at all, look."

Helena glanced at the drawer and then took hold of one, herself. "This one's full of newspaper cuttings," she said.

"Tip them out," Naomi said. "There might be a clue." She spread the paisley shawl over the carpet like a picnic blanket and her mother tipped out the drawer, giving the base a gentle tap to encourage the last few pieces out before sweeping her fingers through the cuttings as if panning for gold.

"Anything?" Naomi said.

Helena picked an article from the pile. '*Open Garden at Barque House*'," she read.

Isla checked through some of the others. "Most of them seem to be about the garden."

"It looks as if she kept every article the paper ever printed about it."

"I'll check the other drawers," Naomi said. She slid them back and forth in quick succession "Empty, empty and empty." She tried the top drawer for a second time. This time it refused to budge more than a crack. "There's something stuck in here, now," she said. "I must have disturbed it when I opened the drawer before. I didn't notice anything." She rattled the drawer up and down and then bent over to peer into the far corners. "Ah, I see it now." Using the fan as a lever she hooked out what had been hampering the free running of the drawer. "It's a tin," she said sliding the offending article towards her. "Devon Fudge," she added as she read the print on the lid.

"It will have gone off by now," Isla said.

Naomi removed a small package wrapped in greaseproof paper. "I don't think it's fudge."

"Be careful, it could be toxic," Helena said.

"It's not drugs, Mum." Naomi said as she passed the tin to Isla and unwrapped the package. "Hmm, it's a piece of cake," she said. "I'm guessing wedding cake. This is gross. The icing's gone all yellow. I hope she didn't expect me to eat it."

"Of course she didn't," Helena said a little impatiently.

"But the will stated that everything in the desk should be dealt with appropriately and this is cake," Naomi said cheekily.

Isla was examining the tin. "There's a little silver horseshoe in here," she said "And a note. '*Mary's cake and lucky horseshoe*'." She passed the note to Helena.

"This is Blanche's handwriting," she said. "We must be getting warm."

"It doesn't help much," Isla said. "No address on the note."

"Are you sure there wasn't anything else in the tin?"

Isla turned the tin upside down leaving the lid to flap about like a fledgling sparrow. "Yes, that's it."

"Throw it away, Nims. It's not worth keeping."

"I think I'll put it back in the drawer for now," Naomi said as she re-united the cake with the tin.

Helena shrugged. "If you like."

Isla had turned her attention back to the pile of cuttings. "There's one here about a wedding," she said. "This is odd. The groom's picture has been cut out."

"Why would she have done that?" Helena said as she scanned the words "Oooh I feel quite peculiar now." She sat down in a hurry.

"What is it?" Isla said.

"It says it's a picture of the recent Glebe wedding. The bride must be Mary."

They crowded round to catch their first glimpse of Mary Rose Glebe. "You can't really see what she looks like," Naomi said squinting at the blurry image of a young woman in a white dress and veil, long hair covering her shoulders. "Do you recognise her?"

Helena shook her head. "No... no I don't."

Naomi imagined the bride having produced a pretty smile for the camera, but her features were now unrecognisable and faded with time. "It's all smudged," she said as she tried to smooth out the creases where the cutting had been folded to fit in the drawer.

"Let me see," Isla said. "Oh dear, it's not a very good picture."

"This is no help at all," Helena said. "What we need is the address book."

"Well, it's not here," Naomi said.

"Where's the phone?" Isla asked. "She might have left it there."

"That would be logical," Helena said. "There's one in the hall and one by her bed. Go and check, Nims. This could have been so simple. Why did she have to add that stupid codicil?"

Isla shrugged. "Mary Glebe must have been important to her in some way. Perhaps an old friend, a nurse? Someone from the past, someone she at least took an interest in or she wouldn't have kept the cake or the cutting. Can you think of anyone, anyone at all?" Helena shook her head.

"No address book," Naomi said as she returned to join them. "But I did find this on her bedside table." She held up a small cloth-bound book that fitted into the palm of her hand.

"What is it?"

"A book of poems by Ella Wheeler Wilcox."

"Never heard of her."

"It looks quite old," Isla said. "Gilt-edged pages. It's been well-thumbed."

"It's not the address book, though, is it?" Helena said.

"Do you mind if I keep it?" Naomi said. "I'd like to read the poems."

"Oh, keep it if you like," Helena said a peevish frown creasing her brow. "I've had enough of this. Let's go home."

"Shall we take the cuttings with us?" Isla said. "There might be a clue in one of the others."

"I doubt it and anyway, I don't have the time to read them."

"I'll do it," she said. "You never know."

"I think I do. *Wild goose chase* springs to mind," she said. "But don't let me stop you, if you really want to do it."

"Was that the doorbell?" Isla said.

"I didn't hear anything," Helena said.

"I'm sure it was. I'll go and see."

"It's probably nothing," Naomi said as Isla brushed past her. "Blanche didn't have visitors."

"It could be the postman."

"I thought you'd informed everyone she'd died."

"There's always one, though, isn't there? When your father left I was still getting letters for him from the optician. It didn't matter how many times I told them he'd gone, the letters kept coming until I started sending them back and then they got the message; I was glad when we left and got our own place."

"It can't have been the postman, she's been ages."

"She'll be back in a minute."

"I've been meaning to ask you, Mum. Do you know who this baby is?" Naomi said removing the frame from the top of the desk to show her mother.

Helena shook her head. "I've never seen it before. It's not one of the family, it must be a friend's child or something. Here, put it back on the desk for now... nice frame."

"Yes, oh well, we can't expect to know everything about Blanche, can we?"

"It would be so much easier if we did. The only thing we need to know is the whereabouts of Mary Glebe."

"I saw Alf Minns yesterday. Do you think he knew about the codicil? He might know Mary Glebe."

"I doubt it. Blanche didn't discuss her private affairs with anyone, not even family."

"He said that."

"So, we just have to keep looking."

Naomi got down on her hands and knees to start a methodical search of the scraps of paper. Helena joined her reluctantly. "No, not this one, or this... that's a good picture of grandpa Harold," she said passing the article to Naomi.

"Oh yes, nice whiskers."

"He was proud of those."

"No mention of Mary Glebe, though. It doesn't count. Reject pile."

"This is going to take forever," Helena said. She sat back on her heels and sighed. "I didn't think this would be so hard."

"What do you mean, Mum?"

"All this, having to let go of stuff, having to allow strangers into our lives, sorting through Blanche's private affairs. What was she thinking?"

"We don't have to do this here. We can take the cuttings home like Isla said. If we don't find anything we'll ask Mr. Hampson to sort it out."

"It wouldn't matter where, when, or who does the looking, we'll never find her. We might as well give up now. It's a complete waste of time. I wish we'd never heard of Mary Glebe."

"I know, but we have to do this or lose Barque House; I'm not about to give up, we've only just started the search."

"I could do without all the extra hassle."

"It's boring, but we need to give it our best shot."

Helena's troubled expression gave way to a rueful smile "What would I do without you, Nims? You're right, of course."

"Isla's coming back."

"It sounds like she's talking to someone. Who can it be? I hope it's no-one important," she said standing up and glancing anxiously about the room. "Look at the mess we've made."

"Who do you class as important, Mum, the tidy up police?"

"Blanche didn't like mess," she said frantically attempting to gather up the cuttings.

"Blanche isn't here. Whoever it is, this is your house now. You can make as much mess as you like and no-one's going to care."

CHAPTER 13

Adrian and Isobel were finally on their way again. The car tank had been flushed out and refilled with diesel. "It didn't take as long as I thought," he said, a conciliatory smile flirting with his lips.

"It's no good smiling at me like that," Isobel said steely-eyed. "It wouldn't have taken any time at all if you'd been more careful. You should get some Ginkgo biloba tablets. They're supposed to be good for improving the memory."

"The only thing wrong with my memory begins with an 'I' and ends in an 'l'," he said. Isobel maintained a dignified silence as he parked the car and they got out. "Anyway," he went on "We're here now, just a short walk to the house."

"I hope she's at home," Isobel said ten minutes later. "These boots are killing me. I wasn't expecting to walk this far. Why did you park so far out?"

"Sorry about that. I didn't know they'd pedestrianised the town centre or I could have parked nearer. It was getting snarled up in the one-way system that muddled me. Let's find out if she's here, shall we?" He took the two steps up to the door, pressed the bell and then retreated to the pavement. They heard its shrill ring echoing throughout the house and faced the door in anticipation.

As they waited, Isobel stepped back to amuse herself by staring at the frontage of Barque House; at the sash windows, curved heads picked out in stone and then at the quoined corners. "I've never appreciated the symmetry of this building," she said. "I should have brought my sketch book."

"We can buy one. I'm sure Alf Minns will stock notebooks."

"Alf Minns, that name takes me back. I expect he's retired now. He must be over eighty."

"We can ask Blanche, she'll know. I seem to remember they were great friends."

"Ring the bell again, darling. Press harder this time."

Adrian stepped up to press the bell again just as the door opened and Isla Ford peered out. "Can I help you?" she said.

"Goodness, it's Dr Ford," Isobel said joining Adrian on the threshold. "I didn't expect to see you here."

"I'm sorry," Isla said pushing her glasses closer to her eyes and peering at Isobel more intently. "Do I know you?"

"It's Isobel Flynn, Pippa's mother, Pippa Chisholm."

"Oh yes, sorry Isobel."

"I don't think you've met my husband, Adrian. Adrian, Isla Ford."

"Good to meet you, doctor," he said.

"Is Blanche ill?"

"No but..."

"We were passing and thought we'd pop in to see her but if it's inconvenient ..." Adrian said.

"You're here to see her?"

"Yes, if that's all right. May we come in?"

Isla stared at the floor for a moment. "Um, well, I suppose so, it's just that, no... look, we're all in the breakfast room, Helena will explain," she said as she stood aside to let them pass. She closed the door and then beckoned for them to follow her. "This way."

"Who's Helena?" Isobel murmured in Adrian's ear as their feet sank silently into the crimson carpet.

"Search me," he said quietly.

"Something's up."

"Like what?" he whispered but Isobel did not have time to reply.

"In here," Isla said ushering them into the breakfast room. As the door opened, Naomi scrambled to her feet to join her mother. "We have visitors, Isobel and Adrian Flynn. They've come to see Blanche."

Helena picked her way through the cuttings like Bambi picking his way through the thicket. "Sorry about the mess. Blanche isn't here," she said. "I'm her niece, Helena Henry. This is my daughter, Naomi," she said taking Naomi's arm "And my niece, Isla," she added, drawing Isla into the circle.

"We know Isla," Adrian said.

"She's our daughter's GP," Isobel said.

"Your daughter?"

"Pippa Chisholm," Adrian said.

"Oh yes, McFarlanes."

"Isla loves the auctions," Naomi said.

"Won't you sit down?" Helena said.

"Has Blanche gone into a nursing home?" Isobel asked as she settled on one of the chairs.

"No, I'm afraid she died a few weeks ago."

"Oh no... we had no idea," she said. "I'm so sorry. We wouldn't have bothered you if we'd known."

"We would have come to the funeral if we'd known," Adrian said. He folded his lips in a disapproving fashion as he took the seat next to his wife and rested his left ankle over his right knee in a cavalier fashion.

"We tried to inform as many people as possible, but it's been difficult, we've mislaid her address book. We put a notice in *The Recorder*."

"She only wanted a small funeral," Naomi said.

"Wasting money on a big funeral was a definite no-no for Blanche. She was very careful with her money," Helena said.

"I know how she liked to operate," Adrian said. "I managed her financial affairs for years until we moved up to Cumbria."

"Now I remember. I'm sorry I seemed so vague before. Blanche called you 'young Adrian'," Helena said. "She was always singing your praises."

"I liked Blanche very much. She was quite a character."

"That's one way of putting it," she said. "Her will is causing us no end of trouble."

"Oh dear… can I help?" he said.

"Not unless you know Mary Glebe," Naomi said.

"Blanche left me the house," Helena explained. "But I can't inherit until I've had tea at Roman Reach Country Club with someone called Mary Glebe."

"We don't know her," Isla said. "We're having trouble tracking her down."

"We've found a newspaper cutting about her wedding, but we don't know where she is now," Naomi said.

"Or even if she's still alive," Isla said.

"How extraordinary," Isobel said.

"She might have died," Helena said. "We didn't think of that, did we? I wonder where that would leave me."

"Don't," Naomi said.

"No, we have to presume she's still alive," Isla said.

"They have a good selection of real ales at Roman Reach," Adrian said. "We're eating there tonight."

"Do you know Mary Glebe?" Naomi persisted. "Did she ever mention her to you?"

Adrian shook his head. "Isobel?"

"Why would she mention her to me?" she said.

"I meant, had you heard of her," he said tetchily. "I still have some of my old files. I could look through them when I get home, if you like; see if there's any reference to her."

"That would be great. We just need a clue as to where she might be," Helena said. "If you find something, anything that might help us find her, could you let Guy Hampson know?"

"He's the solicitor," Isla said.

"Yes, we know Guy," Isobel said.

"We know *of* him," Adrian said. "Our son, Tim, he's a solicitor in Linchester, he's mentioned him."

"Well, we mustn't hold you up," Isobel said as she got to her feet.

"I'll see you out," Isla said.

"Thank you for coming," Helena said. "It's nice to know Blanche had friends."

Adrian nodded "Indeed she did; friends and admirers."

"That could be a clue to Mary Glebe," Naomi said.

"Was there anyone who stood out?" Helena asked.

"Not as far as I know but I don't know why not. I always thought of Blanche as a handsome woman, rather Spanish-looking with all that dark hair," he said.

"My husband has always admired handsome women," Isobel said. She lowered her eyes and patted her plentiful hair in a self-congratulatory fashion.

"And why not?" he retorted. "There's nothing wrong with admiring handsome women. Blanche wasn't known for encouraging men though, kept them all at arm's length, kept most people at arm's length."

"Including us," Helena said. "It's quite shaming that we know so little about her."

"She didn't suffer fools gladly," Adrian said. "You tended not to cross her if you wanted a quiet life, but she had a good brain, could have done much more if she hadn't been so devoted to her parents."

"I've often wondered about that," Isla said. "They didn't want her to leave, was that it? As the younger sister, she was expected to stay at home and look after them?"

"No, it wasn't like that at all. *She* didn't want to leave *them*. She told me her father had tried to persuade her to go away to university but she didn't want that. He reckoned she would have made a fine diagnostician, but it wasn't how she saw her future. She thought she could learn more from him, carry on his research and so she stayed at Barque House."

"I can remember her working with him on some of his research," Helena said.

"She told me loads of stories about the past," Naomi said. "Do you think she regretted her decision later, when they died, I mean that she hadn't trained as a doctor?"

"She didn't strike me as disappointed," he said. "Not unhappy with her lot at all, quite the opposite. She knew what she wanted in life. She certainly kept me on my toes."

"She made her wishes clear in her will, but why did she have to make it so complicated? This whole process is emotionally draining," Helena said.

"It must be," Isobel said. "You must want to get on with everything. We'll leave you to it. Come on Adrian," she added nudging him towards the door. "Good luck with the sorting out."

CHAPTER 14

Jake was down on the beach again that afternoon, he had visited the same spot every day hoping to bump into Naomi. Being so abruptly dismissed had left him bewildered and intrigued. He wanted to ask why she had left in such a hurry but there was more to it than that.

He had often seen her around in the old days, but she had never given him so much as a wave of acknowledgment. She must have known who he was but had obviously decided to have nothing to do with him due to all the gossip around at the time. He couldn't deny he had enjoyed being the centre of attention, then; being invited to all the parties, having his pick of the girls who had homed in on him like meteors to planet earth. All that had palled after Nicola. He wasn't sure why it was so important for him to explain himself to Naomi or why her opinion of him mattered so much. He had the option of saying nothing, of leaving her to think what she liked, but he couldn't. He wanted her to know the truth.

He was searching the tide-line in a lack-lustre fashion when he heard voices coming his way. A middle-aged couple were meandering along the beach, stopping every now and then to pick up shells, arguing as to whether she should collect so many. He was taken back to his childhood … to his mother searching the sand for shells with him in tow. She had spent hours on the beach with him when he was small. They had done everything together until she disappeared from his life.

On these shell-seeking trips he would take his big spade with the wooden handle; he remembered using it as a walking stick as he followed her, carrying the little plastic bucket decorated with Spiderman pictures into which she would place her finds and his. The shells had been all over the house in different guises. She had covered books with them, made shell pictures, cemented them into garden sculptures, onto plant pots. It had all happened so long ago ... and yet he could remember it as if it were yesterday. The couple were getting closer.

"We must bring Phoebe down here. She'd love all the different shapes," he heard the woman say.

"They're just shells, Isobel," the man said. "Bog standard, two-a-penny shells you'd find on any beach on the south coast."

"Don't be such a killjoy, darling," she said stashing her finds in her coat pocket. "I can explain to Phoebe that they were once the houses of living creatures. Look at this one," she said holding up a miniature spiral cone-shaped shell. "How cute is that? It could be a mini magician's hat."

"It's a common wentletrap."

"And this," she said ignoring his lukewarm response, pulling a piece of driftwood out of the sand. "You could really make something of this."

"A fire?" he said.

Jake moved forward. "Do you mind if I take that?" he said. "It would be perfect for the leg of a deer I'm making."

"You're an artist," Isobel said, her eyes shining.

"Jake Hampson, sculptor," he said. "I use driftwood in some of my work ... and willow."

"That's brilliant. I'm Isobel Flynn," she said. "This is my husband, Adrian. I do a bit of painting."

"She's being too modest," Adrian said. "My wife is a well-known artist. Some of her work has sold for thousands at auction."

"Don't listen to him," Isobel said. "It was only *one* of my paintings. The others go for much less."

"I'm still trying to get my name out there," Jake said.

"You're local?"

"Yes, my studio's in my father's garage."

"Hampson, hmm, that wouldn't be Guy Hampson's garage by any chance?" Adrian said.

"Do you know him?"

"We've heard of him," Isobel said. "I'd like to see your work sometime."

"I was on my way there now. I can show you, if you like."

"We have to get back to Linchester," Adrian said.

"It won't matter if we take a little diversion," Isobel said. "I've been looking for something to add interest to the flower bed by the lounge window. Jake might have just what I need."

"What about a flowering shrub?" Adrian said

Isobel gave him a withering glance and took Jake's elbow to encourage him along the beach in front of her husband. "Now, tell me all about these sculptures…"

"I don't think we're ever going to find her," Helena said as they traipsed down the steps of Barque House. "So far we only have the wedding cake and a pile of newspaper cuttings."

"It's a start," Naomi said.

"And we know she's married," Isla added.

Helena did not want to see the positives. "She could be divorced by now," she said.

"Don't make things worse," Isla said. "She certainly had a wedding."

"We can start with that and work forward," Naomi said.

"It might help if we knew Glebe was her married name," Helena said.

"Why wouldn't it be?"

"Blanche might have known her before she was married. Mary might have kept her maiden name or reverted to it if she's divorced. Pippa Chisholm is still Flynn at work but Chisholm everywhere else," Isla said.

"Adrian Flynn might shed some light on it," Naomi said.

"I doubt it," Helena said.

"Why?"

"His involvement was years ago and he only dealt with investments."

"I've just had a thought," Naomi said. "The wedding photograph."

"What about it?"

"We could try *The Linchester Recorder*. They might have kept all the details."

"It will take forever sifting through loads of back-numbers. We don't know the year she was married, or even if she was married locally," Helena said.

"Surely her parents would have been local, or it wouldn't have been in *The Recorder*. We might find a relative who could lead us to her," Isla said.

"They could all be dead by now, or have moved away," Helena said.

"We can have a guess at the date from the style of the wedding dress," Isla said.

"Why did Blanche keep the cake?" Naomi said.

"Who knows. Nothing seems to add up. The cake's a complete red herring," Helena said. "She had probably forgotten it was there."

"Well, we have to do something, or you'll lose the house," Isla said.

"I don't think I'm up to trawling through back numbers of newspapers."

"You could just tell Guy Hampson to locate her," Naomi said.

"I don't know why we have to be responsible for finding Mary Glebe. He's the solicitor."

"He was trying to save us money."

"Or he didn't want to be bothered."

"I'm sure it's not that. He's never struck me as lazy."

"How well do you know him, Mum?"

"Well enough, for years… since before your father left. Why all the questions?"

"Just wondered, I um, I know his son, Jake."

"Oh yes, from years back. I've never met him."

"You don't want to."

"Why not?" Isla said.

"He's bad news," Naomi said.

"In what way?"

"Let's just say his opinion of himself is higher than his morals."

"Teenagers can go wild despite coming from a good home," Helena said. "You can't blame his father for that."

"Can't I?" Naomi said.

"What are you trying to say?"

"Oh… nothing."

"So, are we going to try our luck with *The Linchester Recorder*?" Isla said.

Helena sighed. "It will be like looking for a needle in a haystack."

"I'll do it," Naomi said. "On Monday. It will be my first job."

"You might not have to, if I find something else in these," Isla said tapping the bundle of cuttings sticking out of the top of her bag.

"Do you think I should tell Guy?" Helena said.

"Tell him what?" Isla said.

"That we might ask *The Recorder* to help locate Mary Glebe."

"I don't think you should have anything to do with him apart from the will business," Naomi said.

"This is will business," Helena said.

"You really don't like him, do you?" Isla said.

"She doesn't even know him," Helena said.

"I know his son and that's enough. Anyway, it's probably unethical for you to have a relationship with the executor of Blanche's will."

"Don't be silly, Naomi," Helena said, her colour rising. "I'm one of the beneficiaries. I must have some sort of relationship with him."

"I'm just saying you shouldn't encourage him."

Isla laughed. "You sound like Nana when she didn't want to hear any more of Grandad's jokes."

"Come on now, you're making more of this than there is," Helena said. "I'm not about to run off with him. It's not like that. He's just an old friend, that's all."

Isla thought Naomi looked as if she were about to say something else and then thought better of it. "Are we still going to Pizza Express? she said to lighten the atmosphere. "My treat."

"Oh yes," Naomi said. "Pizza, dough balls, Prosecco, will that cheer you up, Mum?"

"As long as no-one mentions Mary Rose Glebe."

"Done."

CHAPTER 15

Ivy's thoughts were turning towards her evening meal when the doorbell rang. She heaved herself out of her chair and went grumbling to open it. "Never a minute's peace," she muttered under her breath. "Who'd want to disturb me at this time of night? It can't be the window cleaner; he calls on a Wednesday... it's not Wednesday, is it?" she asked herself; after a moment's thought, she shook her head. "No, I'm sure it's not. It's Saturday, that's what it is. Saturday, hmm, the fish man? No, I remember now, he came last week. People shouldn't call when other people are busy. Who is it?" she called as she reached the door.

"It's only me, Mrs. E."

"Oh right, just a minute, Ian," she said, her mood changing in a flash. She slipped the safety chain from its anchor, turned the key and beamed up at him as the door opened. "What can I do for you?"

"We were wondering if you could baby sit tonight."

"Depends what time. I haven't eaten yet."

"We'll throw in a meal. We had a roast last night. There's plenty of left-overs."

"In that case, I'm your woman," she said. "What time do you want me?"

"Half an hour? We're going out for a meal with Isobel and Adrian before they go home."

"Half an hour will be fine. Are they going back up north tomorrow?"

"That's the plan," he said.

"I expect Edith will be pleased to have them home again, I know she's missed them."

"Well, they'll be back soon. We'll put Phoebe to bed before we go."

"You don't have to," she said.

"She's worn out. Pippa's just run her a bath."

"Don't worry if she gets up again. I won't mind."

"You're a star, Ivy. Thanks. See you later."

She closed the door on him and padded back down the hall. "Phoebe's the star, not me," she said to Hiawatha as she patted the wooden statue on its prominent nose. "A real little star. I wish Edith could see how she's come on since she started school. At least she'll see her over Christmas." She nodded to herself. "She'll notice a big change in her by then."

The dining room at the Roman Reach Country Club was deserted until the Chisholm/Flynn party arrived. "Did we ever tell you about Blanche?" Isobel said as she tucked into her starter.

"No … I wish I'd had the asparagus like you, Mum. These portions are minute," Pippa said placing the last tiny square of toast thinly spread with duck pate, in her mouth.

"I thought Nouvelle Cuisine had had its day," Adrian said. "At least they still serve real ales."

Ian caught a glimpse of their table in one of the ornate mirrors adding another dimension to the room but also reflecting the dearth of diners. His eyes lingered on his wife, on her auburn hair, on her mother whose hair was only a little less vibrant and felt a surge of emotion, of gratitude for their unconditional love, so different from his relationship with his brother which always seemed to be fraught with difficulties and a constant battle. At that moment he was content, at one with the world. "Where is everyone?" he asked.

"It's early; it will probably fill up soon."

"So, Blanche …"

"Yes, sorry Mum. No, you didn't. Who is she?" Pippa said.

"One of my old clients," Adrian said. "A real character, lived all her life in East Knoll."

"So, she's died."

"Yes, but she left your doctor with a problem."

"Isla Ford, what's she got to do with it? Has she been left a fortune? I hope she's not about to give up her practice, she's a great GP."

"Isla Ford is her great-niece," Isobel said.

"We don't know if she'll inherit a fortune but Mum's wrong. It's not Isla's problem, it's her aunt who has the problem, Helena Henry, Blanche's niece. She can't inherit the house until she's found someone called Mary Glebe," Adrian said.

"I'm glad there wasn't a problem like that when my mum died," Ian said. "No arguments from Mike, thank goodness, it was all very straightforward."

"We thought you might know her, sweetie," Isobel said. "You're always in and out of people's houses valuing things for the auction."

"I don't think I've come across any Glebes. I don't often go over to East Knoll."

"Well, if you do remember something, tell Dad and he'll pass it on."

"Or tell Isla Ford," Adrian said. "I've promised to look through the old files. There might be a mention of her in there."

"Can't the solicitor trace her?" Ian said.

"I'm sure he could but it will mean another few hundred on the bill," Adrian said.

"Mike could tell you a thing or two about solicitors and their charges," Ian said. "He's just had trouble with a piece of land he wanted to buy, an old MOD site. From what Gaynor said he's been bombarding the solicitor with emails about the bill they sent him. He nearly hit the roof last week when he found out the land had contamination issues and he'd just signed the contract."

"He's not changed, then," Adrian said.

"I don't think he ever will," Ian said. "Not now."

"He might know Mary Glebe," Isobel said. "Why don't you ask him?"

"I'll have to pick my moment, wait until he's in a good mood or he'll jump down my throat. Gaynor's more likely to know her."

"Yes, Gaynor's a good shout," Adrian said. "And she knows how to handle your brother."

"She should by now," Isobel said. "They've been married nearly thirty years."

"I admire Gaynor," Adrian said. "She knows what to say and when to say it; doesn't rattle on about nothing," he added giving his wife a meaningful glance.

She chose to ignore him. "She's had plenty of practice," she said. "And she's a very patient person, good at pouring oil on troubled waters."

"Perhaps we should send her over to Brussels," he said.

Pippa giggled. "I know who you shouldn't send."

"Mike?" Isobel said.

"Too right."

"He was all for getting us out of the EU and now we are, he can't stop crowing about it," Ian said.

"It's not going to be as easy as everyone thought," Adrian said. "The financial implications are problematic for a start…"

"Boring," Isobel said.

"So, what else did you do today?" Pippa said.

"We met a sculptor on the beach. He makes models from

driftwood and willow. I've commissioned two sheep for the garden," she said.

"I thought you had trouble keeping sheep *out* of the garden," Ian said.

"We do. They trample all over the flower-beds and annoy the dogs," she said. "But I like sheep. They're part of the natural order of things up there. Now I'll be able to have sheep in the garden and know they won't be eating my flowers or getting the dogs over-excited."

"Sounds like a win, win," Ian said.

"I'd prefer real ones," Adrian said. "And then I wouldn't have to cut the grass."

Pippa giggled. "You could set up a cottage industry. School House Wool ..."

"Authentic Cumbrian knits," Ian added.

"I know who'd end up shearing them," Adrian said, his expression grim. "On balance, I think I'll settle for the driftwood alternative."

CHAPTER 16

As Guy passed the garage on his way to work on Monday morning, he was surprised to find Jake already hard at work fashioning ghoulish pumpkins from willow. There was a line of spiders in all shapes and sizes on a shelf behind him, a couple of broomsticks he had seen before, curled up driftwood cats with sleepy eyes and raffia whiskers and some others, backs arched, wide-eyed, challenging. There was a queue of willow bats on top of an old filing cabinet next to a laundry basket full of driftwood topped with witches' hats; the hats had been left to hang there while the paint dried to a dull black finish. "These are fantastic, Jake. You're bound to do well," he said.

"I think I need more, more broomsticks anyway."

"What's this?" Guy said holding up a terracotta pot. In it was what looked like a cabbage-shaped flower with tentacle leaves.

"Audrey two."

"Sorry?"

"The man-eating flower from *The Little Shop of Horrors*. I need to make more of those as well. I bought a job lot of flowerpots from a car boot sale a while ago. I knew they'd be good for something one day."

Guy picked up the pot and turned it round. "Oh yes, I see it now. The kids will love them."

"I should really organise some advertising."

"Did you print off the flyers?"

"Last night."

"Give me some. I'll pass them around for you."

Jake walked across to the filing cabinet "I've left all of this a bit late." The bottom drawer wouldn't budge. He banged the top of the cabinet with one hand and yanked the bottom drawer again. It rolled out slowly with a rusty screech and ground to a halt at his feet. "How many do you want?"

"Half a dozen for now."

He counted six from the pile, slotted the rest back into the drawer, kicked it shut and handed them over to his father. "Thanks."

"It's the least I can do; maybe you should have an 'open garage' event," Guy said. "I wouldn't mind."

"Maybe when the craft fair is over."

"Elsa might help, her dog is on his last legs, she could do with something to take her mind off the inevitable."

"I know how much he means to her."

"She's had him all her life… we could have refreshments," he went on ruminatively. "Music..."

"Not your banjo."

"What's so bad about my banjo?"

"What's good about it? Sorry, Dad, I really don't have time to think about that now."

"Okay… will you still be here when I get back?"

"I doubt it."

Guy wished he could do more to help. Half a dozen flyers seemed a bit pathetic. Emma would have known what to do, what to say, what words of encouragement would have been appropriate. "Right, well, I'll let you get on."

Jake smiled briefly and returned to the pumpkins while Guy went on his way thinking about his wife. He wanted to talk about her, wanted to involve her in their relationship, she had been shut out for too long; the problem was that he did not know how to initiate the conversation. So much time had passed. It had to be done right; it wasn't something you could slot into normal conversation. *How was your day, Jake, let's talk about Mum...* wouldn't do it; *fancy a beer later? Mum enjoyed a gin and tonic...* nor that. *Sit down, son, let's talk about Mum...* a definite no-no.

Appearing in court, writing letters to and for clients was his stock in trade; he was good with words he told himself, it should have been easy, but he found it such a difficult subject to broach that he wondered if he would ever manage to tell his son what he needed to know.

Naomi drove to Linchester in her mother's car. She parked in the market street car park remembering, as she always did when she was down that end of town, the story of Jem Hythe.

Linchester's most famous ghost was rumoured to haunt the building in which *The Linchester Recorder* offices were situated. It had been a coaching inn with multiple rooms and chimneys at that time, but now centrally heated open-plan offices filled the interior. The magnificent façade and the chimneys were intact, renovated and upgraded in accordance with the correct regulations and approved by both planners and local worthies without too many heated council discussions or letters to the paper; a small miracle considering wrangling in the past over the colour some Lincestrians had chosen to paint their listed properties.

Naomi reminded herself of how she had first heard of Jem Hythe during a ghost tour of the town she and Holly had made years before. They had been told that one cold November day in Victorian times with an east wind blowing in from the Downs, Jem had been waiting to shin up the chimneys to perform their annual sweep. The hotel owner, having discovered it was his birthday, had taken pity on the boy and had plied him with hot pies while his master enjoyed a pint of ale in the tap room with the ostlers. This impromptu feast had been the author of Jem's misfortunes. Half-way up one of the chimneys he had become wedged. He couldn't move up; he couldn't move down.

His master had no option but to starve him until he was thin enough to ease his way out again, but weak with hunger he had slipped on the way down and fallen to his death. It was said that his wails could be heard throughout the building every year on the anniversary of this tragic event.

Holly had maintained the wailing was due to the wind whining down the old chimneys and not to Jem's ghostly cries; Naomi had half-heartedly agreed, but the story had made an impression on them both. It had encouraged them to buy tickets for the ghost tour the following week, taking in the most haunted places for a second time and scaring themselves silly into the bargain; that delicious sense of scariness they knew deep down was just hysterical nonsense.

With memories flooding back, she walked through the entrance doors and headed for the reception desk directly opposite; she could detect no sign of supernatural activity but there was someone waiting there talking to the young man on duty. It was an old lady in a patchwork coat and purple trainers accompanied by a Mackenzie tartan shopping trolley on which she was leaning heavily. Naomi could hear their conversation quite clearly. "You like iced buns, don't you, Carl?" the old lady said.

"Love them. Thanks, Gran," he said accepting the paper bag she was offering him.

"I know I shouldn't disturb you at work but I got the bus down to see Judie. I was only a step away, it seemed silly not to pop in."

"I'll have it with my coffee," he said.

Naomi held back, not wanting to intrude, but at that moment Ivy Ellison turned around and saw her. "I won't be long, love," she said and then turned back to her grandson. "I'd better go now you've got a customer," she said in a loud stage whisper. "See you at the weekend?"

"I don't know."

"I could do with a hand in the garden."

"I thought you had a gardener now."

"He's worse than useless. 'Trim that bush,' I say and what does he do? Just tickles it round the edges … only if you're not too busy, Carl," she said.

"Where's your stick? Mum will go mad if she knows you've been out without it."

"I don't need it. I've got my trolley," she said taking the handle of her tartan trolley in a firmer grip. "Bye, then… he's all yours, love," she said turning to Naomi before meandering back to the noise and bustle of the town, pushing the trolley in front of her like a Zimmer frame.

Naomi watched her go and then moved forward.

"Can I help?" he said.

She was thinking, early twenties, pale cheeks as if he only strayed from the computer to re-stock his snack supply, eyes a watery green. His neck was scrawny, magnifying the significant Adam's apple protruding from the collar of his open-necked shirt, his mouth meagre, lips stretched over his teeth like glue on the back of an envelope. His one redeeming feature was the blonde hair which parted in the middle and cascaded over his shoulders to give him, she thought, the cute appeal of a Skye terrier. "I don't know if you can," she said.

The pale turned to pink. "Try me," he said.

She pulled the newspaper cutting from her pocket and handed it to him. "I'm trying to trace the bride in this picture."

"This isn't a recent one," he said.

"No … late seventies?"

"We don't keep any of the back numbers here, I'm afraid. They're all at head office. Sorry."

She took back the cutting. "Oh well, never mind, I knew it was a long shot. Thanks anyway."

"You want to find the bride, yeah?"

"I do."

"Is this the only information you have?"

"Well, apart from a piece of the wedding cake."

He smiled politely. "I don't think we could do much with that. You don't have her name?"

"Yes, sorry. We do know her name, it's in the article, Mary Rose Glebe. We don't know where she is now. That's the problem."

"We could print the photo and add a caption asking for anyone who knows the bride to contact us, if that would help."

"Brilliant… when would it go in?"

"If I take it now I could get it in this week's paper."

"Let's do it," she said and handed the cutting back to him.

"I'll need your details," he said.

"Could you send any replies to our solicitor?"

"No problem. There's a place on the form for replies."

She had just filled in the form and paid the necessary fee when the phone on his desk rang. She left him to answer it, mouthed a thank you and turned to go, hoping her mother would agree with her decision. It seemed the best way to pass on any Mary Glebe news without having more contact with Guy Hampson. She reckoned the less they had to do with him the better.

"Morning."

She looked up, startled to see Jake Hampson standing in front of her in chinos and a leather jacket, the slight hint of a beard glinting on his jaw. A sense of guilt at her uncharitable thoughts brought beads of moisture to her top lip. "What are you doing here?" she asked.

"It's a free country," he said and smiled.

For the first time, she appreciated his good looks and immediately told herself it would be better to move on without another word, but instead found herself asking him a question. "How's the work coming on?"

"I'm nearly ready for the craft fair. Are you on the way home?"

"Yes."

"I won't be long, I just need to drop in an advert. If you wait, I could give you a lift back."

"I've got Mum's car."

"Oh, well, perhaps we could meet up later at my studio."

"You mean your dad's garage."

"Yes."

"Why?" she said and immediately wished she hadn't. She didn't want him to think she was interested in his motives or in anything he might or might not be doing in his studio.

"I want to show you how I'm getting on with the driftwood."

"I don't know. I'm busy today," she said.

"This evening, then?"

His persistence intrigued her. She was curious to know why he was so desperate for them to meet again even though she had tried to create the impression of ambivalence. Surely there could be no harm in her checking out his work. Holly would expect her to suss him out. "Fine," she said; the word slipped out with ease. It was too late to retract it now, she had given in. She would have to go. She bit her lip and waited.

"Eight o'clock at the garage?"

She nodded.

"See you then."

As she walked back to the car she immediately regretted her moment of weakness. Why had she agreed to go? How could she have been so feeble? She knew what he was like. She didn't want to be associated with someone like him. Why hadn't she just walked away? It was true she was older and bolder now, not afraid of what he might do to her. The self-defence course she had taken at university had given her confidence; she could look after herself, cope with any unwanted advances should he be foolish enough to try something on, but even so... Holly would laugh when she told her. In the past, they had endlessly picked apart 'the Jake affair' and counted themselves lucky they had not succumbed to his charms.

There was something else. Something quite unexpected. It didn't matter how hard she tried to smother it, she felt a definite attraction towards him. It seemed perverse knowing what she did, the fact that he was vertically challenged and that she was determined not to like him.

She would be on her guard that evening. She had also made herself a promise that if her original opinion of him was confirmed, this would not only be the first, but also the last time she accepted an invitation from Jake Hampson.

Ivy took a taxi home from the bus station. It had been a long day. She was tired, but it had been a good day overall. Parking her shopping trolley in the hall next to Hiawatha, she shuffled off her trainers and tucked her toes into the waiting slippers. Days out were good, but coming home was better.

Judie was still on her mind. They had been friends since primary school and had grown up in a very different Linchester; in the days when, she reminded herself, a cattle market had been held in the town each week with all the attendant lowing, bleating and faunal odours. Buskers in those days had not plugged themselves into backing music, they had relied on the strength of their voices and the musical instruments they brought with them; violins, flutes and later, guitars, drums and maracas. It was a time when the sun did not always shine, but people seemed a whole lot happier than they were these days because, she reckoned, no-one had to worry about all that North Korea and Russian madness, or austerity or global warming or applying and paying for everything online. What had happened to 'never mind the quality feel the width? It was nigh on impossible to select good quality anything without seeing it, touching it, trying it out; such a hassle to send things back if they were not fit for purpose. Virtual shopping was not for her. To her mind a trip to the shops was much more satisfying than pressing buttons on a laptop.

She had been sad when Judie moved to East Knoll after her marriage to Keith, but they had stayed in regular contact ever since, taking it in turns to visit each other until Judie's chest prevented her from travelling further than her own front door. She found it difficult to see her dependent on oxygen. It was sad, but she was still the same old Judie underneath. Ivy smiled as she remembered the laugh they'd had at life and its doings. Time marched on whether you acknowledged it or not and pigtails turned into perms before you knew it.

She wished Edith lived nearer. If she could catch a bus up to Hardale and be back in time for tea, she would do it. They would be able to spend more time together, put the world to rights. They would not have been friends at all, had Ian not married Edith's granddaughter; she was glad they had married, she was glad Ian and Pippa still lived next door and she was glad to have found Edith's friendship so late in life when all hope of new friendships had been extinguished, but she still regretted them not living nearer to each other.

Now Carl was working in East Knoll she hardly ever saw him, but that was boys for you. Claire was good at visiting. "I'm lucky," she said out loud. "Luckier than a lot of other old people.

I'm still in my own home. I can come and go as I please." She only needed help with the garden and although she was critical of his ability as a gardener, Sam Jones did most of the donkey work for her and Carl helped if he was asked. "Good family, good friends and good neighbours," she murmured under her breath. "What more do you need?"

With that happy thought uppermost in her mind, she settled down to tackle the crossword. It was late before she admitted defeat. "Two clues," she grumbled. "Just two." She wasn't unduly bothered. She knew that if she left the puzzle to do something else and then came back to it, the answers would eventually reveal themselves. She heaved herself from her chair, rubbing her wayward hip as she padded into the kitchen. "A couple of fig rolls, that's what I need," she muttered, her stomach rumbling at the mouth-watering prospect. "Fig rolls and a cup of tea, mmm, bound to get the old brain working again."

CHAPTER 17

The fund-raising committee of St. Laurence-on-the-Hill was assembled in Daisy Parsloe's conservatory discussing the forthcoming craft fair. "Who's volunteering for teas?" she asked.

It was airless in the room. The autumn sun had warmed the glass roof and tried to wheedle its way in through the venetian blinds. Owen Reedman's chin brushed the pocket of his Viyella shirt, his eyelids drooped, his head nodded just as his hand slipped off the seat. He coughed and re-adjusted his position, only to nod off again straight away.

"Me," Vi said tilting her head in Owen's direction and exchanging amused glances with Daisy.

Marion Grey was next. "And me."

"I won't be there," Joan Drabble piped up. "It's my brother's sixtieth. Fred and I have been invited to a family meal."

"That's nice," Daisy said.

"It would be, if Fred's brother hadn't been invited, too. He never stops talking, especially when he's had a glass of wine."

"I can't stand people like that," Rachel said. "My aunt was the same. Too fond of her own voice by half. I'll help, Daisy."

"Good, that should be enough. I've made the table plan as usual; mostly the same people as last year but we have one new one, Jake Hampson from East Knoll. He makes sculptures from driftwood. Anyone seen his work?" There was a cluster of shaking heads. "No? Well, there's one of his sculptures outside the High School, well worth a look if you have the time. He said he'd do some Hallowe'en-type things for the children."

"Do you think that's wise?" Rachel said.

"Wise, how do you mean?"

"Well, it's not very Christian, is it, all this Hallowe'en hype?

Fr. Jon might not like having witches and warlocks in the church hall."

"There won't be any witches *or* warlocks and I've already asked him. He says it's ok. Anyway, Jake said he was making lots of different stuff; spiders, broomsticks, black cats and things."

Owen suddenly snorted himself awake. "Is this Guy Hampson's son?" he asked, keen to be involved in the debate.

"Yes, do you know him?"

"I've played tennis with the father a couple of times; don't know the son."

"Did you organise posters?"

"Printed and distributed," he said with a muffled yawn which shape-shifted into a smug smile.

"I think that's everything, then."

"The Raffle," Bella said.

"Do we need a raffle?" Rachel said.

"We always have a raffle," Bella said.

"That's hardly the point. Do we actually *need* one? If we charged more for the tables, we wouldn't. It's so much work," she complained. "Getting the prizes, selling tickets, folding them all up and when it comes to the winners, people can never make up their minds what they want."

"Marion and I will be organising it," Bella said. "You don't have to raise a finger."

"Well, make sure there are some decent prizes. Last time we had about four tins of the same biscuits."

"And John's wine," Joan said. "Wasn't that decent?"

"I'd forgotten the wine," Rachel said. "It's all gone now, thank goodness."

"And so has John," Bella said provocatively her double chins wobbling in unison.

"Good riddance," Rachel said folding her arms. "I wish we'd divorced years ago. I don't miss him one bit."

Owen chewed his moustache thoughtfully. "I could donate some home brew," he said.

"It's a kind thought, but," Daisy said hastily "I think we have enough prizes, don't we, Bella?"

"Yes," Bella said firmly. "Plenty; the local shops have been very generous. The sports shop in Linchester has given us a signed football and some other sports equipment... Ben's cousin's daughter works there."

"The one with the twins?" Joan said.

"That's it."

"They must be quite big now."

"Nearly three," Bella said.

"Do you need any help with ticket selling, folding or anything?" Marion said.

"Daisy and Thyme are helping me."

"Will Thyme be up to it?" Rachel said.

"She's bouncing with energy now the tired phase has passed."

"I wonder if it will be a boy or a girl," Joan said.

"I don't know if they know," Bella said. "She hasn't said anything."

"Fr. Jon seems very pleased with himself," Vi said.

"And so he should be," Rachel said.

"He is," Daisy said. "Diana is over the moon at the thought of becoming a grandmother."

"She doesn't know how lucky she is," Rachel said.

Daisy tapped placatory fingernails on her back, Pink Freeze contrasting starkly with the black cardigan Rachel had slipped over her shoulders in case of draughts. "I think she does," she said. She was aware that Rachel's dreams of becoming a mother had never materialised due to her husband's infidelity and the fact that he had made a family with someone else. By the same token, her dreams of becoming a grandmother would never come to fruition. Fate, she mused, could be so cruel. She couldn't help wondering how different her own life might have turned out if Brian hadn't fallen off that roof, leaving her to fend for herself and bring up their children alone.

"Angela asked me to tell you she's had an idea about the jars of grace we collected over Lent," Owen said.

"Yes?" Daisy said, glad to leave her brooding thoughts.

"She said we could paint them up, buy some tea-lights from the pound shop and sell them at the fair."

"That's a brilliant idea," she said. "If we only spend a few pounds on the whole lot we'll make a killing."

"You might have to invest in some glass paint," he said.

"Even so, if we charge a couple of pounds for each one we'll be well into profit. I'll get them out of the store cupboard. Does she need help with that?"

"Depends how many there are."

"About thirty, I think."

"I'll ask her," he said.

"Right, well if there's nothing else," Daisy checked the room for signs of dissent and found none "Good, then it must be cake time."

Helena returned from work to find Naomi washing her hair. "I thought you did that yesterday," she said remembering the days when she'd had the time to think about washing her hair every day.

"I did, but I'm going out tonight," Naomi said, glad that her face was completely obscured by wet strands.

"Where are you off to?"

"I said I'd go and see Jake Hampson's work."

"I thought you didn't like him."

"I don't but I couldn't get out of it without being rude. I am quite interested to see what his sculptures are like. I can't imagine anyone making anything artistic from driftwood." Naomi rinsed off the last of the lather and wrapped her head in a towel. "There's a quiche in the oven."

"You have been working hard."

"Not me, supermarket special."

"Oh well, I don't care who made it. I'm starving. We were short-staffed today, I only had time for a coffee at lunch-time. I've been on my feet all day. Did you call in at *The Recorder* offices?"

"Yes."

"And …"

"And I didn't find out where Mary Glebe lives if that's what you mean," Naomi said.

"You know it is."

"They suggested getting other readers to help."

"How?"

"They're going to re-print the photo in the next issue, what's left of it and ask if anyone knows of her whereabouts. You know, a headline like *Where is she now?* I thought it was worth a try. I couldn't look through any back copies. They're stored somewhere else."

"I suppose it might work," Helena said doubtfully. "If it doesn't, we'll just have to leave it to Guy." Naomi pulled a face. "What have you got against him, Nims?"

"I don't want you to make a terrible mistake, that's all."

"The other day you said he'd be a good catch."

"I'm allowed to change my mind aren't I?"

"Sure, but I'm a big girl now. I don't need your permission to choose my friends and that's all he is, an old friend. We enjoy one another's company. I don't see it turning into anything more than that, but if it does I hope you'll be happy for me."

"Just be careful, Mum. Ask yourself why he was turned down twice after his wife died. Think about how Jake turned out. There must be something wrong somewhere."

"He was just unlucky with his choices and Jake's fine now. You don't need to worry."

Naomi took off the towel and dipped her chin so that hair covered her face again. "If you say so," she said, thinking that she needed to worry more about their relationship, not less.

As she walked round to Lincoln Road later, Naomi still had the feeling that what she was about to do was a bad idea. She nearly turned back twice, but reckoned if she didn't visit the studio and they met up again, it would be embarrassing. She told herself she didn't have to stay long. How long would it take to look at a few pieces of wood glued together?

She tried to think up an excuse if she needed to get away. The one excuse she couldn't use was that she needed to wash her hair. It shone with vitality. The plait was thick, healthy-looking as it rested over her shoulder. Soft tendrils had escaped to curl around her ears and rest in the nape of her neck, a definite giveaway that it had just been washed; and anyway, *'I need to wash my hair'* was such a cliché. Jake would see through it straight away. The best she could come up with was a family discussion to locate a missing person.

She saw light spilling out under the garage door like the lights from a spaceship in some B-grade movie. Jake must be in there, she thought, waiting to lure her in. She did not want a Close Encounter of the first kind with him, never mind the Third but now she was there she might as well go in; she took hold of the handle and twisted it. The door rumbled up over her head and it was almost a disappointment when there were no humming machines inside, no curious creatures to welcome her, just Jake. "Oh hi," she said smiling at her thoughts. He smiled back.

She stood where she was, trying to make sense of all the cats and bats, broomsticks, pumpkins and spiders. She stared in amazement at the antelope and then the stag with its head down, antlers ready for a fight; she saw a dove flying from the roof, a rusty filing cabinet smothered in bats, several willow twigs and piles of driftwood stacked up awaiting inspiration. Anything less Spielberg would have been hard to imagine. This was in no way the bridge of an alien spaceship.

"I'm glad you came," he said.

"I said I would, didn't I?" She moved towards the stag and, forgetting her hostility for the moment, ran her fingers over its bleached wood back. "This is amazing, so realistic. What gave you the idea?"

"The wood. I'm always led by the wood. I look at the shapes and see what ideas come to me. I've just had a commission to make two sheep. That's easier because I know straight away where I'm going to end up and I can search for the pieces I need."

She turned to his Halloween offerings. "No," she said. "It can't be."

"Can't be what?"

"They're not *Audreys* are they?" she said eyeballing the plant pots complete with exotic flowers.

"You recognised them."

"*Little Shop of Horrors* ... I love that film. Great escapism. I've watched it a few times, especially since Blanche died."

"Blanche?"

"My great-aunt."

"Oh yes. I'd forgotten you were one of the Blacks."

"I'm a Henry," she said.

"Way back, I mean. One of the Black dynasty, like the Adams family."

His tone was light-hearted, but she objected to the inference that there was something creepy about her family. "What's that supposed to mean?" she said.

"When we were kids, me and my mates, we used to make up stories about the old lady. No-one ever saw her. We thought she might be a vampire, you know, sleeping all day and only coming out at night. We reckoned she was busy in the cellar carrying out weird experiments."

"The cellar was full of coal," she said prosaically.

"We crossed over when we got to Barque House," he went on unaware of her indignation "In case she kidnapped one of us, used our bodies for spare part surgery; drained our blood, turned us into zombies or did something equally gross to us."

"That's stupid. Blanche was great; a little eccentric, maybe, but nice. I loved her. I spent a lot of time with her. I miss her."

"It was just kid's stuff. Didn't you ever make things up?"

"Not like that, no," she said getting ready to make her excuses. She had been right about him all along. He was mean, stupid, unfeeling. Not the sort of person she wanted to call a friend.

"I know Dad liked her."

"A lot of people liked her."

"So, what do you think?"

"About what?"

"My stuff."

"It's all right," she said.

He had expected more. He was proud of his work. It hurt that Naomi seemed unimpressed, but it wasn't going to stop him getting to know her better. He pulled open the top drawer of the filing cabinet and produced two glasses and a bottle of white wine. "I thought we could celebrate the sheep," he said.

Naomi felt her anger rising. Did he think she would be his for a glass of wine? Did he think she would stay to hear her family insulted again? Her judgment had been correct in the first place and she couldn't get away from him fast enough. "I need to go," she said.

"Don't rush off," he said as he filled the glasses. "We haven't had a chance to talk."

"Family meeting," she mumbled as the garage door rumbled up for a second time. "Anyway, I don't drink. See you around."

"Come on Naomi don't be like that," he said but she had gone. He put her glass down and drained his. "What did I say?" he muttered to himself. "What ... did ... I ... say?" he repeated louder and more staccato and then kicked the filing cabinet and emptied her glass, too.

CHAPTER 18

It was cold in Cumbria. There had been a brisk northerly wind blowing all night. It was still sighing in the pines bordering the lake at the foot of the fells above the Killingbeck Ridge Hotel, a stone's throw from Edith Gill's cottage. She knotted the silk scarf more tightly around her neck and set the kettle on to boil. A cup of tea was what she needed.

She had thought she might light the fire in her front room until she realised she did not have the energy. The central heating was on. She should have been warm enough, but she wasn't. When the kettle boiled, she made the tea and carried it through to the front room. She did not understand where all her get up and go had gone. She shivered. Perhaps she had a cold coming on.

She settled her slim frame in the armchair by the empty grate and pulled the throw off the arm of the settee, tucking the soft wool around her bony knees. She knew she should eat something but she had no appetite. Perhaps by lunch-time she would feel like tackling that nice piece of salmon Isobel had bought for her before she went down to Linchester. She didn't want it to go to waste. There were potatoes in the cupboard and some broccoli. By lunch-time she might have regained some energy. She sipped her tea instead and wondered when Isobel and Adrian would be back. They had said they would only be away overnight, but they had stayed away for three. She wanted them to be on their way back. She felt lost when they weren't there, vulnerable on her own in the cottage now she couldn't walk far without getting breathless. She had always been happy in her own home, the home she had shared with Ralph for too short a time; she didn't mind her own company, it was just comforting to know Isobel and Adrian were only five minutes away if she needed them, but she would never have asked them not to go. She did not want to be a burden.

As that thought meandered away the phone rang and her spirits soared. Perhaps they were back already "Isobel," she said as she picked it up.

"No, it's me."

"Oh … Ivy. It's good of you to call."

"Are you all right?"

"I'm fine, just sitting down with a cup of tea."

"Nothing like a cuppa to start the day. I thought I'd call for a chat."

Edith smiled. "Thanks Ivy."

"Are you sure you're ok?"

"Well, I'm beginning to feel my age," Edith said.

"Aren't we all. I take a stick now when I go out, or my shopping trolley."

"I don't like to make a fuss."

"No, well, we don't do we?" Ivy said. "It's the way we were brought up. No-one would listen if we did. I thought I'd call to remind you, Morse is on tonight."

"Oh good. I know we've seen all the episodes, but I don't mind watching them again. They're such good stories. What time?"

"Eight o'clock, ITV 3. I was round at Ian's last night, babysitting."

"Ah. How's Phoebe?"

"She was asleep when I arrived, I didn't hear a peep out of her the whole time I was there, so she must be fine. School tires her out," Ivy said.

"They're coming for Christmas, you know."

"Yes, Pippa said. That will be nice for you."

"I'm looking forward to it. I hope it doesn't snow. It's cold enough already."

"Phoebe's never seen snow."

"Well, perhaps a little sprinkling would be all right," Edith said.

"I went to visit Judie the other day."

"How is she?"

"She's in a bad way … can hardly breathe, poor love."

"That's a shame."

"She's plugged into oxygen all the time now."

"We're not doing too badly, then."

"No. We need to count our blessings."

"I am and I'm counting the days until Christmas," Edith said. "I can't wait to see how Phoebe is coming on."

"Ian said she's enjoying school," Ivy said.

"She'll be reading before we know it."

"It's a shame Pippa's pregnancy was a false alarm. It would be nice for her to have a little brother or sister."

"Yes," Edith said. "Isobel always wanted a brother or a sister."

"She had a sister."

"She never knew her, though, did she? She really wanted a play-mate, but it wasn't to be."

"It was sad about Ruth."

Edith sighed. "That was a long time ago."

"Do you ever wonder how she might have grown up?"

"Sometimes."

"Call me if you ever need a chat," Ivy said.

"Bless you, I will. Did Isobel say when they'd be back?"

"No, but I'll let you know when they leave."

"Thanks, Ivy."

"No problem. Look after yourself, Edith."

"You look after yourself," Edith said.

"I will, don't you worry. We'll speak again soon."

Ivy waited for the phone to click and then put it down on the table while she stared out of the window. The phone call had not been a good idea. It just made her miss Edith even more.

Naomi was still annoyed with Jake when she woke up on Tuesday morning. She vowed to return to her original plan of avoiding him and to discourage her mother from building on her relationship with Guy Hampson. As soon as they found Mary Glebe she would not need to have much more to do with him. She had been disappointed that Jake had not changed. He was as she had suspected; shallow, boorish and only interested in one thing. Well, he had chosen the wrong one this time. She could not be cajoled into his trap.

Thinking about Jake and his father brought her own father to mind. How could a father ignore his own child as she had been ignored? To give Guy his due, he had always stood by his son even if his motives had been misguided. She seldom thought of Kevin Henry, but when she did, she wondered if he ever thought about her; not that she wanted him to think about her, she was curious, that was all. She was indifferent to his current circumstances. She could not remember ever having missed him. There was nothing he could add to her life. Her mother had given her a perfect childhood and she was conscious of her continuing love and support. She had no regrets, but she would make sure that any children she might have would gain a father on whom they could rely for love and advice. They did not need a father like Jake Hampson. She felt sorry for any children he might father. She felt sorry for his wife.

She went downstairs intending to make her mother a cup of tea and was surprised to find her already up and dressed. "That's not your office gear," she said as she took in the long-sleeved t-shirt, body warmer and jeans "And you're up early. I was going to bring you a cup of tea in bed."

"Aw, that's nice, but I need to be in early this morning. We're stock-taking."

"I heard Isla's car."

"She left ten minutes ago," Helena said. "What are you up to today?"

Naomi shrugged. "Don't know."

"You could make a start on Blanche's clothes."

"Do I have to?"

"It has to be done some time."

"I know."

"You seem a bit down," Helena said. "Is everything alright?"

"Yes, all good."

"You rushed off to bed so quickly last night I didn't have time to ask how you got on with Jake."

"Oh that... his sculptures are ok, but he hasn't changed," Naomi said. "I won't be going again."

"Oh dear, well, there's no reason why you should. Holly rang while you were out. She wanted to know if you'd had your phone stolen, apparently she's been trying to talk to you for days."

"I'll give her a call later."

"Perhaps you could go up to London to see her now you're not visiting Blanche."

"I don't know, maybe," Naomi said and then she thought for a moment. It was a good idea. It would get her away from Jake. "On second thoughts, I think I will, if that's ok with you. I haven't seen her in months. You don't need me for anything, do you?"

"Don't think so. It's time you had a break. It looks as if it's going to be nice again. Why don't you go down to the beach?"

"No."

Her daughter's decisive tone and stormy expression alarmed Helena, but she did not have time to delve deeper. "We'll talk tonight. Don't worry about dinner. I'll get us a take away. Now, I really must go." She gave her daughter a hug before she headed for the door.

"Chinese?" Naomi said.

"If you like."

"Thanks, Mum. Have you told Kevin about Blanche?"

"It's nothing to do with him."

"Don't you think it's strange he doesn't want to know us?"

"Honest answer? I'm pleased that's the way it is. He was like a damp cloud smothering us. You don't remember what it was like, I do. Does it bother you?"

"Nope... it's just... I can't imagine ignoring any child of mine."

"That's because you're a woman. We're different."

"Alf Minns is close to his daughter. He's proud of her."

"Where is all this coming from?"

"I was just thinking about things."

"You haven't got enough to do. I, on the other hand, have too much. Come and help me with the stock-taking."

"Thanks, but I think I'll go for a run," Naomi said with an almost smile.

"Good, that's good. It will lift your spirits."

"I'm fine, Mum, really. See you later."

Adrian and Isobel were driving down the winding lanes of Cumbria on their way back from stocking up at the supermarket. "Let's stop for a coffee at the Force Inn," Isobel said.

"I thought you wanted to get home."

"I do."

"Then we'll wait for coffee. We're nearly there."

"Do you think Mum's ok?"

"Why wouldn't she be?" he said.

"She is nearly ninety."

"I know."

126

"We shouldn't have stayed so long in Linchester," she said.

"Has she said anything?"

"No."

"We asked Matty to call in on her."

"Yes, but she's not us, is she?"

"Well, we don't have any plans to leave her again for a while," he said. "Ian and Pippa promised to bring Phoebe up to us for Christmas."

"I can't wait. It will be the first time she's been with us for Christmas. Mum will love it. She's already bought her presents."

"We all need things to look forward to. Heaven help us if Labour win the next election."

"They won't," Isobel said taking her phone from her bag.

"I wouldn't be so sure. People might like to have more bank holidays," he said. "I would have liked more bank holidays."

"That's because you worked in a bank," she said.

"Very funny."

"I'm sure Mum would approve of us celebrating the Saints' days."

"No doubt about that."

"They can't think they'll win the election just by offering the great British public more days off work," she said scrolling through the news.

"It's all the money they want to borrow that bothers me," he said with a worried frown. "If they've got the students on side anything could happen. Now the great British public have voted to come out of Europe, who knows what they'll vote for next. I'm fed up with the lot of them."

"Did you read about Flying Scotsman?"

The frown melted away. "I did …"

"*Four trains travelling together to represent the past present and future of the railways,* it says here," she said scrolling down a news feed on her phone. *"An iconic railway moment on the East Coast Main Line.* Hundreds of people were watching apparently ..."

"And I wasn't one of them," Adrian said. He sighed.

"Don't be like that," she said. "Haven't you enjoyed our break?"

"It's always good spending time with Ian and Pippa ..."

"And Phoebe."

"... and Phoebe, but getting away is such a performance; I sometimes think we should encourage everyone to come to us in future. We have to find someone to look after the dogs, we're always torn leaving your mother and this time, finding out about Blanche ..."

"None of us goes on for ever, darling."

"I know that."

"And Mum really doesn't mind us going away."

"She wouldn't say if she did. Don't you feel queasy, looking at your phone when we're travelling in the car?"

"No," she said, eyes still glued to the screen. "I can get the news, the weather, photographs, messages. I don't know what I did before I bought this phone."

"You used to talk to me," he said. "Now you're just like a teenager, always checking WhatsApp."

Isobel looked up in surprise. "You can't be jealous of a phone," she said.

"Of course I'm not jealous. It would just be nice for once to have a conversation with my wife and know she's actually listening to me."

Isobel put the phone in her pocket. "There, happy now? What did you want to talk about?"

"I wanted to have a chat about Edith. She doesn't seem to be eating much, surely you've noticed."

"I have noticed. I told her before we went away that she should see Dr. Lock but she said I was making a fuss over nothing. I left her food in the fridge. What more can I do?"

"Phone him. Tell him we're worried. Ask for advice."

"She won't like it."

"She doesn't have to know. It's for her own good. At least if we've mentioned it to the doctor, I'll feel as if we've done something to help. I'm very fond of Edith."

"And you think I'm not? I love her. She is my mother, for heaven's sake."

"We can't just ignore it," he said.

"It's awkward. I suppose I still think she knows best."

"Now the cold weather's coming, she needs to eat more."

"We can't force feed her."

"I'm not suggesting that, Isobel. There's nothing wrong with her wanting to be independent, but we don't want her getting hypothermia."

"I know what we can do," Isobel said. "We'll call in at the surgery before we go home, see if we can book a home visit."

"Can you still do that?"

"Mum's one of Dr. Locke's favourites, he's always saying so. He never minds being asked to call round; if we ask him to keep us out of it, he will. He can make some excuse, say he was visiting another patient nearby and thought he'd pop in on her, or say he's checking how she's managing with all her medication. If he suggests she should eat more, she will. I'm sure he'll call round unless he's on a city break or something."

"A city break," he said tetchily. "Why would he be on a city break for heaven's sake?"

"He told me once that he likes to re-connect with the outside world from time to time. Living where we do is fine, idyllic even, but we are, sort of, cut off from the real world. He's an opera buff."

"Is he now. I never had him down as a culture vulture."

"What's wrong with that?"

"Nothing … I'm glad to be cut off from the real world. It suits me. I like the peace and quiet."

"I do too, but it's good to get away occasionally, see something different, refresh the mind. Anyway, I don't know why we're arguing about it. The chances are he *will* be in the surgery."

"Let's find out."

CHAPTER 19

As the morning wore on, Naomi's need to escape became overwhelming. She slipped her phone into the back pocket of her running vest and plugged in the ear phones. With a baseball cap pulled down over her eyes she was ready to set off for her run. She hadn't planned a route, but she wanted to get as far away from the town and the beach as she could; way out into the fields that separated East Knoll from Linchester and everything in-between.

She left the familiar streets. As her mind raced, her trainers pounded the tarmac of the newly-laid road in the burgeoning housing estate to the north of the town. She noted that there were very few parking spaces and wondered if the developers were short-minded enough to think they could persuade people not to drive simply by rationing spaces. She continued to make her way through the New England-style houses, admiring the landscaped gardens and newly-planted trees.

It was not possible to stuff the car-genie back in the bottle now she reflected, cars were too convenient. A necessity for some people. There were no shops in the development and no schools. She asked herself how councillors imagined residents would be able to get on with their lives without transport. A bus service had been promised but it would not be running until all the houses had been finished and occupied and they were well behind schedule according to her mother, who had been told about it by Marjorie Dann, whose husband worked for the council. She had heard people complaining about the lack of forethought in allowing the estate to be built so far out of town and then rationing the use of cars. What if, she thought, some of the residents needed carers; where would the carers park. If she became a carer where would she park? Maybe she should get a bike, no a scooter. A scooter would be cool. She could be like Audrey Hepburn in Roman Holiday.

She remembered her grandmother's predilection for Hepburn films and for all her leading men; Gregory Peck, Stewart Granger and Cary Grant were the favourites. Whenever she was off school due to illness or inset days, Betsy would allow her to choose one of the old rom coms from her collection and they would settle down under an eiderdown to watch the chosen one until her mother came home from work. Betsy hadn't moved on to duvets like the rest of the world. On a sleepover at her grandmother's house there had been something comforting about being tucked into a bed with sheets and blankets scented with Damask Rose. In winter, it was particularly delicious when a soft eiderdown and candlewick bedspread were added for extra warmth, creating the illusion of her providing the filling for a Turkish delight roll.

As sisters, Betsy and Blanche could not have been more different; she reckoned she was lucky to have known them both, fortunate that she still had her mother. Jake only had his father. She shook her head as she ran; she did not want to think about him. She did not want to think about her father. She referred to him as Kevin for a reason; he hadn't earned the right to be called, Dad. She had been barely more than a baby when her grandfathers had died. She had never heard their opinions, never shared their memories. Would her life have been different had she spent time with them, got to know them... if they had got to know her? Maybe, but it was useless to speculate. Blanche's death seemed to have stirred up all sorts of disconcerting emotions.

Now she was through the footpath into countryside and the signs of human habitation were gradually disappearing. She ran on past cows and then sheep and finally, empty fields. She stopped at a small church tucked away down the winding track she was following and took a swig from her water bottle. A watery sun appeared to light the dreary skies before disappearing behind a cloud. This pattern repeated itself several more times; she imagined a celestial semaphore. Was the message that she must take heart, face reality head on, that she would get over this feeling of emptiness she'd experienced since Blanche's death and that she should ask Jake what had really happened all those years ago? The two seemed to go hand in hand and yet they were not connected, or were they? Did her happiness rest on the resolution of both?

The sun startled her again with its brilliance. It illuminated the 'A' shaped east wall of the church, bouncing off the flint stones to reveal hidden hues in the stained-glass windows. She was thinking that the church might be open and that she would be able to get a better view of the glass from the inside.

Meandering through grave stones, stopping every now and then to witness sorrowful epitaphs and pious claims, she searched for a point of entrance and finally arrived at a side porch. She was disappointed to find the door closed. She took hold of the hooped handle expecting it to resist but it turned easily in her hand and a moment later she was inside.

It was peaceful in the inner porch, cool, fresh. The walls were white-washed and the floor tiled. There was a noticeboard stating that this was The Parish Church of St. Agatha of Sicily. She had never heard of St. Agatha of Sicily but she liked her church very much. There was a list of services posted there and a request for donations. She went through the half-glazed doors into the main body of the church. The building was empty. Neat rows of pine pews led up to the altar. There was a stone font on a marble plinth near the door. Her fingertips traced the carved leaves decorating the bowl and as she glanced up at the barrel-vaulted ceiling, the sun burst through the windows in the chancel again; it was as if someone had switched on a spotlight behind the vibrant glass.

She stood admiring the giant bookmark panes for some time, absorbing their beauty and thinking of nothing but their jewelled magnificence. It was a while before she felt a restlessness to be running again. She ambled back down the central aisle taking in memorial plaques, embroidered hassocks and the windows either side. The glass panes on these windows were small, clear, melded together with lead, the stone sills host to flower arrangements or brass candle sticks. She thought someone must really care about St. Agatha and her church to keep it in such pristine condition.

She checked the time on her phone, gone twelve. She had been out for almost two hours. It felt like five minutes. Her sense of loss and bewilderment in this new world where nothing was demanded of her had been tempered. She had no relationship in need of nurture, no caring to do, no job, no one relying on her, no stress and yet the irony of it was that no stress had felt immensely stressful.

She had never been religious, but her visit to the church had allowed her to make space in her head; she was ready to step back outside and deal with whatever life had to throw at her. She reached behind her for the five-pound note she had put in her pocket in case of emergencies and posted it in the wall safe before setting off again. It fell into the void without a sound; a silent token of gratitude to St Agatha for her silent counselling.

Gradually, as fields dwindled into verges, cows were replaced by cars, houses took over from trees and the streets of East Knoll were once more in sight, she pulled out her earphones and slowed to a walk. On the spur of the moment she decided not to go home but to call at Barque House instead. She knew she had time to make a cup of coffee there and chill out a bit longer before her mother finished work.

She hopped lightly up the stone steps to let herself in, feeling calm and hassle-free. As she let the door close behind her, she had a sense of being hidden, safe, as if the empty house had embraced her, welcomed her in. She headed straight for the kitchen. It was a few moments later that the doorbell rang and made her jump. She considered ignoring it and then thought again. It might be Alf Minns. She reckoned he must be feeling quite down. She was prepared to share some of her new-found serenity with him. If he needed to chat she would listen, after all Blanche had meant a lot to him, too. Leaving the kettle to boil she went to see if her suspicion was correct.

It was not Alf Minns. To her surprise, Jake Hampson was standing there, his arms full of flowers. As people passed by chatting, laughing, texting, she stood motionless, still as the air before a storm. A flurry of thoughts flooded her mind. What was he doing there, was he stalking her … how else would he have known she was there? If he was, why had he brought flowers? How should she react, cool, reserved, pleased to see him? She slapped down that notion straight away. Cool, that was the way to play it.

"I saw you come in," he said. She stared at him, watched his lips move as time ticked on "… will you, please? I don't think I can do it on my own," he said.

"Sorry?" she said.

"I've never visited her grave before."

"I don't understand."

"It was what you said last night. It made me think, made me realise that if we care about someone as you cared for your great-aunt… and they die, we don't have to pretend it's all fine. We don't have to put on a brave face or ignore how we feel. It's all right to be sad. It's all right to be angry, to still love them, miss them. It's part of coming to terms with things. I've always felt bad that I've never done this before but you made me see that I should do it. I can do it, I need to do it and I'd like you to come with me."

Suddenly she got it. "Your mum."

"She died when I was small. I can just about remember her. Dad never talks about her. I think about her every day and especially when I'm down on the beach, she loved shells. I don't say anything to him, he'd be upset. Anyway, the thing is, it's her birthday today. I wanted her to have flowers on her birthday. Will you come with me?"

"I don't know."

"No strings, I could do with a friend," he said. "Moral support."

She felt ridiculous, foolish that her first thought had been that the flowers might have been for her, an apology for his insensitivity, an admission that he cared, maybe; that he would explain? It wasn't that at all. He was asking for help. The great Jake Hampson, everyone's idol, asking for help. Could this be the real Jake Hampson or was it merely a ruse to catch her in his web?

Whatever it was, she needed him to explain more about himself before she would consider him a friend; before she could trust him, but she supposed it was a start. If taken at face value, it showed he had a soul, compassion, feelings for others. She wasn't his friend, but she would go with him because he needed her and at that precise moment she needed to be needed. It would work for them both. "Ok," she said. "Wait here while I unplug the kettle."

Naomi thought Holy Trinity a curiously large church for such a small town. Re-built in the late eighteen- hundreds from local stone, its attractive round tower and spire could be seen for miles around. The stained-glass windows were much bigger than the ones at the little church of St. Agatha. She remembered them from the occasional wedding she had attended in the past. There had been ample time then for her to study the colourful panes as sugary sweet poems were recited to the guests and words of wisdom offered to the bride and groom. Her favourites were the one depicting the Blessed Virgin Mary surrounded by lilies, holding a crucifix, and the one of St. Christopher carrying the Christ child.

The graveyard was in the extensive grounds, sheltered by yew trees and a stone wall. Jake had said nothing for several minutes and the silence was making her uncomfortable. "The windows here are awesome," she said as they left the path to take a zig-zag route through the headstones.

"Where is it? I can't remember where it is," he said his breath coming in short bursts.

"Be methodical, you'll find it," she said.

"Ah… this is it," he said a few moments later.

They had stopped in front of an upright memorial, polished granite inscribed with gold lettering. Naomi read the inscription out loud. *"Emma Margaret Hampson 1960-1991, beloved wife and mother. Soar with the angels.* That's so sad," she said. "What were you, four, five when she died?" He said nothing. "It's peaceful here, the perfect resting place," she went on. "So still, so quiet."

He laid the flowers on the grass. "Too quiet," he said bitterly. "That's what death is."

"I suppose."

"There are so many things I wanted to ask her."

"Ask your dad."

He shook his head. "He never talks about her. No talking, no laughing. She used to laugh a lot. I'd give anything to hear her voice again," he said struggling to hold it together.

"Yes," she said as he stood there gripping his hands together, head bowed. She stepped back to allow him some space. "I'll wait over there," she said heading towards a wooden bench with a view of the sea.

The sun had disappeared. It was another grey afternoon, typical October, she thought, dismal, damp, oppressive; so different from the brightness of her morning run. She tried to imagine him as a small boy, to imagine his bewilderment, "Don't go there," she mouthed to herself. To let her guard down now would be a big mistake but she knew what he meant about the silence of death. She had felt it herself. Barque House was now silent; and she had her own questions.

Had Blanche ever visited this church? She must have done. Had she known about the little church in the fields; had she known about St. Agatha? Everyone knew about Peter, Paul, Luke and John. They knew about Matthew, Mary, Joseph and all the rest, she mused, but Agatha not so much. She made up her mind to find out about her. She had just taken out her phone to start a google search when he sauntered over. "Ok?" she said.

He sat down on the bench beside her, his hand hovering near hers. She drew it back and slid it under her leg. She did not want him to get the wrong idea about their relationship. There was no relationship, nothing significant in her being with him. She was merely doing him a kindness, as she would for anyone, but while she did not want him to read anything into it she could not help noticing that, sitting side by side as they were, his head was way above hers.

"Thanks for coming," he said. "I appreciate it."

She gazed up at him and noticed again how blue his eyes were and then she looked away, overcome by their intensity. What was he trying to do, looking at her like that? She thought of Nicola. There was no way she was going to be another notch on his bed-post. "No problem," she said as she got to her feet. "Shall we have a look around while we're here? I was at a church this morning. St. Agatha's... out in the fields. Do you know it? It's a sweet little place," she babbled on as they walked towards the main door of the church. "I've never heard of St Agatha but I'm going to find out about her; the stained glass was stunning ..."

"Painting with light," he said "The windows..."

"Yes," she said eagerly. "That's it. That's just what they were like, awesome."

"There are some pretty impressive tombs inside this church. I used to come here to do brass rubbings years ago."

"Oh... cool."

The shadowy interior was revealed as the door swung back; she thought it smelt faintly of beeswax; beeswax, brass polish and books. Their footsteps echoed on the stone flags as they moved into the central aisle. There was someone standing in the carved wooden pulpit, papers resting on the lectern. It was a young woman in jeans and a tee-shirt, a wooden cross resting on her chest. She looked up and smiled a greeting. "Welcome. Don't mind me. I was practising for Sunday."

"We don't want to disturb you," Naomi said.

"You're not. I'm done. I've been asked to preach here. It's my first time. As I was passing, I thought I might get a feel for the place, see what my voice sounded like somewhere different, check out the microphone. Some churches don't have them, or if they do they're not working properly. I'm not good at throwing my voice."

"I didn't know preaching was so complicated," Jake said.

"It gets worse. What to preach, how to preach, to add in a

laugh, to be serious, how to get your message across. I don't want everyone to nod off."

"I'm sure they won't," he said.

"This is a lovely church," Naomi said.

"I was putting flowers on my mother's grave," he volunteered. "It's her birthday."

"You could light a candle for her."

"A candle?"

"Yes, it's like saying a special prayer in remembrance. You don't have to, I just thought, as it was her birthday you might like to reflect on your memories."

He glanced at Naomi, looking lost. She nodded encouragement. "Go on," she said. "If you want to."

"What do I do?"

"I'll get you a taper. I saw some in a box by the door. Most churches have a box somewhere." She climbed down the narrow stairs into the aisle in front of them and they followed her back towards the entrance to a small side table covered in pamphlets. There was a cardboard box at the back, a few tapers rolling around in the bottom and some matches. She handed him the matchbox and a taper. "The candle stand is behind that pillar, over there," she said indicating where he should go. "Just light a taper and hold it to one of the candles."

"And stand well back?" he said.

"Let's hope it doesn't go up like a rocket," she said.

As he sauntered across to light his candle, Naomi admired the wrought iron stand in front of the pillar. Greenery and lilies cascaded from the tall vase set on the top. "Nice flowers," she said.

"I'm told there's a good guild of flower arrangers in this area," Jane said.

"Are you a vicar?" Naomi said. "No offence, but you don't look much like one".

"I'm assistant curate at Upfordham. I should have introduced myself, Jane Chisholm," she said "And you are ..."

"Naomi, Naomi Henry. Do you know Pippa Chisholm?"

"She's my aunt. How do you know Pippa?"

"My cousin knows her. She's always buying stuff at the auctions ... Isla Ford?"

"Oh yes, I know Dr. Ford."

"This is a bit of a random question, but you don't happen to know Mary Glebe, do you?"

"No, sorry, why?"

"It's a long story."

Jane smiled "Aren't they all?"

"She's mentioned in my great-aunt's will. We need to find her. I just wondered."

"You could try the Salvation Army. They're good at finding people."

"We're putting a request for information in *The Recorder* this week. If nothing comes of that, we could try them. I'll suggest it to my mum."

"I've done the candle," Jake said handing the taper and matches back to Jane.

"I need to get back," Naomi said.

"If you're down my way, pop in to St. Laurence's," Jane said.

"Upfordham?" Jake said.

"Yes. Do you know it?"

"I'll be at the craft fair."

"He's a sculptor," Naomi said.

"Oh, you must be Jake Hampson."

"That's right."

"We're looking forward to seeing what you've made. Daisy Parsloe says you've done lots of spooky things for Halloween."

"He has. The children will love them," Naomi said and then wondered why she was acting like his marketing manager.

"I'll ask my boss about Mary Glebe when I get back, see if he knows anything. Shall I leave a message with Dr. Ford if I have any news for you?"

"Perfect, thanks."

"No problem. See you soon, I hope."

"I'm not going to the craft fair," Naomi said as they walked back outside.

"No-one asked you to."

"I don't want there to be any misunderstandings."

"There won't be. Thanks for coming. I couldn't have done it without you."

"I'm sure you could," she said.

"You, being there," he said. "It helped a lot."

She was getting cold now she had stopped running. She would not give him the satisfaction of seeing his soft words get to her. She decided on an uncontroversial, "See you," stuffed the earphones back in her ears and set off home at a jog leaving him standing there as she had before, confused and alone.

He had no idea how to handle the situation. She was not like any of the other women he had met. He usually had to fight them off. She was so distant towards him, seemed to be able to take him or leave him and it hurt… but he thought he knew why she was behaving like that. He thought he could guess what she was thinking. He wanted to explain, to put his side of the story, to put things right between them and then at least one other person in East Knoll, apart from his father, would know the truth. He thought it unfair that he should be judged before he had been given a chance. He could have walked away and ignored it, ignored her, but he couldn't. He didn't want to. It did not matter that she wouldn't be at the craft fair, but it was important that she knew the whole story.

There was something about her. It wasn't just her good looks that attracted him. He asked himself if her disinterest was spurring him on. No, he was past all that; he had learned his lesson the hard way. It was something deeper, something he could not explain ... almost as if some external force was drawing them together. He couldn't work it out, but he knew he had to find a way to make her listen before it was too late. He hoped that when she learned the truth, she would be willing to give their friendship a chance. He would settle for friendship if that was all she had to offer, but he hoped... no, he wouldn't contemplate being lucky enough for their friendship to turn into something deeper. It would be devastating if it didn't, but friendship would be better than nothing. It was all he could hope for.

CHAPTER 20

"Pulchritude," Ivy said out loud as she filled in the last few squares in her crossword. The solution had eluded her for the best part of the day but as ever, she had not been prepared to give up. "Ha, got you," she declared.

She heaved herself out of the chair to see if Sam had finished cutting back the cotoneaster. It was a shame to prune it now it was covered in berries, but there was nothing else for it. She didn't want it encroaching on the path all winter. He hadn't been able to work for a few weeks. If he had left the bush as it was, she would have had to continue pushing her way past it to get to the front door from the gate, risk losing her balance; she needed a broken hip like a hole in the head. Carl had phoned to say he wouldn't be able to help until the following weekend. There was no guarantee he would come then. She felt impatient with her body. Her fingers itched to do all the gardening herself but massaging her misshapen fingers, reality struck hard. She was reaching a watershed in her life.

Claire had started talking about sheltered housing. She had brushed off that suggestion straight away. She knew her daughter was concerned for her welfare but, she reasoned, she could still do her own cleaning; she still prepared her own meals. She could organise a day out, walk to the shop. She had good neighbours; she didn't want to lose them or her house. Sid had always wanted Claire to inherit the house and so did she. She wanted to stay in the home they had shared; the house she had moved into as a young bride. All her memories were woven into the fabric of the place; it had become essence of Ivy and to lose it would be to lose her very being.

Her eyes swept around the room as she scanned the ornaments they had collected, the photographs that held precious memories she had begun to forget; his chair, his books, their pictures. Moving was unthinkable at her age. She would be lost if she moved, her life would be miserable anywhere else, like stewed beef without dumplings, she reckoned. She had just gone on to consider how she could make the garden more manageable and her life easier, when the phone rang.

"Ivy? It's me."

"Edith, your phone's working again."

"Yes. I'm spitting feathers," Edith said, her sing-song lilt accentuated by her indignation.

"What's happened?"

"It's that daughter of mine. She only went bothering Dr. Locke. He's just called round to see me."

"Are you ill?"

"Why *no*," Edith said. "Just old. There's nothing he can do about that. He doesn't have the elixir of life and even if he did, I wouldn't take it."

"So, why did Isobel get the doctor out?"

"She said I wasn't eating enough. I eat what I want. I don't do much these days. I don't need to eat much."

Ivy looked down at her ample bosom and sturdy legs. "I wish I didn't eat so much. What did he say?"

"He took my pulse, did all the usual, you know, blood pressure, all that and then said he'd call again next week."

"And how are you feeling now?"

"Fine," Edith said.

"Well, I'm not. I'm fed up."

"What's happened?"

"Same as you, I'm old. I can't do what I want when I want.

I'm thinking of getting more paving in the garden to make it more manageable."

"I suppose it would make sense," Edith said.

"Who wants to be sensible?"

"Perhaps *you* should see the doctor."

"Don't start…"

Edith laughed. "Talking of doctors, did Adrian tell you about Isla Ford's aunt?"

"Blanche Black? I thought she'd died," Ivy said.

"She has but she left money to a mystery woman. No-one knows where she is."

"Wills can be a mine-field. Have you done yours?"

"Ages ago, there's no mystery to it."

"What have you done?"

"Left it to the family."

"I've left mine to Claire with a little something for Ian. He's been very good to me over the years."

"Isobel said Phoebe was on good form."

"She is, the little darling. We have some great conversations. She's a funny little thing."

"They'll be here for Christmas. Did Ian tell you?" Edith said.

"No, Pippa did, and you mentioned it the other day."

"Oh sorry. I'd forget my head if it wasn't screwed on."

"It's something to look forward to."

"I'm already making lists."

"Lists of what?" Ivy said.

"Food, of course."

"Oh yes, I'd forgotten; you make the Christmas cake and puddings, don't you?"

"I thought I might make the bairn some gingerbread men this year. If I don't make lists I forget what's in the cupboard, what

I need to buy, what I need Isobel to get for me, all that. I bought my presents online, they're all wrapped and ready."

"Sounds like a military operation," Ivy said.

"Why *no*," Edith said. "That makes it sound like a chore and it's not. I love baking."

"Well, I'm glad your phone's back on. I miss our chats when the phone's playing up."

"Me, too."

"What was the problem?"

"They've been re-laying cables," Edith said. "They did apologise."

"I should hope so. Is it likely to happen again?"

"Who knows… they're burying them underground this time, to keep them out of the weather. I expect there'll be more problems before they're finished."

"That sounds about right," Ivy said.

"It will be a big improvement when it's done. Strange how you get so dependent on things. When we were children hardly anyone had a phone and we managed."

"These days, most people have two."

"Isobel's always busy doing something on her mobile. She wanted me to have one but I soon put paid to that suggestion. Why do I need a mobile? I never go anywhere."

"At least you've got the land-line back."

"And good friends with the time to chat."

"As rare as hen's teeth."

"The world is a mad place now."

"People rushing here and there…"

"… no time for writing letters," Edith said. "No one passing the time of day. People used to say good morning to each other in the street years back and now they're plugged in to something

147

or other in their own little worlds. They can't even be bothered to smile."

"A little smile goes a long way and what about the self-service tills at the supermarkets?"

"They don't want you to chat while you're paying for the weekly shop, oh no."

"No, that would be too much to ask. Quick in and out is what they want. Grab your money and get rid of you," Ivy said.

"I'm not surprised there's so much mental illness about. People don't communicate enough."

"We all need to communicate. I don't know what I'd do without Ian and Pippa next door..."

"... and Phoebe."

"Yes, she's a little chatterbox."

"God gave us tongues so that we could talk to each other, not just to lick stamps," Edith said.

"We don't do that now, either."

"You're right."

"What comes around goes around," Ivy said. "I can remember my mum having groceries delivered to the house."

"Yes, and then no-one would deliver anything; they wanted us to drive to those big out of town stores, which is hard if you don't have a car."

"And now you can phone the supermarket to get your stuff delivered. Ridiculous, isn't it?"

"Useful though, provided your phone's working."

"Well now we've put the world to rights, I'm off to make a cup of tea," Ivy said.

"I was thinking of doing that," Edith said.

"PG Tips and a nice sit down," Ivy said.

"Just what the doctor ordered."

"Better than a million pills."

"You're right. What would I do without you to cheer me up, Ivy?"

"Take out shares in a tea plantation?"

"Now, there's an idea."

That evening as she was alone in the house, Naomi decided to look at the poetry book she had found in Blanche's bedroom. She didn't switch on the light, choosing the more intimate glow of the table lamp to illuminate the pages. She settled down on the settee and tucked her toes under a throw, perching a cushion on her lap like a writing slope. She rested the book on top of it and turned the first page. Written on the fly-leaf in faded ink were the words, *For Blanche, on her thirteenth birthday from Mother and Father.*

She thought it a rather stiff dedication for a child but, she reminded herself, despite her up-to-date ideas Blanche had grown up in more formal times.

The poems were easy to read; none really spoke to her until she came to the one called *Wishes for a Little Girl.* A dried flower lay between these pages marking the poem out as special, more meaningful than the others. The petals were papery, faded, but still clinging to the stem. It was a rose, a yellow rose. She thought she could detect a lingering hint of perfume. Putting the flower to one side she skimmed the lines, not expecting to be touched by the words, but she found three of the verses particularly poignant.

... Give her not genius. Spare her the cruel pain
Of finding her whole life a prey for daws;
Of hearing with quickened sense and burning brain
The world's sneer-tinged applause ...

... But make her fair and comely to the sight,
Give her more heart than brain, more love than pride,
Let her be tender-thoughted, cheerful, bright,
Some strong man's star and guide,

Not vainly questioning why she was sent
Into this restless world of toil and strife,
Let her go bravely on her way, content
To make the best of life.

She felt almost embarrassed to be reading what had obviously struck a chord with Blanche; almost like a voyeur, an intruder on her most private thoughts. Tears welled as she contemplated a young Blanche being sneered at, was that why she had stayed away from society?

Had she made the best of her life? Was this how she had wanted to be, more heart than brain, more love than pride? Had she resented being clever, had she yearned to be some strong man's star and guide? She imagined the emotional turmoil the young Blanche might have felt. She wished she had found the book before Blanche had gone. She would never know for sure what she had felt, how she had felt. Questions without answers, like Jake had said. She was so taken up with her thoughts that she didn't hear Isla walk into the room.

"Naomi are you all right?"

As light besieged her, she blinked away tears and hastily dusting her cheeks with the backs of her hands, produced a convincing smile. "Yes, fine, thanks... just reading Blanche's poetry book. Do you think she was bullied because she was brainy?"

"It's possible. In those days, women weren't supposed to be clever and her parents were very Victorian. That can't have helped. She didn't fit the mould."

"People can be so cruel."

"That's life," Isla said. "I got teased for wanting to be a doctor. Even thirty years ago being brainy set you apart from the others."

"I didn't know that."

Isla shrugged. "It didn't bother me. I knew what I wanted to do. I just got on with it. Anyway, never mind all that, I came to tell you I haven't found any clues in the cuttings."

"Bother, well, it was a bit of a long shot. We've still got *The Recorder*. It comes out tomorrow."

"That's our best bet. Where's Helena?"

Naomi pulled a face. "She's gone to play badminton with Guy."

"What *is* your problem with him?"

"His son."

"Is he violent?"

"I don't think so."

"Dangerous?"

"Not as far as I know."

"Does he have mental issues?"

"No, he's a sculptor…"

"I don't suppose Helena will have much to do with him."

"He uses his father's garage as his workshop."

"Ok, so she might see him. What's wrong with being a sculptor?"

"Nothing... oh well, I may as well tell you. Jake got a girl pregnant years ago. He refused to take responsibility for the baby and instead of making his son face up to it, Guy paid for him to go travelling to get him out of the way. That's the sort of man he is."

"Does she know?"

"Probably not. I didn't tell her at the time," she said.

"Perhaps he regrets it now."

"I'm sure he regrets people knowing about it. Why do you think his last two partners ditched him? Mum needs to keep away from him."

"I expect he was trying to help. You can't blame him for something his son did. I get that you want to protect her, but you can't choose her friends."

"I don't mind them being friends, if that's all it is; I just don't want to be Jake Hampson's step-sister."

"Is it that serious?"

"I have no idea, but I can't take the chance."

"She hasn't said anything to me. Talk to her if you're worried."

"I guess I'll have to now she's seeing so much of him."

CHAPTER 21

Helena picked up a copy of *The Linchester Recorder* on her way to work on Wednesday along with a skinny latte. She elbowed her way through the bulging bags of donations and rails of clothes waiting to be priced and grimaced. She couldn't allow herself too much of a break from the backlog of sorting or she would never catch up. People were generous, but she wished they would pace their generosity. Her days swung between having a nightmare backlog of work to be done or worrying about dwindling donations.

Checking the rota, she noticed that Ann was coming in at ten. That was good. Ann was a hard worker. Sue was rostered for the afternoon. She was good at pricing but enjoyed chatting, which was fine if things were slow, but tended to hamper progress when they had as much to sort through as they did today and then there was little Joe; '*little*' was hardly an accurate adjective to describe Joe. He towered above everyone else and had the physique of a lowland gorilla. He was eager and helpful but constantly in need of reassurance. She wondered if he would ever find a 'proper' job. He didn't seem to interview well, which was a shame because he had many sterling qualities. She had told him she would give him a good reference when someone offered him a proper job; he wasn't the brightest, but he was only seventeen and he was strong, fantastic at shifting stock. He was reliable, polite, honest. That counted for a lot in business.

Perhaps she should spend the weekend sorting clothes. She had never had to do that before but if the shop wasn't properly stocked, customers would try elsewhere; there were plenty of charity shops in East Knoll, even more in Linchester. She could not afford for that to happen. She might lose her job and she would need money to sort out Barque House. Margins were always so tight it was a constant struggle to stay ahead of the pack.

She sipped her coffee and opened the paper. She did not expect the photograph to be on the first page or the second, but it was not on the third or the fourth, either. She was about to pick up her phone to call them and ask for an explanation, when she saw the article at the bottom of the letters page. The headline was catchy... *Lost Bride ... Where is Mary now?* She read the short article and when she came to the last few words, she panicked... *If you have any information about Mary Glebe's whereabouts, please contact local solicitors, Hampson Tailor and Palmer ...* she had forgotten to inform Guy that he was to be the contact. She checked the time. Just after eight thirty. Would he be in the office this early? She could leave a message if not. The phone rang out endlessly while she asked herself how any self-respecting solicitor managed to run a practice without an answerphone in his office. She finished her coffee and tried again, still no joy. She reasoned that it was unlikely he would be contacted immediately and anyway, she could not afford to waste more time; later would have to do.

Leaving her phone on the desk, she went through to the store room and tipped out the nearest bag. It was an unusual mix of hats and shoes. She guessed someone must have been popular to have been invited to so many weddings. Putting them to one side she decided they would look attractive in the window. Ann was good at window dressing. She could work her magic with the hats when she came in. The next bag was household goods; then one full of jeans and sweaters, all good quality, followed by a box of books. She was relieved there would be no need to fret over lack of stock for a while, one blessing at least and one item to tick off her worry list. All she needed now was news of Mary

Glebe and then she could relax, contemplate the future and start making plans for Barque House.

When Ivy arrived at the One Stop to collect her paper later that morning, Jerry had *The Linchester Recorder* spread out on the counter in front of him. "Morning Mrs. Ellison. Come for your paper?"

"Yes, I had trouble finishing the crossword yesterday. I hope I'm not losing my marbles."

"Maybe there was a mistake, it happens."

"I don't like to give up. I'll try and finish it when I get back."

"Have you heard about this missing person?"

"What missing person?" He turned the pages around to face her so that she could read the news. "Mary Glebe," she said ruminatively. "Well, I never. That must be who Edith was telling me about. Someone must be keen to find her. I don't know any Glebes."

"It says here, she might be in East Knoll."

"I was over there the other day. My friend Judie has lived there for years. She knows everyone. She might know about Mary Glebe."

"Does she take *The Recorder*?"

"I don't think she does. Give me a copy for her. No, give me two. I'll have one as well."

Jerry took another copy from the stand and folded them up with her paper. "How are the aches and pains today?"

"Not too bad," she said hurriedly as she stuffed the papers into her bag. "I'll see you tomorrow." She thrust the right money on the counter and headed for the door. She didn't want to stop for a chat. She wanted to get home as fast as she could so that she could speak to Judie. She was quite out of breath when she approached Blain Gardens. As she arrived at her gate she noticed Pippa on the drive next door about to get in her car, but instead of calling across as she normally would have done, she put her head down and slotted her key into the lock without even thinking about stiff fingers. When she finally got the door open, she stepped inside, kicked off her trainers, tucked her toes into the waiting slippers, shrugged off her coat in double quick time and forgetting all about the irritating crossword clues, went straight to the phone to call Judie.

"Do you know a Mary Glebe," she blurted out as soon as Judie picked up.

"Is that you, Ivy?"

"Yes. It's important, do you know her?"

"Don't think so."

"Well, I'm posting you *The Recorder*, first class; you should get it tomorrow. Have a read, it's all in there. Someone needs to find her urgently."

It was lunch-time when Naomi staggered off to her mother's shop carrying the bin bags with her. She had been at Barque House for a couple of hours searching through drawers, emptying cupboards, trying to find anything she thought might sell. Joe was rooting through DVDs when she arrived. She rested the bags on the floor. "Hi Joe, is Mum here?" she said.

He looked up at her. "Helena?"

"Yes… is she here?"

"By the shoes," he said.

She picked up the bags and bumped her way through the stands of clothes and toys. Helena was checking the card rack at the far end of the shop. She turned when she heard the rustle of black plastic. "Goodness you've got your arms full," she said.

"I've been to Barque House."

"Is that everything?"

"I haven't even scratched the surface."

"I didn't expect it to be emptied in one go, but it's a good start."

"Where shall I dump them?"

"Go through to the back. I'll come with you."

"There weren't many shoes."

"How many pairs do you need?"

"More than four, for sure."

"Naturally, if we're talking about you. Thanks for doing it."

"No probs … have you checked the Recorder?"

"Yes, oops oh no, I forgot to call Guy again."

"What?"

"I tried to call him this morning but there was no reply. I forgot to tell him we were putting an article in the paper and he was our contact man."

"Couldn't you have left a message?"

"No answerphone."

"That's bad for a solicitor's office."

"I was going to call back later, but there's been so much going on, it slipped my mind."

Naomi scanned the stock room. "What's with all the bin bags?"

"We're a bit behind with things."

"I can help. I don't have any plans for the rest of the day."

"Are you sure you don't mind?"

"I don't have a problem with old clothes. It was just sorting through Blanche's things that bothered me. I don't know why. It wasn't as bad as I thought."

"She would have wanted them re-cycled."

"There are some nice vintage blouses."

"I'll have a good look through. Have you had lunch?"

"Not yet."

"We could grab a sandwich. Joe can hold the fort for ten

minutes and then we can get started on all this. I'm expecting Sue this afternoon. She's good at sorting and pricing."

"I haven't seen Sue for ages; it'll be good to catch up."

"She'll probably have some juicy gossip for you."

"That reminds me, have you ever heard of St. Agatha of Sicily?"

"I don't think so, why?"

"I wanted to find out about her.

"Because…"

"Because I just do."

"I'm surprised you haven't Googled her," Helena said.

"I was going to, but I thought I'd ask you first."

"Sorry I can't help. Now, before I forget again, I'll phone Guy and then we'll get some lunch."

CHAPTER 22

Jake felt out of control, confused, lost; as if he had been dumped on Love Island with no hope of making sparks fly. It was an unpleasant sensation. He needed to see Naomi. He was ready to tell her everything. The way they had left things was far from ideal, but he was at a loss to know how he could improve matters. She had not given him her mobile number, so no texting. He was not familiar with her daily routine, so he couldn't just hang around where he hoped she might be on the off-chance of bumping into her. In fact, he hardly knew anything about her, which made his current turmoil even more illogical.

He let himself into his father's house and sat down in the farmhouse kitchen; it was as his mother had left it, warm, homely, bright, artwork covering the walls and a big picture window looking out onto the garden. He started to play with a tennis ball he had discovered in the gutter earlier, bouncing it on the floor in a monotonous rhythm, up and down, up and down like a yoyo.

He made himself a cup of coffee, bounced the ball some more and then dropped it, strode through to the office, snatched a sheet of paper from the printer and sat down at the scrubbed pine table to try and clarify his thoughts.

He stared at the paper for what seemed like hours, pen between his lips, writing nothing, listening to the hum of the fridge and when that stopped, to birdsong in the garden. He heard a gate slam; a dog was yapping somewhere close by. A lorry rumbled down the road. Naomi's face swam into his mind and swam out. He was listening to her voice telling Jane Chisholm he was a sculptor. There was only one option, he thought as he nibbled the end of the pen, to tell her how he felt about her … but when and how?

Now he had a picture of her standing in the church urging him to light a candle in memory of his mother. He kept her image in his mind until he realised day-dreaming about her would not help. He must focus. He couldn't text, but he could write an old-school note to her. He spelled out her name, *Naomi*. He wrote his name beside it, *Jake*. "Naomi and Jake," he said out loud, finding the sound of their names coupled together very satisfying. He doodled around the two names, framing them in an elaborate heart. He paused again. This time his eyes strayed over to the bird table.

A robin was sitting on the cast iron finial at the top, staring in his direction. He was certain he couldn't be seen, but he sat very still anyway. The robin turned its head, fluffed up its feathers and flew off. He waited for a while to see if it would return. A few moments passed. The robin fluttered back to perch on the arm of the south-facing bench his mother had made her own. He remembered how she would sit there balanced like a cushion against the wooden slats, legs stretched along the length of the bench, so still that she could have been mistaken for a mannequin as she watched the birds, pen and pad to hand, waiting for the opportunity to catch a likeness before suddenly jumping up and running into the house to transform the sketches into watercolours.

Another robin appeared. He watched as they danced around each other and then flew off together. He wished they had stayed a bit longer. He wished his mother had stayed a lot longer. She had died so long ago that his memories of her were limited. There were no photographs anywhere in the house and if the shells had not been there, he reckoned he could have been forgiven for thinking she had never been there at all but if he tried hard enough, he could still smell her perfume, feel the warmth of her smile, see her hair. One of his first memories was of sitting on her knees, twiddling the silky blonde tresses between his fingers as he sucked his thumb. He remembered her hugging him to her. He remembered her saying he should stop sucking his thumb if he didn't want his teeth to stick out. She had told him he was handsome, that he would have all the girls after him when he grew up. He felt her love for him deep inside. He knew how much he had wanted to please her, to spend time with her, to hear her laugh.

He had not understood why his father had taken him to stay with his grandmother and then left him there on his own for what had seemed like a very long time. On previous occasions, his mother had taken him and stayed with him, but she had been ill. He remembered that. He remembered his father lifting him onto the bed so that she could kiss him goodbye. He remembered her hugging him, telling him to be a good boy for Nannie as tears glittered in her eyes. He had asked her why she was sad.

"Because I can't come with you," she had replied.

"Why not?" he had said.

That question was never answered; his father had lifted him down and whisked him away. That was the last time he had seen her.

They had played board games at his grandmother's house, he had helped with a jigsaw, but on that visit something unusual had happened. His grandmother had taken him to her friend's house to play and had left him there for the afternoon. He hadn't minded. Her grandchildren had come for a visit and he'd had fun, but when she returned to pick him up, something had changed. She was wearing a dark coat he had never seen before; her demeanour had been unusually sombre, her eyes reddened, her cheeks pale. He had asked if she was ill like his mother and she had held him to her until his neck ached and he had wriggled free.

For the rest of his stay, his grandmother had tried to be cheerful, but he had noticed her tears when she thought he was not looking. Whenever he had plucked up the courage to ask her what was wrong, she had claimed it was the onions she had been peeling, that she had a cold, even that it was a touch of hay-fever, but he knew instinctively it was something more.

When he returned home, his mother had not been there to greet him, which was odd. Every trace of her had gone; her clothes had disappeared from her wardrobe, he had checked. He remembered asking his father why she wasn't there; he had wanted to tell her about the toad he had found in Nannie's garden, to show her the pictures he had drawn. "It's just you and me, son," he had said. He had been shocked, scared to hear the gruff tone of voice, had feared his father might be ill like his mother and then he thought he might have tonsillitis.

He'd had tonsillitis. It had made him so ill he hadn't wanted to play, he hadn't been able to sleep, and *his* voice had sounded funny; he remembered feeling hot and then cold even though his throat had been burning. His mother had given him ice lollies to suck and his childish mind thought they would make his father better, too. He knew there were some left in the freezer. He went to fetch one and offered it to his father only to see him turn away.

His father had never ignored him before, which had confused him even more and then he had learned the shattering truth. "I'm all right, Jake. Look, there's something you need to know. Mum won't be back. She was needed elsewhere. Don't worry, she's happy. When you look up at the stars, she'll be up there, looking down on you."

For a long time, he had worried that his father might disappear, like his mother. What if *he* was needed elsewhere, who would look after him then? Where was elsewhere? Nannie had gone to Australia to visit her sister and no-one had said when she was coming home. Maybe she wouldn't be coming home. Maybe Australia was elsewhere. If they didn't come back, he would have to find a way to get there but he didn't want to go. Nannie had told him there were big spiders in Australia and snakes. He didn't like snakes.

His nights had been filled with dreams of faceless people. People who were there one minute and gone the next leaving him alone in a strange place. He didn't know how to get home. He had woken up crying on several occasions. Once, his father had heard him and had gone to find out what was wrong. Somehow, he had known that he mustn't reveal what was really upsetting him and so he had made up a story about monsters under his bed. His father had given him a torch so that he could check there was nothing there. He had made him a warm drink and kept him company while he drank it.

As he got older the whole truth had come out and so had the shells. He had found them in a box in the garage when he had been searching for more seed for the bird table. Much later he had taken it upon himself to keep the bird table well-supplied as he knew she would have done. He was certain she would not have wanted the birds to go hungry just because she wasn't there.

He had been told that she had been buried and where, but he had never wanted to visit the grave until that conversation with Naomi. It had stirred up old emotions. Up until then, he had felt detached from her death. He had not understood why a stone with his mother's name on it was supposed to make him feel better.

The anger came later. He had been angry for a long time; with her, with his father with the whole world, but as soon as he discovered his abilities as a sculptor he had managed to channel his emotions into art and the anger had cooled, he dealt with everything much better … until he met Naomi.

His mother's prophesy had been correct, but his good looks had been more of a curse than a blessing. He had attracted the sort of girls he did not want to attract. He had never let them get under his skin. He knew he had been unfair to some of them, but he had not considered others at that time; for a long time, if he was honest. Compassion and empathy were still alien to him. Now he was hiding out in his father's garage trying not to make waves. Pathetic. He screwed up the paper and threw it in the bin.

He had not been able to show his true self to any of his girlfriends, had not wanted to, but he wanted to show Naomi. He wanted to please her now, to spend time with her, to hear *her* laugh. He was scared it would never happen but he could not just give up. What should he write, ask her to contact him so that they could discuss the past, his past? Was that arrogant? Would she be interested? It would be better than doing nothing.

If she did not respond he would know what to think. He would move away and start again where no-one knew him and where he would not, could not, be judged; somewhere he could forget the past and move on.

CHAPTER 23

Naomi had spent the afternoon laughing at Sue's silly stories and some particularly salacious gossip. "How do you know all this?" she said.

"I have my sources."

"You're like 'M'."

"It's the family," she said.

"That sounds like the Mafia."

Sue laughed. "Some of them are pretty scary. Everyone has a story. I just listen. It's amazing who knows who, or rather, who knows whose sister, brother, partner, aunt and so it goes on; I just have a good memory, that's the trick, remembering everything and making sure I keep in touch with the family. I reckon I must know something about everyone in East Knoll; I've lived here all my life."

"Cool," Naomi said. She had never been sure how old Sue was and had never liked to ask. She could have been a well-preserved seventy or a not so well-preserved forty-five. Her clothes were casual but up-to-date, trousers not too wide or too narrow; tops classic, shoes quirky, hair well-cut and dyed blonde and most intriguing of all, she never wore jewellery, not even a wedding band.

She stood back to admire the colour co-ordinated rack she had just completed, tweaked the shoulders on some of the hangers to avoid the jumpers or flimsy blouses from slipping off, shuffled scarves, cotton, cashmere and acrylic into a more attractive muddle and checked the tee-shirts and joggers. "Not bad," she said. "That's the last of the red section done."

"Looks good to me," Sue said from her post behind the till. "Do you need me to write out more price tags?"

"I'll ask Mum."

"She was still dealing with those shoes five minutes ago."

"Stock room?"

"Yup."

Naomi found her mother on her hands and knees bringing some order to a pile of men's' shoes. "How are you getting on, Mum?" she said.

"Slowly ... you?"

"Reds are finished. Sue wants to know if we need more price tags."

Helena sat back on the floor and swept her hair from her face. "We can leave price tags for tomorrow. I'll finish these and then we'll call it a day," she said. "It's time she went home, what is it, half five?"

Naomi checked her phone. "Nearly."

"Are there any customers in the shop?"

"No."

"Tell her she can go."

"I need to catch the six thirty train."

"I'd forgotten you were going up to London. You can go, too, if you like."

"Well, if you're sure you don't mind…"

"Of course, I don't mind. You've been a big help. I can manage this last bit on my own."

"I'll go and tell her." Naomi made her way back into the shop where Sue was tidying the jewellery cabinet. "Mum says you can go now. She'll finish up here," she said.

"School's out, hooray," Sue said. She held up a string of blue-flecked glass beads. "These are beautiful, if I wore beads, I'd wear these, they match my eyes," she said holding them up to her eyes to prove the point.

"Why don't you take them?"

"I'll only come out in a rash. I'm allergic to all sorts; gold, silver, titanium, any metal really. These have a silver clasp, that's worse than anything."

"I'd hate not to wear my bling," Naomi said fingering her numerous bangles.

"I don't mind. I've got used to it now."

"What about your wedding ring?"

"I don't wear it. Phil says I've saved him a fortune over the years. He's such a cheapskate. The only upside is I get given a lot of clothes instead."

"That's fair enough."

Sue nodded as she unhooked her coat from the wall behind her and picked up her bag. "Will you be in again tomorrow?"

"No, I'm off to London for the night."

"A night on the tiles?"

"Just visiting an old school friend. She's cooking me a meal."

"You'll be having a catch-up, then."

"That's the idea."

"Don't do anything I wouldn't do."

"That leaves the field wide open."

She laughed. "See you," she said.

Naomi was just flipping through the row of CDs thinking she might buy one to take with her when the door opened again. "That was quick," she said expecting Sue to have returned to collect something she had forgotten. She looked up with a ready smile; it withered in seconds. It was not Sue.

"No, I don't think so," Guy said. She felt her shoulders stiffen. "Is Helena about?"

He was not dressed formally as he had been when they had met in his office to find out about the will. She noted his turtle-neck sweater and tailored tweed jacket. She liked his style. She liked his mellow voice. She liked the fact that she had to look

167

up at him. She even liked his teeth and then she called herself to order. This was enemy number one. She must not allow herself to be charmed by him. "I'll get her," she said abruptly. He did not seem to be fazed by her unfriendly tone, instead he was smiling an acknowledgment and selecting a book from the stack waiting to be slotted onto a shelf as she made her way to the stock room "Mum, Guy's in the shop," she said and immediately noticed her mother's confusion.

"What's he doing here?"

"He didn't say. Shall I tell him you don't want to see him?"

"No, don't start that again," she said. She jumped to her feet and dodged her daughter with an armful of shoes. "Guy, it's good to see you," she said, genuine pleasure in her voice. Naomi sidled up and nudged her shoulder. Helena shrugged her away, ignoring the warning.

"I have news," he said.

"About Mary Glebe?" she asked.

"I've had a phone call from a guest at the Glebe wedding."

"Really, so soon?"

"Someone in Linchester saw the story in the paper and told her friend who lives here. It seems to have spiralled from there."

"Right; sorry I didn't let you know we'd put the article in the paper. I've been trying to call you all day."

"You should have tried my mobile."

"I didn't think it was urgent. I didn't expect an immediate response."

"I've been with clients. I forgot to switch on the answerphone. Elsa wasn't in; her dog just died. He'd been ill for weeks."

"Poor thing. I noticed she was upset the other day."

"She'd had Dave since he was a puppy; he was a big part of her life."

"Dave?"

"Yes, her father was a huge Bowie fan."

"Right … I've never owned a dog, but I know they can be like one of the family, it's sad for her. So, what have you found out about Mary Glebe?"

"I know her address. I've just posted her a letter explaining about the will and asking her to make contact as soon as possible."

"That's fantastic, a big relief, isn't it Nims? Hopefully we can meet and that will be that."

"I think you know my son, Jake," he said turning to Naomi.

"Yes," she said a frosty expression tightening her cheeks. There was no way she wanted to discuss Jake with his father, or anyone else for that matter. She did not want Guy to think they were friends. She did not want him to think she approved of his friendship with her mother. What she wanted was a blanket ban on both the Hampsons.

Her ungracious attitude had no effect on him. He turned his attention back to Helena. "You're busy," he said.

She dumped the shoes on the floor. "I've let things slide with Blanche and everything," she said.

"Can I help?"

Naomi gave her mother a meaningful glance. "I need to leave or I'll miss the train," she said.

"Yes, you must go." She gave her daughter a hug. "Have a good time. I'll see you tomorrow."

Naomi was so surprised at being dismissed in such a way that she walked out of the shop without turning back. She had done her best to protect her mother from Guy, to give her a way out; it hadn't worked.

When she came back from London she was determined to try again, explain in detail what had happened with Jake and make her mother aware of his father's part in it. Perhaps then she would realise why a relationship with him would be a disaster. It would be wrong on so many levels. She was convinced that when she knew all the facts, her mother would want nothing more to do with Guy or his son.

By nine o'clock that evening, Jake had driven past Helena's house, three times. He contemplated a fourth circuit and then realised he was being ridiculous. He parked his mini further down the road and drummed his fingers on the steering wheel for a while, trying to make up his mind if he was doing the right thing. He came to the conclusion that it was all he had; there was no other choice. He had to get on with it or forget the whole thing with Naomi and he knew he couldn't do that. He stepped out of the car and walked towards the house. He posted an envelope through the letter box and rang the bell before sprinting away to the safety of his car.

He did not want to see who opened the door. He did not want them to see him. He didn't even care who opened it. If it was not Naomi, he was confident that whoever it was, would pass on the note to her. He had decided against begging her to hear him there and then; she might have turned him away. As he drove off at speed, he reckoned it would be much better to agree a time mutually agreeable to them both when he would be calmer, more able to explain himself clearly and she would be prepared to listen, or at least that was the plan.

He wanted her to know he was not the person she thought he was. No, he wanted her to know he was not the person he thought she thought he was. He wanted her to decide to get to know him better; he wanted her to know the truth, even if she did not want to get to know him better. He wanted her to give him a chance. What she did with that truth, was up to her.

He had tried to convince himself that it would be enough for her to know the truth, for him to be given a fair hearing, but in truth it was more than that and to jeopardise the future would be foolish when he had no idea if the future he envisaged for himself, matched the future Naomi had in mind. He hoped she would feel compelled to contact him. If she did not, he would not pressure her. He would know she wanted nothing more to do with him and the truth would stay untold. He would leave East Knoll and never contact her again.

Helena and Isla were checking their tablets, exchanging snippets of conversation from time to time. "Guy Hampson called in at the shop today," Helena began only to be interrupted by the doorbell. They glanced at each other. "Who's that?" she said.

Isla put her tablet down. "I'll go." She noticed the envelope immediately. It stood out against the laminate flooring, white on brown. She stooped to pick it up and scrutinized it carefully, turning it over to check the back flap was sealed before she opened the door to peer outside. The path was deserted. The pavement was deserted; even the road was deserted. She shut the door and went back to join her aunt.

"Who was it?"

"No-one," she said.

"No-one?"

"No-one. Just this letter addressed to Naomi."

Helena took the envelope. "I don't recognise the handwriting."

"Where is she?"

"Gone up to London to meet Holly. She won't be home tonight. I'm sure it's not important. I'll give it to her when she gets back. Anyway, as I was saying, Guy Hampson called in at the shop today. He's found Mary Glebe."

"That's brilliant. Is she up for the meeting?"

"She'd be silly not to be. There's over a thousand pounds in premium bonds, I asked."

"It won't be long before it's all sorted, then."

"Let's hope not. Now we've decided what to do, I want to get on with it."

"You could get an estate agent round to value the house while we're waiting."

"I've made an appointment for tomorrow."

"I thought I'd have a good sort-out at the weekend."

"That's something we should all do. Naomi's room is full of clutter. She dealt with Blanche's clothes for me."

"Did she show you the photo of the baby?"

"What baby?"

"Neither of us could see a family resemblance. It was on top of Blanche's desk."

"Blanche wasn't big on babies."

"You're right. Another little mystery. It's in quite a nice frame, silver."

"Oh, that baby ... yes, she did. I don't know who it is, probably just a friend's child." Helena dropped the envelope onto the coffee table. "I'll make sure she gets this tomorrow."

CHAPTER 24

Naomi found Holly's flat surprisingly large. In an idle moment she had researched rentals in London and knew how expensive they could be. The kitchen had all the usual equipment; cooker, washing machine, fridge with a work-top-cum-breakfast bar spanning the top. A shiny Nespresso machine was plugged in next to the kettle, surrounded by a selection of tiny coffee cans.

At the other end of the open-plan room was a door which led to the bedroom and an en-suite bathroom; in-between was a futon next to a coffee table, then the television and two easy chairs. A weeping fig stood beside the window in an earthenware pot, almond-shaped leaves edged in cream, protected from the glare of the sun by shutters. The varnished floorboards were softened by a deep pile rug, grey with splashes of yellow and black. "This place is amazing. How did you find it, how can you afford it?" she said.

"It belongs to Nicola's cousin."

"Nicola ... *the* Nicola?"

"Mm, Lou travels abroad all the time. She wanted someone to flat-sit. She hardly charges me anything. Lucky or what?"

"Very lucky. What do you do when she comes back?"

"Sleep on the futon or go home. She's never here for more than a week at a time."

"Perfect. What are we having?" Naomi said. She lifted a pan lid and inhaled dramatically. "It smells delicious."

"Coq au vin. My speciality ... basically it's the only thing I can cook from scratch."

"You didn't have to go to all that trouble," she said as she perched on one of the high stools tucked under the work-top.

"I like cooking when I have time, which isn't very often these days; I eat out a lot."

"I'm starving."

"Grab a plate, I'll dish up."

Naomi watched as Holly placed quenelles of mashed potato on her plate followed by the chicken in a sauce glistening with baby onions. "So, how do you like London?" she asked.

"Love it. I don't know how you can stay in East Knoll. Nothing ever happens there."

"Things are happening all the time."

"It's where people go to die," she said smiling provocatively.

"That's a bit harsh. I'm not about to die."

"What about Blanche?"

"She was old."

"Well, London's buzzing with life. Galleries, clubs, shows. I'm out practically every night."

"I prefer fresh air," Naomi said. "And the sea."

"There is that, I suppose. What are you planning to do now Blanche has gone?"

"I've been making enquiries about taking up caring full-time."

"Are you mad?"

"Mum thinks I am. I enjoyed looking after Blanche. I'm sure I could do it for other people; did I tell you about the will?"

"What about it?"

"We have to find someone called Mary Rose Glebe or Mum can't inherit Barque House."

"How come?"

"Blanche wanted them to have tea together at Roman Reach."

"Bizarre."

"You don't know her, do you?" Holly shook her head. "Oh well … and that's not all that's bizarre. Guess who's back in East Knoll."

"Dunno."

"Jake Hampson."

Holly dropped her fork and wiped her mouth with the back of her hand. "Jake, Jake Hampson?"

"Uh huh."

"What's he doing back in East Knoll?"

"He's a sculptor now, makes stuff from driftwood and things. He's got a workshop in his dad's garage."

"I don't know how he dares show his face after what happened."

"I didn't know him very well back then," Naomi said. "Hardly at all."

"Neither did I."

"You knew him better than me."

"Not really. I was only going by what Nicola told the others."

"Do you see her much these days?"

"We're not best buddies, but it would be awkward if I didn't, with me living here."

"What's she doing now?"

"She's a florist."

"What happened to the baby?"

"Didn't I tell you?" Holly said. "I'm sure I did."

"No …"

"There is no baby. She had a miscarriage when we were away at uni. Laura Heath told me. Nicola never talks about it."

"Laura Heath … I haven't seen her since we left school."

"I never liked her," Holly said.

"Oh well, it doesn't change things, does it? He still behaved badly."

"Too right, keep away from him."

"That's going to be difficult," Naomi said. "His dad's sorting out Blanche's estate and Mum seems to like him."

"Didn't you say anything?"

"No, when it happened she was having problems with Kevin, I didn't want to give her more grief and there didn't seem much point afterwards. She would only have worried about me."

"She must know about Jake."

"I don't think she does. She hasn't said a word. Surely if she'd known about it she would have said something. I have mentioned that he's no good; she just thinks I'm exaggerating."

"You have to tell her."

"Do you think?" Naomi said scooping up the last gloop of sauce from her plate.

Holly nodded. "If she's in a relationship with his dad, I do."

"I don't think it's that serious. I hope it's not."

"What if it gets serious?"

"It won't," Naomi said with more confidence than she felt. "I can see why Mum fancies him. He is quite fit for an oldie."

"You can't be sure."

"So, you think I should say something?" Naomi said.

"Definitely and soon. You don't want him getting his feet under the table. Have you finished?"

"Yes, it was delicious, thanks," Naomi said. Holly whipped her plate away and dunked it in the sink.

"Let's go and sit on the comfy chairs."

Naomi chose the futon. She pulled out the cushion from behind her and hugged it like a soft toy. "Have you heard about St. Agatha, Holl?"

"That's a bit random," Holly said.

"Well, have you?"

"Of course not."

"Let's Google her," Naomi said getting out her phone.

"Why?" Holly said.

"I went for a run the other day and found this little church in the fields miles from anywhere, the parish church of St. Agatha of Sicily. It was a sweet little church. You couldn't have got more than thirty people seated comfortably in there. I want to know who Agatha was, what she did, how she died."

"You're bonkers," Holly said.

"Hey, listen to this," Naomi said. "It's shocking. She was a martyr, tortured for being a Christian and because she wouldn't marry this Roman... no... they chopped off her boobs, rolled her over broken glass..."

"Yuck, that's gross."

"Now she's the patron saint of breast cancer patients."

"That figures."

"She was only fifteen," Naomi said.

"What is it with you and scary facts? I remember you dragging me round all those ghost walks years ago."

"I don't remember dragging you anywhere."

"Ok, it was spooky fun, but you can keep your saintly facts. I don't want to think about poor Agatha."

"That's the whole point. It makes you think," Naomi said.

Holly pulled the cushion from Naomi's arms and grabbing her hands, yanked her up from the futon. "The trouble with you is, you've spent too long in East Knoll. Before you dedicate yourself to caring for others, you need a drink."

"Where are you taking me?" Naomi asked as Holly marched her out of the flat and down the road.

"La Casa, my favourite wine bar, there's someone I want you to meet."

"Do I detect a hint of romance?"

"Not really. "

"Who is it, then?"

"The barman," Holly said. She grinned. "You don't look impressed."

"I'm sure he's great, what's his name?"

"Vittorio … he's only behind the bar while he looks for a proper job, it's his uncle's business."

"Don't tell me, let me guess. He's tall and dark with a six-pack. What is it with you and Italian men?"

"He's also only twenty-one and I am not a cradle-snatcher, but he mixes great cocktails."

"I'll let him off, then."

Holly squeezed her arm affectionately. "I knew you wouldn't turn down a Mojito."

CHAPTER 25

Ivy had spent a frustrating day trying to contact Judie. It wasn't until mid-afternoon that she had been successful. Her old friend had been more breathless than usual. "You don't sound too good," she had said.

"My chest's playing up again," Judie had wheezed. "I've been at the hospital for hours."

"Oh dear … and you were so well when I saw you the other day."

"It blew up out of nowhere. The doctor sent me for more tests."

"Well, I won't keep you long. I just wondered if you had news about Mary Glebe. Did you read *The Recorder*?"

"Yes, but I haven't had a chance to do anything about it with my chest like this."

"Well, someone needs to find her."

"Glebe," she had paused. "Hmm … Glebe. Wait a minute, that rings a bell. She coughed dramatically before carrying on. "No, it's gone. Kirsty might know something."

"Well, if she does, she'll have to contact the solicitor. It's all in the paper."

"Now I think about it, there was a Glebe on the council for a while. My brain is useless. Was it Glebe? I'm not sure it was." Ivy had waited as another coughing fit interrupted Judie's musing. "Yes, she was one of those people who think they're a peg or two above everyone else. Deirdre it was; now I remember, Deirdre Glebe, but it can't be anything to do with her."

"Was she married?"

"She was; she married Barry Glebe, remember him? The butcher down by the market. We called her Dreary and, believe me, she was."

"It could be the same family. Her daughter, maybe, someone in her husband's family?"

"I don't know."

"Well, if you think of anyone else, you know what to do, contact the solicitor."

"What solicitor?"

"The one in the paper."

"I know, I'll call George, he used to be chief exec at the council, he'll know. What he doesn't know isn't worth knowing. If anyone remembers the Glebe family, it will be him." Another bout of coughing brought an end to their call.

"You look after yourself," Ivy said. "See you soon."

She had felt so miserable when she came off the phone that despite all her aches and pains she had gone outside to rake over the rose bed by the back door and now she was nursing her painful joints.

It was sad how Judie was deteriorating. Her problems knocked the arthritis into a cocked hat. When she was sitting down doing nothing, she hardly noticed it. Judie really did have something to complain about. What would she do without her? She still had Edith but anno domini was catching up with all of them. Perhaps she should consider Claire's idea, go into sheltered housing where there would be lots of other people her age and someone to keep an eye. She shuddered. Surrounding herself with a whole lot of oldies she didn't know, was her worst nightmare. She liked the company of young people. She wasn't ready to be pensioned off. "Young people keep you young," she muttered. "Everyone knows that."

No-one would persuade her that disappearing into a parallel universe of constant repetition was a good thing. She wanted to stay in the here and now, at twenty-five Blain Gardens. "I've just got to keep going," she muttered. "I'll move when the good

Lord takes me and not before unless I lose my marbles; that wouldn't be too bad would it?" she rambled on and then she had a thought "I reckon it would be a blessing. I wouldn't care where I was because I wouldn't *know* where I was. I'd be happy in my own little world, re-living the past." And then she had another thought. "Or, I could take vitamin pills. Yes, that's the answer. I'll go and see the pharmacist in the morning, get some advice. Ivy Ellison does not cave in at the first obstacle, she goes down fighting."

Jake spent most of the next day waiting for Naomi to call. At first, he was optimistic. The morning dragged. By the time three o'clock came and he had still heard nothing, he felt angry that she was not prepared to give him a chance and then annoyed with himself for feeling angry. He was frustrated that he couldn't work. As more hours passed and he had still heard nothing, his anger collapsed into depression. He was sitting staring into space, playing with a chisel when Guy came home from work. "How's it going?"

"It's not," he said. "I can't concentrate and I've only got a week left to finish everything."

"It sounds to me like you need a beer. Fancy coming down to the pub with me?"

Jake dropped the chisel onto his work bench where it spun like a top before rolling onto the floor. He watched it go, left it lying there as he looked up at his father. "I don't know."

"What's up, Jake?"

"I'm thinking of moving away."

"We've been through all this."

"It's my best option."

"How will you afford it?"

"I'll sell the flat."

"That might take time. The housing market isn't good at the moment. Where will you go?"

"North. The wilds of somewhere … Yorkshire maybe, Northumberland? I don't know. Somewhere I can work."

"You can't run for ever, son. Running away from yourself won't work. Wherever you go your thoughts will go with you."

"Well, it's not working out here," he said bitterly. "I'd rather be somewhere no-one knows me, where I'm not judged."

"Who's judging you?"

"Everyone."

"That's not true," Guy said.

"Ok … Naomi."

"Naomi Henry?"

"She thinks I'm a loser."

"I'm sure she doesn't, as it happens, I saw her yesterday."

"Did you?"

"She was at the charity shop when I called in to see her mother about the will."

"Right," Jake said, his expression unchanging.

"Perhaps the beer is not such a good idea. Spending an evening with you in a bad mood isn't my idea of fun."

"Sorry, Dad, I'm just stressing over everything."

"Nothing lasts for ever."

"Some things do."

"What do you mean?"

"I went to visit Mum's grave the other day." Jake saw his father's shoulders sag and wished he hadn't said anything, but now he had, he decided to carry on and spit out what had been bothering him for years "We never talk about her, Dad."

Guy stared into his son's eyes and saw the hurt, felt the familiar pain of his own pent-up emotions. "No."

"I wish we did. I still miss her."

"I know."

Jake waited to see if his father would be more forthcoming, but when that didn't happen, he lowered his eyes to the chisel and then stooped to pick it up. "Naomi came with me."

"That was good of her."

He lifted his head. "I really like her, Dad."

Guy tested the resilience of a willow whip with his foot. It bent, curved away from the pressure but did not break. "Is that a problem?" he said.

"She doesn't want to know. I'm sure it's because of Nicola. How do I get her to change her mind?

"Tell her the truth."

"I can't"

"Why not?"

"I don't have her number." As soon as he said it, Jake knew it was a feeble excuse.

"That's easily fixed. I'll ask Helena for her number."

"It's not just that. I feel as if I'm stuck in the past... as if we're both stuck in the past."

Their eyes met again and for a split-second Guy was looking into Emma's eyes. He knew the moment had come. The moment he'd been dreading. He sighed. "That's probably my fault. We never discussed Mum dying, not properly. I thought it would be too much for you. To be honest, I couldn't deal with it myself at the time. As the days went by, then weeks and then the months turned into years, I thought you'd find it too embarrassing to talk about her. Teenagers are not the best communicators and besides, there were other more important issues to tackle."

"You mean Nicola."

"A' levels, Nicola, university... look, I know we need to talk. I should have done this a long time ago, but, well, oh, it's hard to explain."

183

"You don't have to."

"I do. I want to. I'm seeing Helena later but…"

"It's ok, Dad. Don't change your plans for me. You're right, I'm not good company. I don't fancy going out anyway."

"We can talk here. I've got an hour. Just give me five minutes to change."

Naomi returned to East Knoll the same evening. As she walked out of the station she didn't make a beeline for home, she went down to the beach instead. It was getting dark. The moon was rising over the town, stars spangling the sky like sequins on a godet. She lifted her chin and filled her lungs with fresh air. There was no wind. The sea was deceptively calm, waves nudging groynes like mares nudging their foals into life, the tide sliding in and then shrinking back over the smooth sand massaging rocks and shells in its path. As the moon rose higher she could detect fishing boat far out in the bay. A stiff breeze blew up and surprised her, the swell now curling back and forth in a rhythmic pattern, covering the wet sand in seaweed and froth.

She thought of Nicola again as she leant against the lamp-post lighting the path down to the beach; of Jake and Nicola. It made her emotional, thinking of them as a couple. She was surprised to find that she was jealous of their relationship; jealous that they had been together if only briefly and then she felt sad, sad for the baby who had not survived. She did not understand the jealousy. She did not want to be with Jake. No-one in their right mind would want to be with someone like him. How he had treated Nicola was shocking. He hadn't cared that she was carrying his child; he had left her, ignored her existence, gone abroad without a second thought. She wanted children but not with someone so callous and uncaring. Neither did she want a man like her own father who had found commitment an ugly word.

Luke had not wanted children. She knew a long time before they parted that children would be their biggest battle. She wanted a large family and that was why she reckoned she would be touched by the loss of anyone's baby, but why should she feel jealous? She had only just met Jake. She was sure she did not want a relationship with him. It must be the moon with its romantic undertones affecting her mood, that and hunger; it had been a while since the Costa panini, but it didn't matter what she felt. She must put her feelings to one side. She must focus on the fact that it would be wrong for her mother to have a relationship with Jake's father. She had to find a way to persuade her to keep him at arm's length and forget her own mooning thoughts.

Just then, a dog barked, down on the beach. She strained to pick it out in the gloom. Her eyes focused into the distance. She could see a man in a dark jacket strolling along the sand. He lifted an arm and threw something into the waves. The driftwood was silhouetted in the moonlight as it soared, arched and then fell arrow-like into the water. She heard splashes as the dog raced after it. Driftwood... Jake. Like all roads leading to Rome, her thoughts insisted on returning to him despite her common sense telling her to forget all about him.

She remembered him asking her to go with him to his mother's grave. She had warmed to him a little then, until she had remembered Nicola, but despite Jake, she was glad to be back, away from the fumes and the raggle-taggle of people on the streets selling whatever they could, souvenirs, lucky heather, fake perfume; away from the constant noise and anonymous lives of the capital. Holly was welcome to it. City life was not for her.

She turned for home, ready to explain to her mother why she should not allow herself to fall for Guy Hampson, when her phone rang. "Hi Mum. I was just thinking about you."

"That's nice. Where are you?"

"On my way home."

"I'm on my way out. I've left a casserole for you. It's in the oven."

"Thanks, you off somewhere exciting?"

"Just out for a drink. I'll see you later."

"Hang on a minute, who with? Who are you going out with, Mum… Mum?" Her mother did not answer, but Naomi thought she could hazard a guess. "It's Guy, isn't it?"

"I have to go. I might be late back."

"Wait, I want to talk to you …"

"We'll talk tomorrow. Enjoy your meal."

"Mum … Mum …" Naomi begged, but the conversation was over. She sighed, she should have said something before. She had a nasty feeling that it might be too late now to halt the progress of their friendship, but she had to try, to give her mother all the facts before she arranged another date with him and things became even more complicated.

"It was a whirlwind romance," Guy said. "Emma didn't like to make plans. She loved surprises, spur of the moment trips, the unexpected."

"Where did you meet?"

"Quite by chance. I'd dropped off my car at Brierley Motors to get its MOT sorted and she was walking past. The handle of her carrier bag broke. I stopped to help her pick up her shopping and saw she had a Terry's chocolate orange."

"That was it, then," Jake said knowing his father's predilection for the sweet treat.

"We arranged to meet that night and then every night for the next few weeks. I knew at once that I wanted to marry her. She made me feel special, interesting, as if I could conquer the world, but being as cautious as she was impulsive, I said nothing and then one night she invited me round to her flat for a meal. There were candles everywhere. She had cooked a special dinner and after we'd eaten she asked me to marry her."

"She asked *you*?"

"She did."

"You said, yes."

"I'm ashamed to say I didn't. I said I'd think about it. My legal training, I suppose. My head needed to cross all the 't's and dot all the 'i's before I committed to anything, even though my heart really wanted me to."

"Wasn't she upset?"

"No, she laughed. When I got home that night I couldn't sleep. I tried everything, whisky, cocoa…"

Jake smiled "Counting sheep?"

"Even that and a few hours later, I called her to accept."

"So, she was romantic."

"Oh yes; she was romantic, warm, compassionate, funny, artistic, beautiful …"

"I can remember her blonde hair. I know she loved the birds."

"Nature, she loved everything about nature. When she got ill she refused treatment. She didn't feel too bad at that point. She said poisoning her body was not the way she wanted to go. She thought natural remedies would cure her. As she got weaker I begged her to listen to her specialist, take the chemo he suggested but she wouldn't."

"Couldn't you have made her?"

"Believe me, I tried but I loved her, Jake. In the end I had to respect her wishes."

"Even though it meant I would lose my mum."

He sighed. "She said she would rather have a few good months with you than years of being ill and losing her hair and then die anyway. She thought that would be too traumatic for you. She wanted you to have happy memories of her."

"I can remember sitting on her knees. I remember her feeding the birds, taking me down to the beach to collect shells."

"Oh yes, the shells."

"I didn't get the chance to say goodbye. That's why I wanted to visit her grave."

"And did it help?" Jake nodded. "That's good. I'm sorry I let you down."

"You didn't."

"I did," he said. "She made me promise to help you through your grief, to talk about her, to tell you how much she loved you."

"I know she loved me."

"I felt guilty I hadn't kept my promise, but I couldn't talk about her then. I didn't want to. When I looked at you I saw her in your eyes, your hair, your mannerisms, I still do. The thought of her not being there, made me too sad. I didn't want you to see me upset. It was a man-thing. I wanted to be strong for you, stiff upper lip, all that, but it was more than that. I was afraid if I started talking about her, I'd lose it, break down ..."

"It's fine. You've told me now."

"I'm glad I have. It feels good. We'll talk about her from now on. Ask me anything, anything at all and I'll give you the best answer I can."

Naomi arrived home to an empty house. She dumped her bag in the hall, helped herself to the casserole and watched some television before she decided to have a bath. She tipped a generous glug of jasmine oil under the gushing taps, making sure the temperature of the water was just right before stepping into the scented warmth, allowing the oil to anoint her limbs as she lay back to ponder how much longer her mother would be. It was already ten thirty and she was tired, relaxing to the point of sleep. She had been chatting with Holly well into the early hours after their visit to the wine bar the previous evening where she had drunk more of Vittorio's cocktails than she had intended, but she didn't want to drop off until she had told her mother everything.

She really seemed to like Guy and she had a niggle of guilt that she was trying to break them up. She reassured herself with the thought that it was a question of being cruel to be kind. She had to reveal his true character before her mother became too attached.

As she removed herself from the fragrant but now not so warm water, she had not wavered in her resolve to air Guy's unworthy actions. She pulled her bath robe around her and padded back to her room, staring into space as she brushed her hair and then plaited it in an absent-minded fashion, whilst pondering how her mother might take the uncloaking of the Guy Hampson paragon. She reflected on the best way of explaining to her what must be said and how she could sweeten the bitter pill. She decided there was no way other than to tell it how it was. She hopped onto the bed, making herself comfortable as she waited for her mother's return.

She awoke to the sound of hushed voices. She rubbed her eyes and strained to hear more... the front door closing, her mother's footsteps on the stairs and a door opening. She jumped up, re-tying the belt of her robe as she hurried to her mother's room.

Helena turned in surprise as she appeared in the doorway. "Gracious, Naomi, you startled me. What are you doing creeping about in the middle of the night? I thought you were asleep, are you ok?"

"I'm fine. I just wanted to talk to you."

Her mother yawned. "Can't it wait until tomorrow, I'm exhausted."

"No, it's important."

"Ok." Helena sat on the bed and patted the duvet beside her. "Come and sit down." She waited for Naomi to join her. "That's better. Now, what is it?"

"Where have you been?"

"You know where I've been."

"Out with Guy."

"I am over eighteen," she said. "You must get rid of this silly phobia about him. He's a perfectly nice man. He drove us to a pub somewhere out in the Styx. You'd think I'd know all the pubs around here by now, but this was a new one to me, The Wheatear, do you know it? There was a live band. Did you know Guy played the banjo?" Naomi answered neither of those questions. Helena sighed. "Why don't you like him, Nims?"

"I don't think you can trust him."

"He's a solicitor for heaven's sake."

"That only means he can pass exams," Naomi said. "It doesn't make him honest or…"

"Or what? I've known him for years. If there was anything dishonest in his past, or his present come to that, I think I'd have heard about it. Sue would have let something slip. She knows all the gossip."

"You don't know about this."

"All right, so, what do you know that I don't?"

"Are you sure you want to know?"

"Yes, if it means you'll let me go to bed."

"This is serious, Mum."

"I'm listening."

CHAPTER 26

Alf Minns was reading Moby Dick. In a busy working life books had not played a big part. Now he was on his own, less active in the shop and his evenings dragged, he often sat down to read. He reckoned most modern books were not worth the paper they were written on. He borrowed books from the library on a regular basis, but he always returned to Moby Dick. He reckoned no-one could write a yarn as well as Herman Melville.

Having lived by the coast all his life, he had a healthy respect for the sea and all creatures of the deep. Once, when he was a child, he remembered seeing a beached whale at Knoll Point. The news had spread like wildfire until it reached the local school. Mr. Dobson had become quite exercised about raw nature arriving in their little community. So much so that he had taken the whole class down there to view the spectacle before it was carted away. They walked two by two, sketch pads and pencils in hand. Some of the girls had screamed at the size of the whale. Some had cried in pity at the bloated body. He recalled that Blanche had not screamed or cried. She had wanted to know how much it weighed. She had wanted to touch it but Mr. Dobson had refused to allow her anywhere near it.

The boys had marvelled at its tail. He remembered Bernard Green being punished for slipping away from the others when Mr. Dobson's back was turned and trying to poke a pencil down its blow-hole. Queenie Doyle had ratted on him and he had been ordered to write, *I must do as I am told,* one hundred times in his best handwriting before he had been allowed home that night. His father had sent him to bed with no supper when he found out. That's the way it was then, he mused. Nothing namby-pamby about his schooldays. It had done them no harm. People were too soft nowadays.

He took off his glasses and rubbed his eyes remembering how that Friday and for many of the Fridays following, Mr. Dobson had read the class extracts from the story of Moby Dick. That was when he had been hooked by the fight between man and nature. From the curious names of the protagonists, *Starbuck, Queequeg* and *Tashtego,* to Captain Ahab's whalebone leg, he had been and still was, captivated by the tale and its intricate whaling detail.

He put the book down and stared into the flames of the gas fire, tongues of mauve, orange and blue licked up the honeycomb bars to mesmerise him. His fight with his conscience could not be compared with Captain Ahab's tussle with Moby Dick. It was not a question of revenge, more of setting the record straight before he passed on; but his decision had to be the right one. He could choose to let the truth die with him, say nothing, be content that what people did not know would not hurt them or, he could reveal the facts, reveal the past and risk the fall-out. He needed to examine his motives. The truth would change lives for ever, he was sure of that, but he hoped it would not spin them round and round in one vortex as it had done to the crew of the *Pequod.*

Blanche had urged him to explain, had said she didn't mind if he did, that he had to make his own decision. That had somehow made him feel it was his duty to do so. Blanche had been clever, had always been cleverer than him. She had been clever at getting people to do things without them knowing she had influenced them in any way. He had noticed it happening several times over the years.

He remembered how she had persuaded her father that it would be best for her to carry on her studies with him, without ever stating such an aim. Instead, she had expressed a willingness to discuss possible courses for which she could enrol at university, while at the same time treating him to subtle flattery. In the end, he had declared that she would learn far more with him on a one-to-one basis than in a class of other less able students, which is exactly the outcome she had wanted in the first place.

He chuckled at her wily ways and wished for the umpteenth time, that she was still there. He had searched his conscience and was almost sure it was the right thing to do, but he kept coming back to the one question that bothered him and to which he had found no answer. It was his chat with Sol that had thrown up the pertinent question; Sol had asked him if he was doing it for others or for himself.

He was the only person left who could explain what had happened, but he was under no obligation to do so. He reasoned that what people did not know would not hurt them, but they had a right to know, that was the thing. He would have wanted to know, had things been the other way around. He carried on weighing up the pros and cons for a while longer and then when his head started to throb with all the indecision, he knew he had wrestled with it for long enough. He stopped the fight. He would go with his gut instinct and tell all.

Naomi was having second thoughts. She was questioning her motives. Did she want her mother to know about Jake because she thought it was the right thing to do, or just because she wanted to hurt Guy and ruin her mother's relationship? That would be a bit dark if not unfair. Her mother was not naïve. She was not a bad judge of character. Maybe she should just leave things as they were. She didn't want to be the cause of her mother's unhappiness if they split up. Guy's only sin had been to help his son escape a messy situation. Wouldn't any parent want to do the same? She stared at her hands and said nothing.

"If you're just going to sit there and say nothing, you may as well go back to bed and let me get some sleep," Helena said.

"Do you really want to know?"

"I've already answered that."

"I know, but…"

"It's obviously something important, so, yes, I do."

"Ok, so, do you remember when we were at school and everyone wanted to go out with Jake Hampson?"

"Everyone except you."

"I wasn't interested and I didn't even know him then. I knew who he was, but from what I'd heard, he was a bit full of himself. Anyone could tell that from the way he drove his mini around as if he owned the world. Anyway, he got this girl pregnant… Nicola."

"Right."

"She wasn't one of our group. She didn't come from round here. Holly knew her better than me. Anyway, Jake got her pregnant and then he disappeared, just left her to it. His father didn't encourage him to stand by her, he sent him abroad instead." she hesitated for a moment while she attempted to read her mother's expression. It was neither shocked nor horrified which she found surprising "He went straight off to uni after that and we all forgot about him until he turned up here again. Holly told me Nicola had a miscarriage."

"Maybe that was for the best."

"How can you say that?"

"She was very young and not with the father. She may have come to resent the child."

"I think it's sad. I expect Nicola was sad about it. I would have been sad, if it had been me."

194

"I'm glad it wasn't you."

Naomi hadn't expected the conversation to go this way. She had expected her mother to think, as she did, that both Guy and Jake had behaved badly. "So, now you can see why I don't want you to get involved with Guy Hampson. He's flaky. You can't trust him."

"I'm glad you're looking out for me, Nims, but I knew all that already."

"You knew… how?"

"Guy told me at the time."

"Why didn't you tell me?"

"Nicola wasn't one of your friends and neither was Jake. I didn't think you'd be interested and anyway, Guy had asked me not to. He didn't want the whole world finding out. It's very sweet that you care about me, but you've been worrying over nothing," Helena said.

"I wouldn't have been worried if you'd told me," Naomi said more than a little miffed that her revelation was not a revelation at all.

"I told you, Guy asked me not to say anything."

"What if I'd wanted to go out with Jake. You would have let me go without a word?"

"You didn't want to go out with him."

"That's not the point."

"I also know that Jake was not the father of the baby," Helena said. "Nicola had been sleeping around but not with him. She just picked on him because his father had money."

"How do you know that?"

"Guy explained everything. He had been prepared to do his bit."

"He would say that, wouldn't he?"

"Why would he make it up?"

"To make himself look good."

"He's not like that, Nims. We weren't in a relationship then. He would have had nothing to gain by lying to me. He told me the parents got together and Nicola eventually admitted the truth; she hadn't a clue who the father was. Jake was just a convenient fall-guy. He had been due to fly to Australia to visit some of his mother's relatives a few days later anyway; it was just coincidence he went when he did."

"Oh." Naomi's head was spinning. She felt bad for not being nicer to Jake. He was the one who deserved her sympathy, not Nicola. Nicola was the bad guy, not Jake. It must have been awful for him to have been blamed for something he hadn't done. She could feel warmth creep up her neck and into her cheeks as she recalled how harshly she had judged him "You should have said something," she said.

"I didn't want to break my promise to Guy. I understood why he didn't want people to know, damage limitation. You know how fast gossip spreads around East Knoll. I would have told you if I'd thought that was why you were so anti. It sounds like Nicola's the one you can't trust, not Guy. You need to put Holly straight."

"Yes, I'm so sorry, Mum."

"It's fine, you didn't know. I'm sorry you've been worrying about it all this time. When you get to know him better you'll see Guy is a really nice man and a good friend."

"Am I likely to get to know him better?"

"I hope so. I enjoy his company. It might turn into something more permanent, it might not, but for the moment it's good. Oh, I didn't tell you, the tea party has been arranged for Saturday. We'll finally get to meet Mary Glebe."

"Can I come?"

"You and Isla can both come. Exciting, isn't it?"

"I wonder what she's like."

"Me too; it won't be long before we find out." She gave Naomi a hug. "I am touched you wanted to protect me, Nims. Don't be too hard on Jake. Look, I'm really tired, can I go to bed now?"

Naomi sauntered out of the room but not to bed. She twiddled with the end of her plait as she made her way downstairs to get a drink and do some serious thinking. From what her mother had said, Jake was not the person she had imagined for all those years. How could she hope to have a relationship with him now after the way she had treated him? She had made it plain that she didn't want to get to know him better, not even as a friend. He would think it a bit weird if, the next time they met, she was overly friendly towards him. It would be embarrassing for them both.

It was bizarre that her mother should be in some sort of a relationship with his father. It was just as well she had given Jake the cold shoulder. No, she couldn't possibly have a relationship with him now. It would be like going out with her brother; that was sick. What would Holly say if she did? How would she take the news that Nicola had passed on fake news? There was no doubt she would challenge Nicola the next time they met. Holly wouldn't be Holly if she didn't.

Maybe she had mis-read the signals from him. Maybe there were no signals to read. She felt a sense of disappointment that their relationship had finished before it had begun, which she thought perverse since she had persuaded herself she didn't want anything to do with Jake Hampson.

Her thoughts continued in confusion, until she heard Isla come in. "You're up late," she said. "I thought everyone would be in bed... are you ok?"

"Yes," Naomi said. "How did you get on?"

"One suspected heart attack, a baby false alarm and an old chap with pleurisy. I hope that's it for now," she said.

"Actually, I was trying to work out what to do with my life."

"That's a tricky one."

"I've decided to become a full-time Carer; I applied for a CRB check, online yesterday."

"Really?"

"It was looking after Blanche that gave me the idea."

"Good carers are hard to find. I couldn't do it, but if that's what you want to do, go for it."

"I know I could do it. I think I'd enjoy it. It has to be better than working in an office nine to five."

"I guess. Is Helena in bed?"

"Yes, and I feel a bit stupid for making such a fuss about Guy. I got it all wrong."

"So, you're not going to bad-mouth him again."

"I'll just let them get on with it, whatever *it* is. She was pretty vague about the nature of their relationship."

"What about Jake?"

"I'm not interested in Jake," she said concentrating on sweeping crumbs from the table into her cupped hand and tossing them into the bin. "I've just boiled the kettle if you want a cuppa."

"That's just what I need. Did she give you the letter?"

"No… what letter?"

"It was delivered by hand the other day. I don't know what she did with it."

"I'll ask her tomorrow. She said the tea party is on. We're both invited."

"Are we? When?"

"Saturday."

"I should be able to do that. I'm not on call next weekend."

"It will be interesting to find out who Mary Glebe is, or at least to know how she knew Blanche."

"They must have been close, or she wouldn't have been left the premium bonds," Isla said.

"I have a hunch."

"Another one?"

"She was her manicurist."

"A manicurist? You're joking."

"Did you ever see her hands?"

"Yes, but I didn't notice anything special about them."

"They were beautiful hands," Naomi said. "Not the hands of a ninety-year old, you know, all veiny and wrinkled. The skin was so soft and her nails were beautifully manicured. She told me she creamed them every night and slept in cotton gloves. She said it was a trick her mother had taught her, and it had obviously worked; she had no age spots, no wrinkles, nothing, just lovely smooth skin and perfect nails."

"I wish mine were like that," Isla said. "I need to wash them so often between patients I get through gallons of hand cream. Look at my knuckles," she said waving them in Naomi's face. "I've got dry skin, broken nails, the lot."

"Blanche was proud of her hands."

"Why are we talking about hands?" Isla said.

"To prove that Blanche could have left her money to whoever it was who made her hands look pretty."

"She was a mass of contradictions, for sure," Isla said. "You wouldn't think that sort of thing would bother her. You wouldn't think she'd want to waste money on her hands."

"No ... she never wore make-up, did she?"

"No."

"Her hair was amazing," Naomi said.

"I can't remember it ever being any different. She never went to the hairdresser. Dad said he saw it down once when she was drying it in the sun. It went way past her waist," Isla said.

"Wow."

"She certainly didn't care about clothes."

"She only had four pairs of shoes for heaven's sake, *four pairs*, can you believe it?" Naomi said.

Isla laughed. "I can. I only have a few pairs. How many pairs do you have?".

"Hmm ten, twenty? No, more than that. I haven't counted my boots…"

"Ok, so by your standards, Blanche was low on shoes," Isla said. "Clothes and shoes don't make someone who they are. It's more complicated than that."

"I know, but she didn't like spending money and yet she shelled out for works of art, a top if the range kitchen..."

"With the help of the insurance company."

"… she wasn't sentimental," Naomi went on "And yet she kept that piece of wedding cake."

"And so, you reckon it follows that, however unlikely, she left the premium bonds to the person who did her nails," Isla said.

"Exactly and because they were important to her," Naomi said. "I'm guessing Mary Glebe is young and bubbly with blonde hair."

"She could just as easily be middle-aged with a wig," Isla said.

"She probably thought Mary could do with the money."

"We'll probably never find out."

Naomi yawned. "Oh well, it doesn't matter as long as we can live in Barque House. I'm off to bed."

CHAPTER 27

Adrian had finally rolled up his sleeves and tackled the files stored in the loft in his search for references to Mary Glebe. So far, he had come up with precisely nothing. There was no mention of her in any of his correspondence with Blanche Black. "Adrian." He ignored his wife's call and checked through the last batch of papers but drew another blank. "Adrian." Her voice was becoming ever more strident as he took his time putting everything back in the plastic boxes he had raided. Auburn hair followed by indignant green eyes appeared through the loft entrance. "Didn't you hear me? I've been calling for ages. You really need to get your ears tested."

He shuffled round to face her. "What did you want?"

"I thought we could take Mum out for lunch."

"Where do you want to go?"

"Anywhere, I don't mind."

"The Killingbeck Ridge?"

"No, somewhere more informal."

"The Two Peaks?"

"Too far."

Adrian gave her a long hard stare. "Where, then?"

"She likes going to the tea-rooms in the village."

"For heaven's sake, Isobel, you could have said that in the first place. It's not my idea of a lunch out but if she's happy with beans on toast, it's fine."

"Don't be so snobby. They do nice pies. You like their pies."

Adrian tutted impatiently. "Fine. I'll finish up here and then we'll go. Have you told her we're taking her out?"

"No and I'm not going to. She'll only make some excuse not to come. She sits in that house all day, never goes out, never does anything. She didn't even go to church this week. It's getting silly."

"She's old. She might not want to go out."

"I think it will do her good."

"Perhaps we should take lunch in to her."

"No, she must go out, that's the whole point. I'm sure she'll perk up when she gets out of those four walls." Adrian knew it was useless to argue. He had learned from experience that once Isobel had made up her mind, it was made up. "I'm taking the dogs for a quick walk first." She disappeared back down the ladder, only to return moments later. "Did you find anything about Mary Glebe?"

"Sadly not. I reckon they'll have to get Guy Hampson onto it."

"It took you so long to get up here he's probably done it by now anyway. Mind you don't trip on your way down."

With her back safely turned, Adrian rebelled. "*Mind you don't trip,*" he mouthed. "Don't fuss, Isobel," he said out loud.

"I'm not fussing. I just don't want to have to drive you all the way to the hospital."

"I got up here all right. I'm sure I can get down again, no problem. Take the dogs. I'll be ready by the time you get back."

"Not again," Ivy grumbled to herself as the phone rang out endlessly. "They must have cut her off. That phone company is hopeless." She wanted to tell Edith her big news; that Judie had discovered a clue which had led to the discovery of Mary Glebe's whereabouts. The thought of being the first to break the news had overheated her. A stroll round to Ian and Pippa's to report the fault would cool her down. If the phone was out of order, she reckoned it was up to her to alert the other members of the family.

She heaved herself out of the chair and then sat down again.

She'd feel a bit daft if Edith had gone to get her hair done, or Isobel had taken her shopping and there was nothing wrong with the phone. Perhaps she should try later. On the other hand, the phone *might* be out of order again and it would be fixed a whole lot quicker if they made a fuss. She owed it to her friend to do something about it whether she looked silly or not. The over-riding reason was that she wanted to tell her about Mary Glebe.

That thought tipped the balance and she got to her feet a second time, kicked off her slippers, tucked her feet into her purple trainers and picked up the house keys.

She was pressing the bell on Ian and Pippa's front door before she remembered they might be out. Phoebe was at school every morning now but Pippa still had Fridays off. Sometimes she went to the gym. Sometimes she met her friends for a coffee. Sometimes she did a big shop. Was it even Friday? Of course it was. She had played bingo at church the day before and the bingo was always on a Thursday, so it must be Friday.

At that point in her reasoning, the door opened and Pippa stood there in jeans and a t-shirt, hands protected by pink marigolds. "Oh, it's you, Ivy. I was just making playdough for Phoebe. She loves pretend cake making and it's less messy than the real thing." She giggled. "Come in. Is everything alright?"

As the door swung shut behind her, Ivy blurted out her indignation. "That phone company should be paying us to use their service, not the other way around, that's if you can call it a service," she said. "I dread to think how much money they've had off me over the years ... and we should get compensation on top of that. This is the third time I haven't been able to get in touch with Edith. It's too bad. Can you call your mum and get her to check out the line?"

"Are you sure you waited long enough for her to answer? Gran always takes ages to pick up."

"I know that," Ivy said. "I waited and waited and still no luck. I had something very important to tell her."

"Did you?"

"It's about this missing person."

"Who do you mean?"

"Mary Glebe. We've been trying to find her."

"Oh, the Blanche Black business. Why are you and Gran involved?"

"Never mind that, it doesn't matter. I'm more interested in getting Edith's phone back on; I don't like to think of her without it."

"Ok. Look, sit down for a minute," Pippa said hoping to calm Ivy's obvious agitation. She peeled back the rubber gloves "I'll try her number. If I can't get through, I'll text Mum," she said. "She can give Gran a message if the phone's playing up again."

Isobel and Adrian arrived at Edith's cottage just before twelve. "Shall I go in and fetch her … Isobel?" She looked up from her phone. "Who are you texting now?"

"Pippa. She said Ivy wanted to know if Mum's phone is ok, apparently it's on the blink again."

"What, Edith's phone … *again*?"

"Yes."

"You spoke to her last night."

"That doesn't mean it can't have gone wrong since."

"We didn't have a hurricane overnight, or did I miss something, apart from you complaining about my snoring."

"You know we didn't and there's no need to be sarcastic," she said brushing past him to unlock the door. "The phone could still be out of order."

"In which case, it's a good job we're here. I'll give the phone company a rocket if it is. That'll be three times in as many months. They waste cash on glossy ads and pay their top men obscene amounts of money, but when you want repairs done it's another story."

Not wanting to let go of her mobile, Isobel jiggled the keys in one hand, trying to find the right one. They slipped from her fingers onto the path. "Bother... now look what you've made me do."

"How is that my fault?" Adrian said as he bent down to retrieve them. "I'll do it, there you are," he said handing her back the keys as he pushed the door open and walked inside.

Isobel trailed behind him, checking to see if she had received more messages. "It's only us, Mum," she called.

The kitchen door was open. A fresh batch of scones was cooling on a wire rack on the work-top. "She's not in the kitchen," he said.

"I can smell scones."

"Indeed, you can," he said eyeing up Edith's baking before putting out a hand to help himself.

"Well don't snaffle one. I'm sure she'll give us some to take home and she will have counted them. She's probably having a nap," she said opening the sitting room door quietly and peeping in. "Yes, it seems a shame to wake her."

"She'll be cross if you don't."

"Ok."

"She needs to eat some lunch and so do I, so get on with it," he said.

Edith was sitting in her chair in front of the fire with the throw over her knees, a book and an empty mug on the table beside her.

Isobel knelt on the carpet and took hold of her mother's hands. "Wake up, Mum, we're going out for lunch... Mum? Mum..." her voice trailed off and she turned to look at her husband, eyes wide with fear. "Adrian..."

"Hmm?" he had taken the poker propped up against the mantelpiece and jabbed at the fire. The glowing embers, far from leaping back into life, had gone out one by one. He sighed and dropped the poker onto the tiled hearth where it clanged like a school bell. "Sorry," he muttered. "What's up?"

"Come here."

"What now?" he said annoyed that his efforts had come to nothing. He straightened his back and twisted round. One glance at her face told him that something was very wrong. He was at her side in seconds. He scanned his mother-in-law's face, eyes shut, skin paler than pale, blue lips twisted into a smile. He bent over to see if she was breathing. He took her wrist to check for a pulse and when he detected no signs of life, he felt a strange surge of emotion in his chest. His legs gave way and he half-fell onto the sofa.

Isobel waited for his reassurance "She's not…"

"I think she is," he said.

"Oh no… we should call an ambulance," she said.

"It's too late for that," he said. "It must have been her heart."

She sat back on her heels for a moment and took a deep breath. "I wish I'd been here for her."

"It's how she would have wanted to go, peacefully, at home."

"I know, but she was all alone."

"It can't have happened too long ago. We were probably at the door. The scones are still warm."

"Yes, but all *alone*," she said bleakly.

"She didn't mind being on her own. She loved this house. She always said she was closer to Ralph here than anywhere else. She had a good innings. I'll phone Dr. Lock."

"In a minute. I could do with a brandy first."

"Your mother didn't drink."

"There'll be a bottle in the kitchen for medicinal purposes and Christmas cakes."

He got to his feet, a tight smile tweaking his lips. "That sounds like Edith."

Isobel nodded. "Adrian…"

"What is it?"

"I didn't know this was going to happen."

"No-one did."

"I didn't have a chance to tell her how much I loved her."

"I'm sure she knew, darling."

"I just kept going on and on about her not eating enough."

"You did that because you loved her, she would have understood."

She leant towards the silent form "Sorry, Mum," she whispered. She kissed the cooling cheeks before settling her head on her mother's knees as she had often done as a child remembering how her mother's hand would lie gently on her hair; remembering how loved she had felt, how safe… and now it was over. How could it have happened so suddenly with no warning, no preparation, no goodbyes? "It was too soon," she said.

"I know," he said.

"Bye, Mum," she whispered. "God bless, I'll miss you… give Dad my love."

He watched, a lump as big as Etna choking him. He tried to swallow it down and when that didn't work, he coughed it away. "Are you alright?"

Isobel stayed where she was, head resting on the throw, cheeks now wet with tears. "I will be."

"Well done," he said. He took hold of her shoulder and squeezed it affectionately. "I'll get you that brandy."

Ian stood outside Ivy's front door hesitating before he rang the bell. He was worried that the news about Edith would upset her. They had become great friends over the short time they had known one another but he reckoned it was better she heard it from him than from anyone else. He pressed the buzzer and waited.

Ivy opened the door almost at once. "Yes … oh, it's you, Ian. Do you need a baby sitter again?"

"Not today. Can I come in for a minute?"

"Come on in," she said as she backed away from the door. "Shall I put the kettle on?"

"I think you should."

"It is nearly three o'clock. I don't know where the day goes. Sit down, I'll bring it through."

He walked into the lounge and flopped down on the sofa only to jump up again a few moments later. He walked across to the window and then he went back to the sofa to perch on the arm.

Ivy appeared with two mugs. "Here you are my love," she said passing him his.

"Thanks," he said.

"The cup that cheers," she said taking her usual seat "Except that we've got mugs. You're home early," she added waiting for him to say what he had come to say.

"Yes," he took a sip of his tea "Um… we're off up to Cumbria," he said having decided to break the news as gently as he could.

"That's nice. Edith will be pleased to see you." She wondered why he seemed so ill at ease and then caught the expression on his face. "What is it, Ian?"

"Something's happened. Edith won't be there, Mrs. E."

"Why not?"

"She died this morning."

Ivy felt the room spin. Her head filled with cotton wool. She could hear distant bells. She put her mug down on the coffee table and looked up at him. "Dead... no, she can't be."

"I'm afraid so ... this morning."

"No," she said again, shaking her head. "No, no, it was just her phone. She told me. They were working on the cables."

He moved across to squat down at her side. "I don't want it to be true, Mrs. E, but it is," he said gently.

"It can't be, not Edith," she said.

"I'm so sorry."

"But I speak to her nearly every day. She said she was fine."

"They think it was a heart attack."

"A heart attack," she repeated. "I don't feel too good," she said. "My head's spinning."

"Shall I get the doctor?"

"A glass of water," she said. "Just a glass of water. I'll be fine in a minute."

He fetched the water and returned to her side. "Thanks," she said taking a large gulp. "Are you sure there's no mistake?"

"There's no mistake."

"Was she on her own?"

"Isobel and Adrian were there to take her out for lunch. They thought she was asleep. It was very peaceful."

"That's a blessing." Ivy put the glass down as her hands started to shake uncontrollably.

"Let me call the doctor," he said.

"No need, it's shock," she said. "I'm in shock." her chin wobbled, tears rippled from her eyes like mercury, settling in the creases of her jowly cheeks. "Poor Edith. I'm going to miss her."

He felt his eyes prick. He couldn't let her see how near to tears he was himself, it might make her worse and he could not risk that happening after he left when there would be no-one to help her. He turned away to pull out his phone as she fumbled up her sleeve for a tissue. "I'll call the doctor," he said. "Better to be safe than sorry."

"What will I do without her?" Ivy said, more to herself than to him. "We used to watch Morse, you know. They don't make programmes like that these days. Morse liked crosswords. I like crosswords. When Edith came to stay we did the crosswords together. We chatted for hours. She was a good friend, one in a million. You don't get many friends like that in a lifetime; we were on the same wavelength. We laughed at the same things." She stared at the phone and her chin wobbled. "The phone won't ring so much now, no more chats …"

Ian finished the call and put his phone back in his pocket "Come on, Mrs E. She wouldn't want you to be sad. She would want you to remember the happy times, all the good memories."

"Good memories, yes," she said. "That's right."

"Someone's coming out from the surgery to see you this afternoon."

She wiped her nose vigorously. "Thanks Ian," she said.

"I really need to go now. Will you be all right?"

"Yes, yes, you go, don't worry about me."

"Are you sure? I could wait another few minutes."

"You get off, love," she said in a much more Ivy-like tone. "Pippa needs you. I'll be fine."

CHAPTER 28

Naomi overslept on Saturday morning which meant she only had an hour to get ready before it was time to leave for the rendezvous with Mary Glebe. She trotted down the stairs in her pyjamas. Her mother was in the kitchen. "Why didn't you wake me?" she asked.

"I was just coming to do it," Helena said handing her a glass of freshly squeezed orange juice. "You've got plenty of time to get ready."

"I was going to wash my hair. You know how long it takes to dry."

"Use my hair drier."

"Mum, I never use the hair drier."

"But you could, just this once. Anyway, your hair's fine as it is." Naomi examined her appearance in the little mirror on the window sill and frowned.

"I *am* going to wash it," she said.

Helena smiled benignly. "I've got something else for you. This came while you were in London," she said as she handed over the envelope. "Ouch," she said wincing and rubbing her wrist. "I don't know what I've done to myself. This wrist really hurts."

"You've probably been lifting too many boxes at the shop. Get Isla to look at it." She glanced down at the envelope. "Oh yes, she told me about this." She put the glass down on the worktop and tore it open.

"Who's it from?"

"I don't know," she said. "It's just a mobile number."

"Let me see," Helena said.

She handed the slip of paper to her mother and took a sip of juice. "Weird or what?"

"It is weird," she said handing it back. "Did you ask someone for their number?"

Naomi thought for a minute and then shook her head. "It's a complete mystery."

"Not another one," Helena said. She had hoped to raise a smile, but Naomi looked preoccupied. "It's definitely for you," she went on "Look, it's your name on the envelope. You don't recognise the writing?"

"I can't be fagged to think about it now," Naomi said. She dropped the paper on the table and picked up the glass. "You can throw it away. I'm off to get ready. Don't go without me. Oh, by the way, can I borrow the car later?"

"Tonight, you mean?"

"No after the tea party. I thought I might go to the craft fair at Upfordham."

"Ok. I'm sure Guy will give me a lift back."

"Thanks, Mum."

"You're most welcome," she said. Something in her daughter's nonchalance made Helena think she knew more than she was letting on. She waited until she heard water running in the bathroom and then picked up the slip of paper. She studied the numbers again. She tapped them into her mobile and waited. "*Hi, this is Jake's phone. Leave a message. Might call you back, might not.*"

Why would Jake be giving her his number? Naomi didn't even like him, or at least she said she didn't. Maybe she liked him more than she was letting on, or maybe she didn't like him as much as he liked her. She shook her head. Whatever the situation, Naomi obviously didn't want to discuss it. She dropped the paper in the bin and went to get herself ready.

The Rev. Jon Driver surveyed the church hall. The rafters were festooned with bunting, the empty tables waiting to be filled with home-made cakes and jam, pottery, paintings, local photographs, not to mention Angela Reedman's popular cards. He was looking forward to seeing what Jake Hampson had come up with but most of all he hoped the day would be a success for everyone. He knew how much hard work the fund-raising committee put into events and it would be disappointing for them if only a few people turned up.

His wife's arms curled around his waist like a sash. He twisted round to face her. "What are you doing here?"

"I heard you go out and thought I'd come too. I know this is the lull before the storm. When everything kicks off you won't have a minute and anyway, I'm meeting your mum in half an hour."

He laid gentle hands on her baby bump. "What are you two doing today?"

"We're going to Ikea to look for furniture for the baby's room."

"Oh yes, so you are."

"We'll be back later, to help."

"You're on the raffle with Bella."

"Yes. I'm looking forward to seeing all the stalls set up. I love these craft fairs. They're one of my favourite events."

"I'm hoping Jake Hampson being here will encourage more people to come this year. I saw his sculpture at the High School … impressive."

"I checked the weather forecast. No rain today," she said.

"Brilliant."

"I think we should buy some of Angela's cards."

"And Marion's cakes and some raffle tickets, or there will be trouble."

Thyme took his face in her hands and kissed his mouth. "I'd better go to the bank, then."

"Ah, young love." Daisy was standing at the door smiling as Jon and Thyme sprang apart.

"Morning Daisy. The hall looks good," Thyme said.

"We're not quite ready. I need to set out the tables and chairs for refreshments and get the urn going."

"Where do you want the tables?" Jon said.

"On the stage. We thought we'd shut the curtains, so people can sit down and have their tea in peace without the children rampaging about. Ben put up some fairy lights for us last night and there'll be tea-lights in jars on all the tables."

"Sounds magical," Thyme said.

"I'll help with that," Jon said.

"Are you staying, Thyme?"

"Not now, but I'll be here to help later."

"Oh yes. You're off to Ikea, aren't you? Diana told me."

"I hope there'll be scones left by the time we get back."

"I'm sure Mum will buy you meatballs at Ikea," Jon said.

"I'll still have room for scones," she said.

"I don't know how she manages to eat so much these days," he said. "She'll end up producing a Sumo wrestler."

Thyme pulled a face. "I hope not."

"Don't take any notice," Daisy said. "It's healthy to have a good appetite when you're pregnant. I'll save you some."

"Thanks, Daisy. Good luck with everything," she said and blew her husband a kiss.

"Have a good time," he called "Don't get carried away with the spending."

"No danger of that," Daisy said. "Thyme is very sensible."

"She knows I was only joking. I hope she doesn't get too tired."

"Your mother will keep an eye on her; they'll have fun."

"It's great they get on so well."

"It's lucky for you," Daisy said. "My mother-in-law was a

nightmare, especially after Brian died; she was no help with the children. Somehow it was my fault he fell off the ladder. It didn't occur to her that her son should have been more careful."

"Mothers and their sons, eh?"

"Diana's not like that."

"No, she's always encouraged me to take responsibility for myself."

"Oh well, water under the bridge. Did Jane tell you about Blanche Black?"

"Did you know her?" he said.

"No, I'd heard of her, of course and her father. All the old dears talked about Dr. Black when I moved into the village."

"You mean this problem with her will?"

"Yes, I wonder if they've found the mystery woman yet."

"If they haven't found her I'm sure it won't be long before they do, especially if there's a lot of money involved."

"I've never been left a fortune," Daisy said.

"Neither have I and I'm never likely to be, more's the pity or I could give a big donation to the church."

"It wouldn't matter how much you donated, we'd be sure to find something else that needed attention. This building gobbles up money."

"And that, Daisy, is why we are here," he said putting an arm around her shoulders. "Come on, let's sort out these tables."

Guy watched his son stagger towards the hired van with an armful of broomsticks "Do you need help loading up?"

"Thanks, Dad."

"How about unloading?"

"Daisy Parsloe will be able to help with that. I spoke to her yesterday."

"Right, so, what do you want me to fetch?"

"Anything from the bench. I put most of the stuff in crates."

"Have you had any more thoughts about moving away?"

"Still mulling it over."

"Whatever you decide, I'll go along with it. You only get one life."

"It hasn't been great so far."

"I'm sorry you feel like that. The only way is up, son. Things will get better. I won't be coming to the fair. It's the tea party today you know, Roman Reach."

"Oh yes," Jake said loading up his father's arms like a fork lift truck and then helping himself to more crates "You're not expecting trouble, are you?"

"Not really, it should be interesting."

"Who's invited?"

"Mary Glebe, Helena, Isla Ford ..."

"Naomi?" Jake asked.

"Yes, she'll be there."

"I hope they all get on."

"It doesn't matter if they don't. We only need Helena and Mary to turn up and drink a cup of tea."

"It's that simple?"

"Yes." Guy dumped the crates inside the van. "Is that it?"

"I just need a few props and then I'm off. Thanks for helping."

"You're welcome. Good luck with the sales."

"I'm not expecting too much but if the weather holds out, there should be a reasonable number of punters there."

"The more people who see your stuff, the more you'll sell."

"That's the plan."

"Jon Driver will be hoping for a good turnout. That church needs a lot of renovation. Bob Pryce should have done more. He'd given up with retirement looming."

"I remember him. You used to take me there for the Christingle service," Jake said.

"You remember …"

"Only because there were sweets involved."

"Do you um, remember Mum being with us?"

"I wish I did."

"It was her idea. Holy Trinity didn't have a Christingle service in those days."

"I'm glad we can talk about her now. It brings her closer, back to life in a way, kind of like when I asked you to choose the crayons for me to colour in my colouring books."

"Ah those colouring books," Guy said. "I spent a fortune in Alf Minns' shop on colouring books."

"So, if you think of Mum's life as one of those books… no, you're going to think this is cheesy."

"I won't."

"Well, your memories are the crayons I need to finish the pages."

"She would have liked that analogy."

"She enjoyed sketching birds in the garden, I can remember that."

"She did … and she did some brilliant sketches of you, too."

"Really? Where are they?"

"Up in the attic with all her art stuff," Guy said.

"I'd like to see them some time."

"You will; she was a very talented artist, a great mum, a good friend, an amazing person. She would have been proud of you and your sculptures."

"Would she?"

"Definitely; you'll find your own amazing person one day."

"I thought I had, Dad. I really thought I had."

217

"Hmm, well, running off somewhere isn't going to make that happen."

"What do you suggest I do?"

"Go with your gut instinct. Be honest. Tell her."

"What if she blanks me?"

"You'll have to take that chance. *Faint heart never won fair maiden*, you know. She's not a mind-reader; unless you tell her how you feel, she'll never know. You can't make people love you, Jake, but if it's meant to happen, it will."

CHAPTER 29

Helena, Isla and Naomi arrived at Roman Reach in good time for their meeting with Mary Glebe. The country-club style hotel was a local landmark with its castellated walls and extensive grounds. In summer the lawns were covered in meringue castle marquees, popular for functions. Teas were served in a small reception room on the first floor, dinners in the large dining room on the ground floor; the two rooms could not have been more different. To reach the tea-room, they had to pass the dining room and climb an impressive wooden stair-case. "Have you ever been in here?" Helena said as they approached the dining room door.

"No," Naomi said.

"Is it very grand?" Isla sked.

"It's worth a look," Helena said.

They paused by the open door and Naomi and Isla peeped in. "It's a bit posh," Naomi said taking in the waterfall chandelier, leather armchairs and white-clothed tables laid with silver cruets. It was a north-facing room, shadowy, cool and it would have been cheerless had it not been for the canary yellow walls and mirrors reflecting light from the windows. The marble fireplace was home to an extravagant flower arrangement; hydrangea blooms, gladioli, lilies interspersed with some architectural foliage.

"Those flowers are beautiful," Isla said. "I expect they have a florist to re-do them every week."

"They're not real," Helena said.

"How do you know that?" Naomi said. "They look pretty real to me."

"Guy and I had a meal here a few weeks ago. He told me.

I didn't believe him. When we got up to leave, I checked, they're silk."

"I bet he loved that," Naomi said.

"He thought it was funny," Helena said.

"They must have a real fire in winter," Isla said. "Imagine Christmas dinner, smouldering logs, chandelier sparkling …" she was interrupted by the ormolu clock on the mantelpiece chiming the hour in a tremulous flurry.

"Look at the time," Helena said. "Come on, we don't want to keep them waiting."

They clattered up the stairs in single file entering the tea-room to a burst of sunshine. Unlike the dining room, there was no fire-place in this room and no mirrors, just bare floorboards and white walls. "We're first," Isla said.

Naomi glanced around the room approvingly. "This is much more me," she said.

The room faced south and despite the white-out, it was warm, sunny with a good view of the grounds. Brightly-painted chairs were grouped around the melamine-topped tables, which with the empty high chairs lined up in a corner like taxis, lent an informal, youthful ambience to the room. Giant butterflies had been attached to one of the walls and a collage of tin cans camouflaged the back of the door.

"Well, it's different," Isla said.

"I am *loving* that door," Naomi said as she clocked the colourful display.

"Where shall we sit?" Helena said.

"Anywhere," Naomi said and then headed straight for a table by the door "Here," she went on, eyes glued to the countless cans "Coke, Pepsi, Seven-up …"

"… Stella, san Pellegrino," Helena added.

"And lemonade," Isla said.

"So, when do you think they'll arrive?" Naomi said.

Helena shook her head. "Don't know." She checked her phone. "They should be here by now."

"Maybe Mary has chickened out."

"Why would she do that?" Isla said. "It's for her benefit."

"It seems unlikely," Helena said.

"Ok, so, where is she?"

"Stuck in traffic," Isla said.

"Let's order a pot of tea while we're waiting," Helena said.

Naomi took off her jacket and hung it round the back of her chair. "I'm going to miss the craft fair if they don't hurry up. It closes at four."

"I'm surprised you're going after what you said about Jake," Isla said.

"This has nothing to do with Jake, ok?" Naomi said her cheeks warm with dissembling. "I was hoping to buy some early Christmas presents."

"That's not like you," Helena said.

"No, you're usually panicking on Christmas Eve because you haven't done all your shopping," Isla said.

"This year I want it to be different, what's wrong with that?"

"You don't have to stay," Helena said.

"I do if I want to meet Mary Glebe. That's the whole point."

"I'll go and find a waitress," Isla said getting to her feet just as they heard footsteps approaching at speed and a flustered Mary Glebe made her appearance closely followed by Guy Hampson. Naomi noticed at once that she was tall. Isla noticed her ankle boots; Helena noticed her cropped hair was dyed blonde; she liked her smart woollen dress, which made the most of her meagre curves. They all recognised her.

"Sorry we're late. I got held up," Guy said. "Helena, Isla, Naomi, this is Mary Glebe."

Mary Glebe embraced them with a warm smile. She sat down on the nearest empty seat next to Isla, leaving Guy to sit next to Helena. "I'm really surprised to be here. I had no idea Miss Black would leave me something in her will."

"We had no idea you were Mary Glebe," Helena said.

"Glebe is my married name, but as Minns is the name over the shop, most people still think of me as Minty Minns. No-one ever calls me Mary. I've always been Minty. Mary is my hospital name," she said.

"Well, I'm glad it's you," Naomi said "And not some random…"

"Beautician?" Isla said.

"Beautician, where did you get that idea?" Helena said.

"Nowhere," Naomi said giving Isla a dark look.

"She reckoned Mary Glebe was the person who did Blanche's nails."

"I don't understand."

"It's nothing," Naomi said. "Forget it."

"It's good you all know each other," Guy said. "It makes everything much more pleasant. Now, has anyone ordered tea?"

"We were just about to when you arrived," Helena said.

"I'll do it now," he said. "Tea and cakes for five?"

"Just tea for me," Minty said.

"And me," Naomi said. "I need to dash off in a minute."

"I'll have cake," Isla said.

"Me, too," Helena added.

"Fine. Tea and cakes for three," Guy said as he stepped away from the table. "I'll organise it."

"So why do you think Miss Black left me the premium bonds?" Minty said when he had gone. "Mr. Hampson said he didn't know."

"No idea," Helena said. "But she must have had her reasons."

"She had a reason for everything," Isla said.

"It was very generous of her."

"Are you going to keep them or cash them in?" Naomi said.

"I haven't had time to think about it. I'll ask Dad what he thinks."

"Maybe that's why she left them to you," Naomi said. "Alf was her best friend."

"That must be it," Helena said. "She didn't want to embarrass him by leaving him something, so she left it to you instead. He's coming to Barque House to see me later. I'll ask if he knows."

"You didn't tell me," Naomi said.

"Didn't I? I thought I had."

"Why does he want to see you?"

"What is this, *Who Wants to be a Millionaire?*" Helena said.

"I just wondered, that's all."

"He said he had something to give me."

"It's probably something Blanche lent him." Naomi said. "He tried to return a book on roses. I told him to keep it. You didn't want it, did you?"

"No… that's probably what it is."

"Dad misses her," Minty said. "They used to chat about the old days."

"When we get settled at Barque House, he can call on us any time, can't he, Mum?"

"Sure, I'll make a point of telling him."

"Did you see a lot of Blanche?" Isla said.

"Not for years. I did in the past, when she called in at the shop. She was never very chatty."

"No," Helena said. "She wasn't great on small talk."

"It was more Dad than me. He'd known her back in the day. We always exchanged Christmas cards. When I got married he said we should send her a piece of my wedding cake."

"The cake," Naomi said glancing at her mother and then Isla.

"She kept it," Isla said

"We found it in her desk," Naomi said.

"No… that was over twenty years ago. It must have been all mouldy."

"It wasn't," she said. "It looked ok. It smelled good."

"We didn't test it," Isla said.

Minty laughed. "I don't blame you."

"Do you have children?" Helena said.

"Somehow it was never the right time. I'm too busy running the business."

At that point Guy returned with a waitress carrying a tray of cups and saucers and the teapot. "The cakes are on the way," he said just as a waiter appeared with a plate of cream cakes.

"I wish I'd said, yes, now," Naomi said. "I had no idea cream cakes would be on offer. I thought, being a health spa, the choice would have been carrot cake, carrot cake or carrot cake. I'm not a massive fan."

"Shall I get another one?" Guy said.

"No, it's fine. I only have time for the tea, anyway," she said taking the cup her mother had just poured out for her.

"We've all been wondering why Blanche wanted us to meet," Helena said.

Minty nodded "I was really surprised when you told me about it. All of this came out of the blue."

"It's probably because she was such good friends with Alf. She thought he might be lonely when she'd gone. She wanted you to continue that friendship," Guy said.

"You mean she was thinking of him?" Helena said.

"They were good friends," Minty said.

"It's a nice thought," Isla said.

"But we all know Minty," Naomi said.

"Only from the shop," Isla said. "She must have wanted you to get to know each other better."

"Perhaps we should meet up here every year to remember her," Minty said. "We could get Dad to come too."

"That would be brilliant," Naomi said. She rattled her tea-cup back in the saucer and retrieved her bag from the floor. "Sorry, I have to go."

"Ok," Helena said. "See you later." She watched as Naomi unhooked her jacket from the back of the chair, slung it over her arm and went on her way with a silent whistle, swinging the bag behind her in a carefree fashion. "She's going to the craft fair at Upfordham," she said to the table at large.

"Jake's over there today," Guy said.

"She *says* she's doing some early Christmas shopping, but I think there's another reason."

He gave her a quizzical glance. "Really?"

"I think she'll be checking out broomsticks and spiders."

"Ah," he said with a knowing smile.

"Broomsticks?" Minty said.

"Yes, what do you mean?" Isla said.

"Something in her life could be about to change," Helena said.

"Is that good?" Minty said.

"I hope so. We'll have to wait and see."

CHAPTER 30

Poor Edith. Ivy could not accept what had happened. She wanted to call Edith, to speak to her, to hear her voice. When the doctor called after Ian rang him about her funny turn, he only told her what she already knew. She had been suffering from shock. It had been the same when Sid died. The doctor had told her to rest and that she should go to the surgery to get her blood pressure checked in a few days. She still didn't feel one hundred per cent. It had come as a terrible blow. It must have been awful for Isobel to find her mum like that ... and Edith had been so looking forward to Christmas.

Poor Edith. She felt tears threatening again. She was going to miss her friend. She was going to miss their chats. Every time she watched Morse she would remember her. Every time the phone rang she would remember her. Every time she checked her emails she would remember her. Edith would never be forgotten, she vowed, fiercely.

Phoebe didn't understand, bless her. She had heard her asking Pippa when they were going to see Edith and Pippa was finding it difficult, she could tell. Ian was very supportive but they had been close, Pippa and her Gran. The void Edith had left in all their lives would never be filled. They would have to learn to live with it; they would all have to learn to live with it.

She sighed and put the newspaper to one side unread, the crossword still full of blank spaces. She had phoned Jerry at the shop to tell him. He had been sympathetic, told her if she needed anything he would bring it round for her. She had appreciated the gesture and so she had told him, but Edith would not have wanted him to be put out because of her and so she had refused his offer.

She heaved herself out of her chair and limped into the kitchen to make herself another cup of tea. Staring out of the window as she waited for the kettle to boil, she was thinking that losing someone you loved was the most unsettling experience. The lack of response, the sense that it was all too soon; the realisation that it might be your turn next.

When she lost Sid she had wandered about like a lost soul for weeks. She hadn't been able to read or watch the television. She hadn't done a crossword for months. She had begun to wonder if she was going mad. It was Vera who had helped her through that, but Vera wasn't there this time. She had been taken too soon, never met Pippa, never held Phoebe in her arms; taken just when Ian needed his mother the most. Life could be so cruel.

She wasn't scared of death, it was what happened in between that bothered her. It made her even more determined to stay in her own home and keep healthy. It cheered her to think that Edith had stayed in hers. She had gone the way she would have wished, which brought her some comfort. She also knew Edith would not have approved of her giving way to misery. She could almost hear her saying with that sing-song voice of hers, *"No tears now, Ivy. I'm ready to go. I've had a good life. Ralph's waiting for me and Ruth. It's time I went to join them."*

Steam billowed from the kettle. Her eyes misted over; she sniffed and blinked, reasoning that when bad things happened, you just had to get on with it or go under. That's what they had done during the War, got on with it. She dashed the last tears away. She knew Edith would have pinned on a smile and carried on as normal even if she had been crying inside. She sniffed again and stiffened her back. She would follow her friend's lead. She would do that, of course she would, but not yet; not until she'd had more time to grieve. Her shoulders sagged, and she let out a cavernous sigh.

227

Poor Edith; she hadn't even had time to hear about the finding of Mary Glebe. She reckoned it would be a while before she was ready to grin and bear it.

The fair was still going strong when Naomi arrived. She had been desperate to apologise to Jake for having misjudged him but now she was not so sure it was a good idea. Her delight on realising it must have been his number on the anonymous slip of paper had taken her by surprise, but she had not wanted a question and answer session with her mother about the state of their relationship and so she had feigned ignorance.

When she was ready for the tea party and Isla was examining her mother's sore wrist, she had snuck back into the kitchen to take the discarded paper from the bin and make a note of his number on her contacts list before throwing it away again. If her mother happened to notice it was not still in the bin when she returned to the house, she would make too many assumptions.

She had her own ideas as to why Jake had given her his number, but she could be wrong. Until she had spoken to him she would not know for sure and she did not want to look stupid or needy or a push-over.

As she paid her entrance money to get into the fair she decided to act cool. She moved nonchalantly around the hall even though her mouth was dry and her heart playing leapfrog in her chest. She glimpsed the stall selling framed photographs and watercolours by local artists. She passed what must have been a table full of home-made cakes. It was now a sad collection of empty plates and discarded price tags declaring *'Four for a pound' 'Fifty pence each' 'Fruit cake with cider' 'Marion's flapjacks'*. She moved on, making her way through knots of children trying their luck on the Tombola and then the crowd parted; she saw him surrounded by eager faces, sitting astride a broomstick, bringing one of his Harry Potter Nimbus 2000s to life for his young audience.

She stayed at the back of the crowd, watching as he interacted with the children, making them laugh, taking their money. With her heart thumping ever faster, she tried to make up her mind whether to move to the front of the crowd to talk to him or turn tail. She felt embarrassed to be there, idiotic to think he might want to see her, or listen to what she had to say.

She was about to retreat when she found her path blocked by a determined Daisy Parsloe. "Raffle," she said shaking a bucket full of folded tickets in her face. "It's nearly time for the draw. Last chance; we have some fantastic prizes... over there," she said pointing in the general direction of the jazzy curtains shielding the stage.

Naomi's eyes were drawn to a table stacked up with an amazing array of goodies; bottles of wine, a basket of fruit, a signed football and a very large rabbit with floppy, pink-lined ears. "How much?" she asked.

"A pound each or six for a fiver."

"I'll take six, please," she said turning her back on Jake and digging deep in her bag for her purse.

"Teas are being served on the stage, behind the curtains... I know. They are awful, aren't they?" Daisy said misreading Naomi's worried expression. "I'm hoping we raise enough today to replace them and we need a substantial amount towards the repairs of the building too. It's waitress service, just find a seat and someone will come and take your order," she went on as she tore off the tickets "You're not local, are you?"

"No, East Knoll," Naomi said and immediately wished she hadn't.

"Really? What a coincidence. Jake Hampson comes from there. Do you two know each other?" Naomi shook her head.

"Over there," she said swivelling round to show Naomi the stall. "The one with all the children round it. He's been popular all afternoon. The skeleton fingers have gone down well. You wouldn't know they were just well-chosen twigs, would you? He said he'd painted them with glow-in-the-dark paint; you can't get the full effect in here, but I expect there will be fun and games tonight when the lights go out."

"Awesome."

And then Daisy did what Naomi had feared she might do. "Jake," she called across the children's heads. "There's someone here from East Knoll."

She did not wait for him to respond. She did not collect her raffle tickets. She made for the safety of the curtains faster than a jaguar with a jet-pack. She did not even consider Daisy's reaction to her flight. It was either that or wait for the floor to swallow her up. Safe behind the curtains she sat down at the nearest table breathing hard. She took out her phone pretending to check messages while she waited for her heart to return to a more normal rhythm. She was hoping to ward off unwanted contact while she worked out a way to escape from the hall without either Daisy continuing their conversation or Jake seeing her.

This was mad, illogical. Why had she said she did not know him? Why hadn't she just gone up to him, apologised and got it over with, and why, oh why, she asked herself, had she come to the fair in the first place? Not to do Christmas shopping, for sure. Another lie. She felt small, foolish and completely humiliated.

What would Blanche have thought of her actions? Blanche who always knew her own mind and who had a logical reason for everything. Blanche, who had been single-minded and straight-talking, not prone to telling untruths. She had let her down. She had let herself down. All she could hope for now was that when she finally escaped from the church hall, she would never see Jake Hampson again.

CHAPTER 31

"Here we are," Guy said as he dropped Helena off outside Barque House.

"Oh look, there's Alf Minns," she said.

Alf was striding towards the car, a paper bag clutched in his hand. "Looks like he's got something for you," Guy said giving Alf a friendly wave.

"I wonder what it is."

"Something from his greenhouse, um, tomatoes? He's a nice old chap. See you later."

Helena got out of the car and waited for Alf to catch her up.

"I hear you've had tea with my daughter," he said.

"Yes, let's go inside," she said.

He pulled off his cap and tucked it in the pocket of his jacket. "Blanche left her some premium bonds."

"She did."

"I thought she might," he said.

Helena led the way into the lounge "Did you?"

"I didn't know it would be premium bonds, but I thought she might have left her something."

"Can I get you a drink, tea, coffee, something cold?" she asked.

"No, thanks, I'm fine. You'll be wanting this," he said.

She took the bag from him. "What is it?"

"Her address-book."

So much for tomatoes, she thought. "We thought it was lost," she said. "You had it all the time."

He crossed his legs as he sat on the sofa facing the fireplace, an apologetic smile lighting his eyes. "She asked me to look after it."

"Why?"

232

"She didn't want a huge funeral, didn't want you calling everyone listed in there. She only wanted *who* she wanted to be there and to have it arranged *how* she wanted; no wake, no fuss." He chuckled. "She was good at dishing out orders."

"I see ... and it would have cut down on costs."

"That was how she was. She was generous in other ways."

"How do you mean?"

"She helped Sarah and me."

"She lent you money?"

"No, not money."

"How do you mean?"

Alf stared into the empty grate. "It's not what you might expect from someone like Blanche."

"Don't worry, I'm beginning to understand what a complicated character she was. None of us really knew her, she wouldn't let us in."

"Complicated is a good way of describing her."

"So ...?"

"Sarah wanted a child. Dr. Black had tried everything to help her. She took more pills and potions than one of these Russian athletes. She got pregnant, no problem, but each time she lost the baby. I said we should give up the idea, but she wouldn't. She wanted to be a mother so much."

"It must have been miserable for you both."

"It went on for years. Whatever I did to try and fill our lives with other things, didn't help. Eventually as the years passed and she realised it was never going to happen, she lost interest in everything; she didn't want to talk, didn't want to see her friends, didn't want to help in the shop. Some days she wouldn't even get out of bed, said her life was useless, said she couldn't go on. It broke my heart to hear her talk like that. In the end I went to see the doc to explain how low she was. Not having a baby was driving her crazy. I thought she was close to ending it all."

"That must have been awful for you. In those days they weren't good on mental health."

"It's not much better now, if what you read in the papers is true."

"Long waits for treatment, yes, but they are better; we have all these talking therapies now."

"Sometimes talking causes more problems than it solves," he said. "Anyway, we were lucky, the doc was sympathetic, said he might be able to help. He asked if I would be prepared to assist him with some research. I said I would if it would help Sarah. He asked me to undergo some tests. I agreed. I didn't want to lose my wife and I was so desperate to see her happy I would have done anything."

"I know how close you two were. So, what happened, you did the tests?"

"Oh yes. Over the next few weeks he tested everything, and I mean everything, heart, lungs, waterworks, even my brain and then he declared me a perfect subject for the trial."

"I'm not quite sure where this is going. What has Blanche to do with it?"

"I'm coming to that. He said he would make Sarah a baby."

"What? In a test tube?" she said half laughing.

"He said I could be his guinea-pig; I didn't know what he meant at that point. I didn't question him. He was the doc and 'doctor knows best' was drummed into us as children. It wasn't for us to argue or ask the ins and outs and if it worked, well it would be worth it. Sarah was getting worse I had to do something. I agreed for him to go ahead."

"How could he do it without Sarah?"

"That's the thing," Alf said, now looking down at his shoes. "Sarah wasn't well enough. It had to be Blanche."

"Blanche? I don't understand."

"She was going to carry the baby. The doc swore me to secrecy," he went on "And then sent me away and told me to wait for confirmation that everything had gone to plan. If it had, I could tell Sarah, explain what was happening and swear her to secrecy, too. He said, when he gave us the nod, she must start telling people she was pregnant. It wasn't a secret we'd been trying for a baby."

He stopped as if, she thought, he was expecting her to comment but she had nothing to say. She had moved over to examine the leaves of the aspidistra. She reckoned it was just as well she had her back to him. Her expression would have given away what she was thinking … if she knew what she was thinking. The only thought she had was that he must be making it up, but why would he do that? It made no sense. Her fingers ran lightly over the textured leaves as he went on.

"The weeks passed; Sarah didn't improve. I wanted to tell her what I'd done but I knew if I told her and the experiment hadn't worked it would have hurt her even more. When the doc gave me the all clear, I told her straight away. It took her a while to understand what I was saying. At first, she didn't believe me and then she thought I was trying to tell her that Blanche and I had been having an affair. It took me a while to convince her we hadn't. When I explained it was the only way we were ever going to have a child and I persuaded her there was nothing going on between Blanche and me, her mood changed, she came around."

"It must have seemed very strange to her," she said.

He gave her unyielding back a wry smile. "It wasn't easy to get her to accept what I was saying and then to persuade her not to tell anyone, but she wanted people to think it was her baby, that's what swung it, trumped any misgivings she may have had. She would finally have her longed-for baby. She started knitting clothes, buying nappies, making plans. It was as if a switch had been turned on in her head. I had my old Sarah back. The doc had told me we must say it would be a home delivery. He would let us know when Blanche went into labour so that Sarah could stay at home to wait for him to bring the baby as soon as it arrived. If anyone asked, she could tell them truthfully that the doc had delivered the baby at home. That way no-one would ask awkward questions. No-one would have any idea about Blanche's part in it."

"I can't believe Blanche agreed to it," she said.

"She was happy to do it."

She turned to face him. "Happy?"

"Yes. She had volunteered. The way she saw it, she was helping her father's research and us. She wasn't interested in men or marriage. She explained to me years later that as she had a perfectly serviceable womb, she reckoned she might as well make use of it to help someone else."

"That's taking 'waste not want not' to extremes," Helena said as she returned to her seat.

"She was way ahead of her time. She hadn't been forced into it. I know that for a fact. She did it for the best of reasons and I was more than grateful to her, we both were; overcome by her generosity, we were."

"It was more than generous."

"Anyway, she was well throughout the pregnancy. It was an easy birth. The baby was healthy."

"How could she part with her baby?"

"Somehow, she managed to stay detached."

"I don't think I could."

"No, well, Blanche wasn't like the rest of us. She didn't ask for anything in return. We registered the baby in the usual way with Sarah as the mother and me as the father and then we all went on with our lives as before, except that we had our Minty and Sarah was ever so happy. I was, too."

"I can't believe it," she said.

"There's more," he said.

"What, more children?" she said expecting him to contradict her.

"Yes. She didn't stop with Minty."

"You mean she did it again?"

"Yes."

"For someone else?" He nodded. "Who?"

"She did it for Betsy."

"For … my… mum?" Helena said the words haltingly as the colour drained from her cheeks. She repeated them quietly, as if to persuade herself that it was true. "For my mum." She stood up and walked over to the window, eyes fixed on the third curtain hook from the edge of the velvet drapes. It was broken, no longer attached to the velvet, hanging from the rail like a monkey from a branch. She didn't want to look at him, didn't want him to see how shocked she was, how much she didn't want to believe his story.

"That's right. That's why the doc referred to me as his guinea pig. They had agreed that if it worked for Sarah and me, they would do the same for Betsy."

"But that's outrageous."

"We all knew the score."

"My mother could have children. She had Martyn."

"She did, but it had been a difficult birth. She had to have an operation and after that she couldn't have more children. Your father had been injured in the War ..."

"I know."

"He was left, you know …"

"Right … no … wait a minute … that means …"

"It means that you are Blanche's child."

"She was my mother, of course, she must have been."

He waited while she took in the startling news. "Blanche wanted you to know the truth but she made me promise not to say anything until after she'd gone. I was going to write you a letter and leave it with my will and then I thought it would be easier for you to understand if I explained everything in person. I could answer any questions you might have, explain my part in things, tell you about Blanche; it seemed the best way."

"Wait a minute, so, Martyn's not my brother, he's my cousin and Isla's not my niece," she said. "Didn't my father have something to say about what was going on?"

"He knew Blanche was pregnant. She told him she had been taken advantage of by one of the medical students who were in and out of the house. She begged him to help her avoid a scandal by taking the baby. Betsy backed her up and managed to persuade him to accept you as their own."

"Why wasn't I adopted?"

"That would have drawn attention to what we'd done. The authorities would have got involved. We didn't want to risk having the children taken away. The doc said the fewer people who knew, the better. He was worried he would have been struck off, if it had got out … you know, what he'd done. We were hurting no-one, we had kept it in the family so to speak, but we were scared we would have been in a lot of trouble for registering Sarah as the baby's mother when she wasn't."

"And Betsy instead of Blanche." He nodded. She felt anger bubbling inside her; anger and a sense of resentment of being left out of the secret "I wish they'd told me," she said. "They should have told me. You should have told me. To have spent all these years thinking I was someone I'm not, living their lie … your lie."

"Blanche didn't want to be a mother. She did it for her sister. She had no maternal feelings and she wanted nothing from you, but she always intended to leave you the house. That was no secret. She didn't want to leave it to Martyn. I told her it would seem strange to everyone else that he didn't have a share, but she wouldn't change her mind. She thought she owed it to you and she wanted it done that way. She knew Minty would have the business. I'm sorry, but that's the truth."

"So, the only thing that stays the same is that Naomi is my daughter."

"That's about the top and bottom of it."

"Does Minty know?"

"Not yet. I'll tell her when I get back. Blanche wanted you to get to know each other, you are sisters after all; she thought you should know, which is why she made that stipulation in her will. We agreed you should know about each other, but I thought it would be down to me to find a way to get you two together. I had no idea about the codicil. She didn't consult me. Maybe she thought it would be easier this way. Either that or it was her insurance policy."

"To make sure you told us." He nodded. "It's madness," she said. "I can't take it in."

He massaged his chin in a ruminative fashion. "With Sarah gone and your mum and after the will, I thought it was time for me to put things straight." He paused, as if trying to give her time to prepare for the next logical conclusion before he had to spell it out for her.

She took in a sharp breath. "What... oh heavens, that means you're my father."

CHAPTER 32

"It means I'm a biological fact, not your father, just part of Blanche's gift to your mother," Alf said.

His revelation proved too much for Helena. She leapt up and walked across to the mantelpiece staring into the grate as if there were hot coals to warm her already flushed cheeks, flames leaping, magical shapes forming, but there was no magic, merely bald facts and an empty grate. "Her gift," she said bitterly.

"That was how she saw it. She was no different after all this happened. She was still your aunt, doing all the things she had always done. Your relationship was how she wanted it to be. You might think her selfish, but you grew up in a loving home. You didn't need her. She didn't need you. Your mother needed you, she had always wanted another child. You were all happy."

"That's true, but if I'd known I could have made more of an effort to spend time with her… or with you."

"It wouldn't have changed anything. It would have hurt your mum and Sarah. Blanche enjoyed her own company. She avoided any sort of emotional outpourings. I know. I tried to thank her several times in the early days. I offered her money, I had a bit put by for a rainy day, but she was having none of it."

"Didn't she care what reaction her 'gifts' might have on Minty and me? You can't play with people's lives like that."

"She realised you might not understand her motives. She knew it might throw you, of course she did. She had feelings, loved her sister, adored her parents but she didn't need anyone else. She wanted to help, simple as that. It was an act of love. We stayed friends for so long because we came to understand each other and respect the boundaries. I've never met anyone quite like her. I don't expect to. She was a one off. It would be wrong to judge her."

"That's easy for you to say."

"It's what I believe."

"It's amazing how you can know someone all your life and not know them at all."

"How would you have described her?"

"Intelligent, eccentric, careful with money, secretive, difficult …"

His lips curled into a grin. "There you are, then, you did know her."

"She didn't know me."

"She knew you needed a safe place after the divorce, that's why she lent you the money to buy a house for you and Naomi."

"You knew about that?"

"We talked about most things but, like I said, not everything. Some topics were out of bounds. She made it clear when she didn't want me to know more and I backed off."

"She expected me to pay her back with interest and I did, every penny."

"She knew you would and now she's given you her house. A fair exchange, wouldn't you say?"

"Ok, so she had a generous spirit."

"She enjoyed those months she spent with Naomi."

"Naomi enjoyed them too."

"Will you tell her?"

"I don't know. If I tell Naomi I'll have to tell Isla. We might not be related in quite the way we thought, but we are still family. I don't want to spoil what we have."

"Niece, nephew, aunt, whatever, they're only words to describe connections. It's the bonds that develop between people that create families, not how society labels them."

"I've always been close to Isla."

"That's good."

"She gets on with Naomi," she said.

"None of this will change your feelings for each other. Why would it? You are all connected to Blanche one way or another and you all get on. Hopefully you always will. Blanche's gift has changed very little."

Helena mulled over his words. She wasn't sure she agreed. Blanche's 'gifts' had altered fundamental parts of her life which had previously been unchallenged. She needed to consider everything in more depth before she told anyone else. "What about Martyn?"

"That's up to you."

"What sort of contact am I supposed to have with Minty?"

"As little or as much as you both want."

"I need to think about it."

He rose from his chair. "I understand; I'll go now."

"I am glad you told me."

He smiled and held out a hand for her to shake. "It needed to be done. Look, I know this must be difficult for you, but if I hadn't volunteered, if the doc hadn't offered his expertise, if Blanche hadn't done her bit, Sarah would have died of a broken heart, I'm sure of it … and you wouldn't be here. I did what I did to make my wife happy and then to help Betsy. None of us meant to hurt anyone."

"I get that. It is what it is. The emotional side is more difficult."

"I don't expect you to see me any differently now you know. Your father was your father, not me." His hand was warm, his handshake firm, like Guy's. Guy had been the last thing on her mind but now she remembered that she had arranged to meet him that evening. As she walked Alf to the front door and responded mechanically to his remarks, she wondered if she would ever be able to tell Guy about Blanche's 'gift'. The door closed and she was relieved to be on her own so that she could try and make sense of her feelings. She leant against the wall and then slid down to crouch on the carpet like a wild animal caught in a snare.

What would Guy make of her unconventional beginnings? How could she tell him ... *should* she tell him, or should it remain as it had for so many years, a family secret and what should she say to Isla?

How would Naomi take Alf's revelations? She had become close to Blanche over the past few months. Would this make her question the nature of that relationship? Would it leave her with issues of trust or would it make Blanche more fascinating? Her aunt's actions could be interpreted in so many ways. Naomi was Alf and Blanche's granddaughter, Alf's only grandchild; he was her only surviving grandparent. Should she ignore that fact; would Naomi pick up on it?

Helena struggled with her emotions, unable to decide if she felt annoyed, upset, sad, or just plain angry at being misled for so many years. She wished her mother was still alive. She wanted to talk everything through, to be reassured, to be told it would be alright; that Alf Minns was a senile old man who had got it wrong, but the discomfort in her stomach and the turmoil in her mind told her that she was fighting a losing battle.

He was telling the truth. She had just had tea with Mary Glebe, his Minty. She had seen the wedding cake and now she understood its significance. Barque House had been left to her. How could she doubt that it was the truth, the whole truth and nothing but the truth? To accept it as the truth was her challenge now; to accept that she had sprung from very different roots from the ones she had always accepted as hers. That thought led her to having a vision of herself as a seedling re-potted. Was she Bill, or was she Ben, she thought. How ironic. She laughed hysterically. It was not long before the laughter turned into a paroxysm of weeping. In that moment she wished Alf Minns had taken their secret to the grave.

Dusk was falling before she regained some equanimity. She rose to her feet and turned on lights, walking around the house as if for the first time, opening doors, staring at pictures, trying to come to terms with the fact that her grandfather's experiment had resulted in the conception of two babies; his grandchildren, sisters destined to grow up apart from one another, shrouded in such secrecy that neither of them knew the true circumstances of their birth. How could he have played God and not expected repercussions? It was too late for him to defend his actions now. Betsy and Blanche had kept quiet. If only they had shared the secret. They had lived in a less open-minded society but even so … the morality of the whole situation bothered her. In the past the views of more than one person were needed to create morality. Modern morality was less constrained. It involved working out the version of any situation that suited you best. No-one would be bothered. The modern-day Blanche would have been lauded for her altruism. Was that right, was it better or worse, was it even morality?

Blanche's gift had been self-less, she accepted that. Had her grandfather been selfish in his experimentation or had he paved the way for others, brought untold happiness to couples in the future who desperately wanted children?

The silence of Barque House was deafening; the house that had been her mother's … and her mother's. The house that she hoped to make her home and which she now knew should have been her home all along.

It would have been bad enough if there had been only one baby, but there were two. Now it was her turn to test her morals.

Naomi was innocent of her roots; she had an aunt Minty, not an uncle Martyn. Her great-aunt was her grandmother. It was for her to decide whether to perpetuate the lie or tell her daughter the truth.

CHAPTER 33

It was raining in Hardale; raining and raining. Solid meaningful rain that replenishes tarns and runs off mountainsides to plump up waterfalls and soak sheep sheltering in the lee of stone walls, wool hanging in waterlogged spirals like fleecy fusilli. It seemed to Ian as if it would rain for ever. The mood was sombre at Edith's cottage in the village. "I don't know what we would have done without Phoebe to keep us smiling," Pippa said. "It's like Cold Comfort Farm in The Old School House. Even the dogs are quiet."

"Your mum's upset," he said. "They must sense it … you know, that something's going on."

Pippa was close to tears as she scanned her grandmother's kitchen, a room she had known for ever but not like this; not without her grandmother in it. The blue and white china was still in the cupboard, the draining board wiped clean as usual, a tea-towel hanging from the cooker door, scones on a baking tray. "Everything's the same, but not quite the same," she said. "I don't know what I expected. It's almost as if she's just popped out to the shops."

"Or church," Ian said.

Pippa sniffed. "Yes," she said in a small voice.

"What shall we do with the scones?"

"Are they still edible?"

He took one from the cooling tray and nibbled a corner. "Hmm … a bit dry but ok," he said helping himself to a larger bite.

"Find a plastic bag. We'll take them with us." She opened the fridge and crouched down to look inside. "There's not much in here. Milk, butter. A piece of salmon and some broccoli that's seen better days."

"Your mum said she didn't have much of an appetite."

"I remember when I was little, the shelves were full of all sorts of delicious food."

"I remember her cakes," Ian said.

"It's so weird."

Ian flopped onto the kitchen chair. "This is what it was like after Mum died, so quiet in the house you could hear yourself breathing, that's what got to me. The clocks had stopped. I kept thinking she would walk in through the door any minute and ask me why I hadn't wound them up. It took me ages to come to terms with her death."

"I know, it was sad; this is sad, but Gran was tired, worn out. She didn't want to stay any longer. She kept telling me it was time she joined Ralph. Did you know she thought she saw him at our wedding? She often talked to him when she was on her own."

"Really?"

"She didn't like to tell anyone in case they thought she was barmy. She spent most of her life without him, but she kept his memory alive."

"And we must do the same for her."

"We will, deffo. You know that. I don't feel so bad now, here in her house. It holds so many happy memories; it's when I'm around Mum I feel awful."

"Your mum's not herself. She spent most of yesterday in her pod with the dogs."

"It's really shaken her."

"Well, it would," he said.

"Did you know she asked me to look for the will?"

"Where do you think it is?"

"Probably in here," Pippa said as she stretched up to remove a Huntley and Palmer biscuit tin from a shelf full of cookery books. "She kept her birth certificate in here, so I guess the will could be in here, too. This is quite a rare one," she said admiring the jester emblazoned on the tin along with a knight in armour and couples in historic dress.

"Is it worth something?"

"Over a hundred."

"Does your Mum know?"

"Probably not."

"You'd better tell her."

"I will. I'll ask her not to get rid of anything until I've had a good look through the house." She prized open the tight-fitting lid and removed a long white envelope. "This must be it, yes, it says 'Will'. I think that might be a clue … bother, it's sealed."

"You can't open it."

"I wasn't going to," Pippa said, her fingers itching to lift the end flap.

"Your mum should open it. She's probably left everything to her anyway."

"She always said she would leave the house to Tim. She worried that he hadn't been able to buy a property for himself and she knew we were ok. When we've finished here we'll go straight back to The Old School House, find out."

"Don't rush your mum, Sweetpea. Let her open it in her own time."

"We've got to know if there's anything special Gran wanted us to do."

"You mean her funeral."

"I meant with her ashes."

"I expect she's already told your mum. She'll want to be with Ralph, won't she?"

"He was buried in the village."

"There's no hurry for any of that."

"No, I know, it's just …"
"You need to do everything you can for her."
She smiled up at him. "I knew you'd get it."
"I love you, Sweetpea, simple as that."

CHAPTER 34

Naomi's mind would not settle as she sat there fingering her phone, hiding behind Daisy's awful curtains. They were not awful at all, in fact to Naomi they were a godsend. They were judicious, convenient, discreet and perfect to hide behind. The table she had chosen was set apart from the others next to a stack of chairs piled high like a troupe of acrobats. She was glad she wouldn't have to make polite conversation with the other tea-drinkers. She needed to calm down, to think. It wasn't long before she became aware of someone approaching. "Hello, it's Naomi, isn't it?" The waitress wore jeans and a frilly apron. "Jane Chisholm. We met at St. Saviour's, you were with Jake."

"Oh yes … the apron threw me for a minute. I didn't expect to find you serving teas," Naomi said.

"We all have to muck in."

"I suppose you do."

"What can I get you?" Jane said.

"Just a cup of tea please."

"Jake's stall is doing really well."

"He was surrounded by children when I arrived."

"He's really cracked it with the broomsticks. He'll have to take orders if this carries on," Jane said. She noticed Naomi's pre-occupied frown "You seem a bit down. Is everything alright?"

"I feel silly to be honest. I only decided to come at the last minute. I didn't think he'd be this popular. I wanted to talk to him about something."

"The whole fair has been manic."

"Good for your funds."

"Not so good if someone needs a chat. I'll fetch your tea and then perhaps I could join you. I'm due a break."

"Ok," Naomi said in a half-hearted fashion.

"Great ... milk?" Naomi nodded. "I'll be back in a mo."

Naomi stared into the tea-light on her table and watched the little flame burning bravely while she listened to the sounds of the fair. Children's laughter, numbers being called out from the tombola, parents trying to persuade toddlers that it was time to go home. There was folk music playing softly in the background. She didn't recognise any of the words although the tunes were familiar. While she had been sitting there, she had decided it would be impractical not to see Jake again. She tried to work out what she should say to him when they did eventually meet. Should she come right out with it and apologise and then leave? Would he want to know? He must have seen her with Daisy but he hadn't beckoned her over. Maybe it would be best if she drank her tea and left without speaking to him. It would be less embarrassing, for sure. She looked up as she heard Jane coming back.

"Here you are, one nice fresh cup of tea for you and one for me. Sugar's on the table."

"No thanks, no sugar."

"I keep trying to give it up," Jane said stirring in a generous teaspoonful.

"Are you sure you've got time to talk?"

"I can snatch five minutes."

"Have you been serving teas all day?"

"Just this afternoon. Long enough for me to know I don't want a career in catering."

"I had a Saturday job in a café when I was at school," Naomi said. "The only good thing about it was the free cakes."

"Our vicar used to be a cook. He's written a recipe book, *Holy Roasts*, have you seen it?"

"No."

"There are some copies for sale on one of the stalls." Naomi made no response. "How's Jake doing?"

"I think he's ok."

"He was putting flowers on his mother's grave when I saw you at East Knoll. He must have been devastated when she died."

"She died years ago when he was little."

"Oh, I thought it was a recent thing."

"No …look, I don't know much about Jake's life. We're not in a relationship," Naomi said.

"Sorry, it's just that you looked so comfortable together and I thought, well never mind what I thought. Just friends, then."

"Not even that," Naomi said defensively.

Jane laughed. "Oh dear, I'm usually quite good at this. Something must have gone wrong with my relationship radar."

"It doesn't matter."

"I hope I didn't embarrass you."

Naomi shook her head. She sighed. "We both grew up in East Knoll. I knew of him years back, but we were never friends. We only met properly a few weeks ago. I thought he'd done something bad in the past. I wasn't very nice to him. He must have known what I was thinking but he didn't try and explain himself."

"Perhaps he didn't think he had to."

"I don't know, anyway, as it happens, I was wrong. He didn't do it and I'm not sure where we go from here."

"Let me get this straight," Jane said. "Jake Hampson is an acquaintance of yours who had a bad reputation which wasn't justified, yes?" Naomi nodded unhappily. "None of this would matter if you didn't like him. You wouldn't be trying to mend bridges. Perhaps you like him more than you think you do."

"I'm so confused. I can't work out how I feel except that I want to apologise for thinking the worst of him."

"So, what's stopping you?"

"I don't want him to get the wrong idea."

"The wrong idea?"

"Yeah … I don't want him to think I'm chasing him."

"Why did you come this afternoon?" Naomi shrugged. "You wouldn't have come if you weren't interested; you wouldn't be feeling bad about getting the facts wrong and you certainly wouldn't need to apologise. You would just keep your head down and carry on as before."

"Perhaps it's too late. He didn't seem pleased to see me."

"And perhaps he didn't actually see you. I told you, he's been very busy all day. He doesn't know you've found out the truth about him. He still thinks you think he's a bad person. Why would he be pleased to see you? Did you try and speak to him?"

"No."

"I think you should."

"What if he blanks me?"

"You'll know he's not interested. You can go home and forget about him."

"I feel like a complete idiot."

Jane sipped thoughtfully from her cup. "If I could get him away from the stall for a minute so that you could talk somewhere quiet, in private, would that work for you?"

"Why are you even trying to help? You don't know me."

"I like helping people, it's what I do."

"I don't want to spoil his afternoon. I'll drink this and go home."

"Do you want me to give him a message?"

"No thanks … um… well maybe … yes," she said as she suddenly thought of a brilliant way to sort out her dilemma once and for all. "Have you got a piece of paper?"

"Serviette?" Jane said leaning across to snatch one from a nearby table.

"Pen?"

"I'm a priest, not a magician," Jane said with some amusement. "I'll borrow one from Daisy." She returned to find Naomi staring into the tea-light again. "One pen," she said. "Daisy gave me these raffle tickets. She said you dashed off before she could hand them over."

"Yes, sorry. I was a bit stressed. I never win anyway." Naomi stuffed the tickets in the pocket of her skinny jeans, took the pen, scribbled something down on the serviette, rolled it over several times and handed it back to Jane. "There. Just give him that."

"What shall I say to him?"

"Nothing he'll understand when he reads it."

CHAPTER 35

Adrian was mooching about the garden when Ian and Pippa returned to The Old School House. "We're back," she called.

"So I see; did you find the will?"

She waved the envelope at him. "This is it. Where's Phoebe?"

"Painting with Mum."

"Messy," Ian said.

"She's amazingly good," Adrian said as he sauntered over to them. "She's painted a picture of dogs that actually look like dogs."

"I'm glad she's keeping Mum occupied. She needs something to take her mind off Gran."

"You can't think of anything else when Phoebe's chattering away. Let's go and find them."

Isobel was sitting at the table in the pod, Phoebe at her side perched on two cushions plonked on the seat of a chair. She looked like a mini monk, dressed in a sheet that had been hastily transformed into a painting overall with the aid of some clothes pegs and a large safety pin. "Just look at you," Ian said. "A proper little artist."

"I'm not little," Phoebe said. "I'm a big girl. Belsie said so."

"I did and so you are," Isobel said.

Pippa looked at her daughter's indignant face and smiled. "Silly Daddy. I know you're a big girl. What have you been painting?"

Phoebe pointed at a large sheet of paper drying on an easel. It was covered in multi-coloured brush-strokes. "Trees," she said.

"And this," Isobel said holding up another sheet of paper daubed in brown splodges with what looked like legs and tails.

"Fantastic, Poppet."

"Shall we go outside, now?" Ian said. "Mummy wants to talk to Belsie. Put your brush down."

Phoebe put down the brush and raised her hands so that he could lift her from the chair. She puckered her lips to plant a gooey kiss on his forehead. "Love you Dad," she said.

"Love you, too."

Ian de-frocked the little monk. Phoebe giggled. "See you later alligators," she said as they walked off together.

"I've got the will," Pippa said when the door shut behind them.

Isobel peered at the envelope over the top of her glasses. "No time like the present," she said taking it from her daughter's hand and slitting it open with a craft knife she took from a drawer under the table top. She pulled out the document. "Yes, this is it," she said.

"What does it say?" Adrian said.

"Give me a minute, there's a whole load of guff to read first … right … so … um … she's left the house …"

"Left the house to …?"

"Tim," Pippa said.

Isobel removed her glasses and stared at Adrian in disbelief. "In trust for Phoebe."

"No," Pippa said. "That can't be right."

"It is," Isobel said. "Dad and I are to manage it for her."

"That is so generous."

"Tim won't like it," Adrian said. "He always thought she would leave it to him."

"I know." Isobel replaced her glasses and scanned the rest of the pages. "She's left me her jewellery," she said. "Money for you, darling," she said looking at her husband. "Money for Ian and Pippa; Tim and I share what's left."

"Very fair," Adrian said.

"I hope Tim sees it that way," Isobel said.

"I didn't expect anything," Pippa said. "But Dad's right, Tim always thought he'd have the house."

"It looks like she changed her will three years ago," Isobel said. "I didn't know she'd done this. She didn't say a word."

"Three years ago," Pippa said ruminatively "… that would be just after Phoebe was born."

"I just presumed she wanted to leave Phoebe a little nest-egg, but she must have wanted to be sure she would have somewhere to live if she needed it," Isobel said. "You know how special she was to Gran, after Ruth."

"I don't know what I'd have done if she hadn't explained about Ruth when Phoebe was born; I was in such a state after they told us she had Down's Syndrome. To know that Gran had been through it as well, really helped. I can remember saying it was unfair and she told me Phoebe was special. That's when I started to realise how special she is. Gran was always there for me."

"She was there for all of us," Isobel said.

"Edith was a one-off," Adrian said with unusual emotion. "Never any trouble, great mother-in-law." He gulped. "I'll miss her."

"We'll all miss her," Isobel said. "What will Tim say?"

"He'll be disappointed," Adrian said.

At that moment the door to the pod opened and Pippa, who was nearest the door, swivelled round with a ready smile for her daughter, but it was not Phoebe. "It's you," she said in surprise. "Are you psychic? We were just talking about you." She kissed her brother on both cheeks, hugging him as if she would never let him go.

"Steady on, sis," he said removing himself from her grip and smoothing stray hairs back into his trademark pony-tail. "What were you saying about me?"

"Tim," Adrian said grabbing his son's shoulders and treating him to a man-hug. "Where did you pop up from?"

"Why didn't you say you were coming?" Isobel said as she fell off her stool in her keenness to smother him in kisses.

"Careful," Tim said hauling her to her feet. "I only decided this morning. I wanted to be up here with the rest of you. So, something's going on … anyone about to tell me?" Isobel looked at Adrian and they both looked at Pippa. "Is it something bad?" he said.

"No," Adrian said. "We've just been reading Gran's will."

"Oh," he said.

"You're not going to like it," Adrian said.

"This one was written three years ago," Isobel said. "It's not the same as the old one; we didn't know she'd changed it. You're not getting the house."

"Gran left it to Phoebe," Pippa said. "I'm really sorry, Tim."

"It's fine," he said.

"I feel bad."

"Well, don't. I helped her draw up the will. She explained why she wanted Phoebe to have it."

"You knew?" Tim nodded "Why did she want her to have it?" Adrian said.

"So that she always had somewhere she could call 'home'."

"Hmm, we thought it might have been that," Isobel said. "You don't mind too much, do you?" She draped her arms over his shoulders. "I would hate for us to fall out over it."

"I don't mind, Mum, I agreed with her."

"Phoebe is a very lucky girl," Pippa said.

"Gran just wanted to know that whatever happened in the future she would always have the cottage to fall back on."

Adrian nodded. "Good lad. Fancy a beer? I know Ian will want one."

"Why not? We can drink to Gran."

"A very wise woman," Adrian said.

"No," Isobel said, firmly.

"What do you mean, 'no'?" Adrian said.

"I mean she was wise, yes, but she hated beer. We'll open that bottle of champagne we bought for Christmas. She was looking forward to her annual glass; we can drink it for her."

"It won't be the same at Christmas without her," Pippa said.

Adrian gave her a hug. "She'll be with us in spirit, you know she will. I'll fetch the champagne."

"She'd be cross if she thought we were moping about," Isobel said.

"I know, but ..."

At that moment the door burst open and Phoebe burst in with two large Rowan leaves, drooping feather-like from her hands. "Tim, Tim, Tim," she said. "Look what we found."

"Well done," he said.

"I'm painting them for Gran."

"For Gran?"

"She needs them."

"Ok ... what colour?"

"Gold," Phoebe said.

"That's very exotic," Isobel said.

"You could paint them yellow," Pippa suggested.

Phoebe shook her head. "No, Mum ... xotic ... angels have xotic wings," she said firmly.

There was an awkward silence and Pippa noticed her mother's eyes fill with tears as she bustled about looking for paint. "That's a lovely idea, Poppet. Where's Dad?" she said.

"He's on the phone."

"To Uncle Mike?"

"Don't know, Mum."

"Never mind … let's put your painting overall back on."

Adrian returned with the champagne and some lemonade for Phoebe. "Glasses," he said giving Tim a meaningful nod.

"I'm on to it," he said. "Dining room?"

"As ever."

Pippa followed her brother "I'll help," she said.

"I'm painting," Phoebe said importantly.

"You are," Adrian said. "What are you painting this time?"

"Angels' wings," she said.

His eyebrows arched in surprise. "Angels' wings?"

"For Gran."

"Oh, I see."

"Got it," Isobel said brightly, waving a small tube in the air. "Now, where did we put your brush?"

CHAPTER 36

Naomi wanted nothing more than to sneak into her room when she got back to the house, but all the lights were on. As she stepped into the hall Helena appeared at the kitchen door. "I'm so glad you're back, Nims. There's something I must tell you. It's urgent."

"What is it? Is someone ill?"

"No, nothing like that," she said grabbing her daughter's elbow. "Come in here," she added as she whisked her into the kitchen and shut the door. "You'd better sit down."

"Now I'm really worried. What's going on?"

"You know I said Alf Minns wanted to see me?"

"Yes … is he ok?"

"He's fine. He explained why Blanche wanted me to meet Mary Glebe."

"Minty, you mean."

"If you like."

"Well, why did she want you to meet?"

"Perhaps I should start where he did. His wife couldn't have children and so …"

"He had an affair with Blanche. I knew it," Naomi said, eyes shining, Jake all but forgotten. "It was a moment of madness; he was too loyal to leave his wife."

"No, you've got it all wrong. Sarah couldn't have children and so …"

"Minty's adopted."

"No, just listen, please. Sarah couldn't have children and my grandfather said he had found a way to help her using a surrogate."

"I didn't think they did things like that then."

"Obviously they did."

"Who was the surrogate?"

"You won't believe it."

"Not Blanche."

"It was Blanche."

"Blanche," Naomi screeched.

"I know, it's shocking isn't it?"

"Wow … go Blanche."

"You're not shocked?"

"No way. Why would I be?"

"Because it's bizarre, what you would call 'random'."

"She didn't tell me about that."

"She didn't tell anyone. It was a big secret."

"So why did Alf tell you?"

"Blanche wanted me to know."

"She wanted you to know … why?"

"Well, apparently she did it again. My mother couldn't have more babies after Martyn, so Blanche stepped in but this time there was an added complication."

"What? Grandpa didn't like it?"

"The complication was that after the War, Grandpa couldn't have children either, due to his injuries."

"So …"

"So, Alf Minns … you know … helped out," Helena said.

"Helped out? Oh crikey, that's mental. Good old Alf."

"You are completely missing the point."

"How do you mean?"

"Well, the baby, that is, me, was Blanche and Alf's child but I was brought up as Betsy and Bob's child."

"You weren't adopted?"

"No."

"Is that legal?"

"Probably not, but never mind that, the point is that Isla thinks I'm her aunt and I'm not. I could only be an aunt if I was Martyn's sister or Alice's sister. I'm Martyn's cousin."

"We're still related," Naomi said. "Martyn is Blanche's nephew. She thinks of you as her aunt. I'm still her cousin, probably second cousin, well something anyway."

"There's also Minty."

"Oh heck, yes. If Blanche was her mother and your mother, you must be sisters. *That's* why she wanted you to meet. That's why she kept the wedding cake ... her *daughter's* wedding cake," Naomi said with a triumphant smile. "This is awesome. Hang on, what about Alf?"

"Exactly."

"He's my grandad." Helena nodded. "He's *your* dad," she crowed.

"He doesn't want me to think of him like that. He said my father was my father. He's Minty's father. He described himself as being part of Blanche's *gift* to my mum. It's a complete mess, isn't it?"

"I think it's cool. You're like me."

"How do you mean?"

"Kevin was just a biological fact. He might as well be George Clooney for all the notice he takes of me. I wish Alf was *my* dad."

"I'm sorry you feel like that," Helena said.

"Don't you like Alf?"

"Not about him, about Kevin."

"I'm not. I don't miss him."

"What about Blanche?"

"Blanche, well, that was a surprise. She always seemed so straight-laced, apart from the way she loved her hands."

"We're back to beauticians now," Helena said. "I don't know, I thought you'd be shocked."

263

"I loved Blanche and now I think I love her even more for making our family unique."

"But it was dishonest."

"I don't think anyone would be bothered now. It happened years ago; it was really brave of her."

"What should I tell Isla?"

"The truth. Her side of the family is boringly ordinary. We are *extra*ordinary. Come on, Mum, what's the problem?"

"It's alright for you. You're who you think you are, all the paperwork is correct. I've never been who I thought I was. What's everyone going to think?"

"Nothing, because you won't tell them. It's none of their business. It'll be *our* skeleton in *our* cupboard," Naomi said.

"Oh, my days …"

"What now?"

Naomi gave her mother a wicked grin "So, there *were* ghosts at Barque House."

"Ghosts? How do you mean?"

"Blanche was haunted by the babies."

"Ah you mean the wedding cake, the photo …"

"Yes, you and Minty, the babies who never were."

"For heaven's sake, what's Isla going to say?"

"You won't find out until you tell her."

"What if it freaks her out? We all get on so well."

"It won't freak her out, Isla doesn't get freaked out. Why would it? It's a good thing." Naomi put her arms around her mother and hugged her tight. "You're a great mum and a great aunt. No-one can challenge that, or change it. Is she in tonight?"

"No, she went to the cinema with a group from the surgery."

"Just you and me, then."

"Sorry, I'm out with Guy. He's got tickets for the theatre; one of those Alan Ayckbourn plays. Season's Greetings, I think he said it was. I could do without going. I'd cry off except that I know he's been looking forward to it."

"Will you explain about Blanche?"

"I haven't decided."

"Perhaps you should. He'll be able to tell you if there will be any legal problems in the future."

"Oh don't ... do you think there will be?"

"I'm not a solicitor."

"Perhaps I could mention it hypothetically."

"I'm going to have a bath, fact. Is there anything in the fridge?"

"All sorts. I did a big shop yesterday."

Naomi opened the fridge door. "That's me sorted, then. Bath, pizza and a night in with Netflix."

"You are an amazing daughter do you know that?"

"I've always known it, but seriously, Mum, this news is better than Prosecco and chocolate. Just what I needed to cheer me up."

"Why, what's happened that you need cheering up?"

"Oh, nothing, absolutely nothing, but it's ok. You're ok, I'm ok, Blanche was ok, Isla won't mind when you tell her, and I've got a grandad I didn't know about ... bonus. It's all fine," she said with such utter confidence that Helena laughed, even though she had a suspicion her daughter wasn't telling her the absolute truth.

CHAPTER 37

It was six o'clock before Jake had packed up what was left of his stock and stashed it in the van. Daisy followed him out of the hall with his last few bits and locked up behind him. "We've all had a good day," she said. "It will be curtains for those awful curtains, thank goodness. Thanks for joining us. I hope you'll come again."

"I don't know. I'm thinking of moving away from the area; if you email me, I'll see if it's a possibility." His wallet was stuffed with notes and coins rattled in his pockets. If he hadn't been so tired and disappointed that Naomi still didn't want to know him, he would have been quite pleased with himself.

"Don't forget to pass on the raffle prize."

"I'll see she gets it." He had already decided to get his father to pass on Naomi's raffle prize; he could give it to Helena and she could hand it over to Naomi. It would be too awkward for him to deliver it, himself.

As he drove out of the church car park he wondered what she had been doing at the fair after telling him she wouldn't be there. To add to his confusion, she had not even spoken to him. She had told him she didn't want a relationship with him and although he was disappointed, he was trying not to take it too much to heart; it still hurt. She had made herself clear. She wasn't interested. He reckoned too many people didn't say what they meant or didn't mean what they said. Naomi was not like that; he admired her honesty however much he wished he had touched her heart.

He cut his speed and he was just checking to see if there was any traffic coming before he pulled out into the road, when Jane Chisholm appeared out of nowhere to stand in front of his windscreen, both hands up. He slammed on the brakes hard. She was gesticulating for him to wind down the window. "What the …"

"I'm really sorry Jake. I had to get you to stop."

"What's up?"

"I forgot to give you this," she said handing him the serviette cigar.

"What's this?" he said.

"Naomi said you'd understand," she said stepping back so that he could be on his way.

"Thanks." He did not understand. He dropped the serviette on the passenger seat and put his foot down. A serviette? What did he want with a poxy serviette? He was determined not to stop again before he got home. He was hungry. Perhaps he'd buy a takeaway when he got back to East Knoll. His father wasn't expecting him for a meal, he could head straight for the flat and chill out.

He tried to forget Jane's offering but as he slowed at every junction, he found his eyes homing in on it. Why had she wanted him to have it? What did it mean? From what he could see there was nothing remarkable about it; it was just a bog-standard white serviette rolled into a cigar-shape. It seemed strange that she had left it with Jane … odd that she had left the fair without trying to speak to him. He did not understand women. The sooner he escaped from East Knoll the better. The idea of giving up on women to concentrate on sculpting somewhere with craggy cliffs, empty beaches and only seabirds and the rolling tide to break the silence, was becoming ever more attractive.

Ian and Pippa had left The Old School House after tea despite her parents' protestations that they should stay on. "Do you think we were wrong to come back tonight?" she said as they neared Linchester.

"Wrong? No, of course not."

She swivelled round to see if Phoebe was still asleep in her car seat and smiled as her daughter emitted a gentle snore. "It wasn't good for Phoebe to be there."

"No, the atmosphere was pretty grim," he said.

"Anyway, they don't need us. Tim's staying another night," she said.

"Your parents don't often see Tim. It will be nice for them to have quality time with him and besides, I wouldn't mind checking on Mrs. E. She was in quite a state when we left."

"I just want to be home to think."

"What's bothering you?"

"Apart from the obvious, you mean."

"I know you're upset about Edith."

"I was thinking about the future. What are we to do with Gran's cottage?"

"That's not our decision."

"It will be."

"Not necessarily. Your parents might set up a trust to administer it. They might sell it and invest the proceeds, I don't know but you don't have to worry about it right now."

"It's just that …"

"What?"

"I didn't like to say anything before because of Gran and what happened last time, you know, it might be tempting fate, but I think … I only think, so don't get too excited … I might be pregnant."

Ian was glad they had turned off the main road into Blain Gardens. He pulled into the kerb straight away and stopped the car. "When will you know for sure?" he said.

She looked at him eyes aglow. "I just need to do a test to confirm it, so don't say anything to Mike."

"I'm not going to say, 'mum's the word', but I'll be thinking it," he said with a grin. "It's great news, Sweetpea."

Without the motion of the car to rock her, Phoebe awoke with a start. "Great news, Mum," she said.

"We're nearly home," Ian said quickly. "It's great to be nearly home."

Phoebe kicked the back of his seat in her excitement. "Nearly home," she said and giggled.

Pippa giggled and turned to contemplate her daughter, cheeks flushed from sleep, glasses askew, the bright eyes behind them full of joy at being 'nearly home'. She straightened the glasses and tapped Phoebe's nose affectionately before she turned to face him. "Oh, Ian, what if there's something wrong …"

He put a gentle finger to her lips "No," he said and then he took her hand and squeezed it tenderly. "We said we wouldn't do this. Whatever happens we'll deal with it, ok? If the test's positive, let's keep it quiet until after the funeral. No point raising hopes too soon."

"No," she said.

"What, Mum?" Phoebe said.

"Nothing," Pippa said. "Nothing at all, my poppet. Everything's fine and it's great to be nearly home with my little family."

"You, me and Dad," Phoebe said.

"That's right, clever girl," Pippa said.

"No, Mum, you've forgotten Millie. You, me, Dad and Millie."

"Quite right," Ian said. "We mustn't forget the dog."

"What was it Gran said to us at our wedding?" Pippa said.

"I remember, no show without Punch," he said.

"Who's Punch?" Phoebe said.

"No-one," Pippa said. "It was just Gran having a joke about Millie not wanting to be left out."

"I love Gran," Phoebe said.

"We all love Gran," Ian said." And we're not going to stop loving her just because she's not here."

"We'll love Gran for ever," Pippa said.

"And ever and ever," Phoebe said. "Amen."

"Amen?" Ian said.

"That's what Fr.Philip says."

"You are a funny girl," Pippa said.

Phoebe giggled. "Amen, Amen, Amen."

CHAPTER 38

Naomi had nodded off in front of the television. The doorbell woke her with a start. It took a moment for her to realise she was not in bed. She checked the time on her phone. Nine-thirty. She checked her messages. Nothing. He hadn't phoned while she was asleep. He hadn't even bothered to text.

The bell rang again. She flipped her plait over her back, re-tied her bath robe and went to the door. "Who is it?" she called.

"Jake."

"Jake … Jake Hampson?" she said, stretching time to check her reflection in the hall mirror as her heart upped its beat. What she saw was not edifying; face scrubbed clean of make-up, cheeks pale, eyes heavy with sleep. She rubbed her eyes as she waited for his reply, biting her lips and pinching her cheeks to add more colour to her complexion and then, catching another glimpse of her face, she realised it looked no better; if anything, it was worse. The blotchy cheeks and reddened lips made her look as if she was coming down with something nasty. There was no way she would let him see her like that.

"Yes."

"What do you want?"

"Jane gave me the serviette," he said. "Can we talk?"

"You want me to let you in?" she said. She could barely breathe her heart was thumping so hard in her chest. Confusion, fear, excitement but most of all anticipation swirled about in her head. She didn't have to let him in. She did want to let him in. Should she let him in … what would happen if she did let him in? She had to make her decision quickly. It had to be the right decision … but what was the right decision? She searched for inspiration and then '*when in doubt – wash*' popped into her mind. Paul Gallico was genius. She would take her lead from Jennie the cat. It was good advice. "Could you come back in half an hour?" she said.

"Half an hour?"

"Half an hour," she called, leaving him out in the cold as she dashed upstairs to get properly dressed and do something with her face. She wanted to look good because she owed it to herself, so that she could face whatever he had to say with confidence. She hoped he would give her a chance to apologise, she wanted to do that at least, to let him know that if he needed a friend she would be there for him, she knew she had no right to expect more, but she could hope. Who was she kidding she thought, as she dropped her dressing gown on the bed and reached for her make-up. She wanted more, but she wasn't going to beg and whatever the outcome of their meeting, she wanted him to notice how good she looked.

Jake walked back to the van. He switched on the radio and studied the serviette again; her mobile number was written on a corner in biro. To him it wasn't just a series of numbers, it was a code. A code that would unlock the way to his future happiness. He was hoping against hope that he had not misunderstood her meaning. They needed to talk. He wanted to explain everything. Her reaction would seal his fate as far as moving away from East Knoll was concerned. If she didn't want anything to do with him, he would leave. He could not stay and risk them meeting up by accident. It would be too painful. As the minutes ticked by, he became more and more nervous. Fifteen minutes, twenty, twenty-two, twenty-five, thirty, at last. He jumped out of the van and headed back down the road.

He rang the bell again and stepped back to wait. This time the door opened at once. "Come in," she said.

Her efforts to make herself more appealing were not lost on him. Her dark hair, still plaited, rested over one shoulder in a glossy braid; her face, subtly enhanced by make-up, was as beautiful as he remembered, her dark eyes as enigmatic, a hint of humour lurking in their depths but he still wasn't sure if his arrival was welcome. "You got my note," he said. "Jane gave me yours."

"Not so much of a note, more of a number," she said. "I thought I'd return the favour. I was away when yours arrived."

Suddenly his mood lifted. He smiled. At least she had explained the delay. Hope was beginning to quell his nerves. "I thought I'd written my name down, too."

"No, but I quite liked having to guess who'd sent it."

"I, um, I came to give you this," he said handing over her prize.

"Ski goggles?"

"It's your raffle prize."

"Okaaay…" she said.

"Do you ski?"

"No," she said unsure as to where this conversation was headed.

"You must give it a try. It's such a buzz. I learned when I was at uni."

"Maybe I will," she said. "One day."

"We could go together," he said.

"So, you came to give me the goggles and invite me on a skiing trip."

"No, I really came to explain about Nicola."

She caressed his arm with her fingertips. "There's no need to explain. I know what happened, Mum told me."

"I thought you'd decided I must be some kind of a monster. You seemed to have made up your mind about me."

"I wanted to apologise for that. I shouldn't have believed all the gossip."

"I've been thinking about moving away," he said.

"And are you?" she asked the dark eyes unfathomable.

"That depends."

"On what?"

"On you."

"Me... why?"

"I really like you Naomi."

There was sincerity in his voice, in those blue eyes. She believed him. In that moment the confusion lifted. She was certain about how she saw her future, had always known if she was honest. She wanted him to stay. She wanted to learn more about him. She wanted to start again, to leave her presumptions and prejudices behind and maybe, just maybe, she wanted him to teach her how to ski. "That's good, because I really like you too," she said leading him into the sitting room.

"So, there's hope for me?"

"Hope?"

"For the future, for us. You know what I mean."

"I think we should talk, discuss everything first, don't you?"

"I want to talk. I want to tell you what happened," he said.

"Glass of wine?"

"I thought you didn't drink."

She smiled, a pink tinge creeping up her neck. "Whatever gave you that idea?" she said coyly.

"You did."

She looked vague "Did I? Maybe I was in the middle of dry, whatever..."

"Maybe you were in the middle of giving me the brush-off."

She laughed. "Don't remind me. Anyway, that was then, and this is now."

He took the glass she had poured for him. "I deserved it."

"You mustn't say that. I'm so sorry I thought the worst."

"It wasn't your fault. You weren't to know. I shouldn't have behaved the way I did."

"Nobody's perfect," she said. She sat down and took a slug of wine. "I'm all ears."

"I've been thinking about this a lot recently," he said. "I didn't deal with Mum's death properly. I was angry. Dad never mentioned her, I missed her. I didn't understand why she had left me. At first, I thought it must have been my fault that she'd gone; that I'd done something wrong and then as I got older and learnt the truth, I pretended not to care. I went a bit wild."

"That summer, Nicola..."

"Yes... I'm not making excuses, well, I am, but I shouldn't have done all those things. Over the years I've tried to come to terms with Mum's death and failed until you made me see I needed to admit I was still grieving and that I could do something about it."

"If only I'd had an idea what you were going through."

"You were with Luke."

"How did you know that?"

"Everyone knew. You wouldn't have wanted anything to do with me and anyway I didn't want people to know how I felt, it seemed pathetic; I was ashamed of feeling like I did. I couldn't talk to Dad and it wasn't something I could share with my friends. They were all about drinking and showing off. I just joined in. I would have looked weak if I hadn't."

She thought how different he was to the Jake she had thought he was. Her heart went out to him "You can talk to me," she said. "I'll always listen."

"It's taken me all this time to understand myself. That day we met on the beach was the luckiest day of my life."

"You don't know anything about me."

"I know you are kind, thoughtful, beautiful, honest. I want to get to know you better," he said, his arm sneaking around her shoulders "If you'll let me."

She did not pull away. "Hmm," she said peeping at him from under her lashes "I'll have to think about it."

CHAPTER 39

As they walked out of the theatre later that evening, Helena was still mulling over the pros and cons of sharing the Blanche secret with Guy. "It was a good play," he said.

"Alan Ayckbourn is clever, insightful..."

"And funny. Families are funny things," he said.

"What makes you say that?"

"I was thinking about Blanche. I still can't work out why she wanted you and Mary Glebe to meet."

"She had her reasons."

"She always did."

"I know why," she said having decided that if she intended to make Guy her number one man and she did, she had to include him in the secret circle. "Alf Minns and Blanche..."

"Were close friends, we all know that," he said. "It's no secret. They didn't have an affair if that's what you're driving at."

"No ..."

"He had an affair with someone else, then... your mother?"

"You think he had an affair with my mother?"

"Why else would you mention him in connection with your family?"

"Ah, that's the thing," she said

"What do you mean?

"It's all about families," she said enigmatically. "All about labels; mothers, aunts, cousins."

They had arrived at his car. He opened the door. "Now I'm confused," he said.

"I'm not sure any of it was strictly legal," she said. She was having doubts that this was the right thing to do, involving him in the messy business. Perhaps it would be better if he only had half the story; just enough but not too much.

"I'll guess, then shall I?"

"You'll never guess, never in a month of Sundays."

"Let's see," he began in a bantering tone. "I was wrong. Blanche did have an affair with Alf. He got her pregnant with you and then they asked your mother to pretend you were hers."

"Not quite."

His brow creased. "Yes, it was a stupid suggestion."

"I told you, you wouldn't be able to guess."

"Are you going to tell me?"

"I don't know… maybe."

"Ok, it's up to you. Whatever it is, it doesn't affect us."

"Sometimes the past can catch up with you," she said.

"What are we talking about now?"

"Jake and Naomi."

"Do you think they will ever make a go of it?"

"I've got a feeling they might."

"He's talking of moving away," Guy said.

"No, he can't do that," she said. "Not before she realises how she feels. What can we do to give them a push?"

"Do they need a push?"

"He sent her a note, which wasn't a note at all. It was just his mobile number."

"Just the number, no explanation, no signature?"

"No, nothing."

"Did she know it was from him?"

"She did, but she didn't let on," she said.

"Is that why she went to the craft fair?"

She nodded. "She said she wasn't going and then she did, so I put two and two together. She was supposed to be looking for Christmas presents but I'm sure she went to see him."

"Fingers crossed they sort it out," he said. "I don't want him moving away."

"Do you think he'll go?"

"I don't know, he might."

"She might go with him."

"It's possible."

"She thinks we're getting serious," she said.

"Are we?"

"I like us being friends, don't you?"

"I'm happy if you're happy," he said.

"You never give anything away, do you Guy?"

"I'm a solicitor, what do you expect?"

"Nearly home," she said. "Are you coming in for a coffee?"

"That would be nice," he said. "Wait a minute. That's Jake's van parked over there, I recognise the number plate; he can't be returning it until tomorrow."

"So, I was right," she said. "They are sorting things out. Shall we go in?"

"I don't know, um, what do you think?"

"Oh, for heaven's sake," she said. "You're enough to drive a woman mad. I say, yes, we go in. I want to find out what's been going on." He locked the car and followed her. "I'll pretend I've forgotten my key," she said, hand hovering over the bell push.

"That's why I love you," he said. "You're so decisive."

"Someone has to be," she said as she rang the bell and then spun round to face him. "What did you say?"

"I love you, is that all right?" Helena felt like a teenager as he took her in his arms and kissed her decisively. "I've loved you for a while, if you want the truth."

"Why on earth didn't you say?"

"You seemed happy as you were and I don't have a very good track record with women."

"That's a bit defeatist," she said.

"I'd got to feeling I might be jinxed."

"Well, I'm about to be decisive again," she said as she slipped a hand into the crook of his arm and urged him away from the house. "Let them keep their secrets. We'll go back to yours for coffee instead."

Naomi unwound herself from Jake's arms and jumped up from the sofa. "Was that the bell?" she said.

"I think it was."

"Mum must have forgotten her key. She does sometimes."

"She won't mind me being here, will she?" he said.

"Don't look so worried. Why would she?"

"You know ... what happened."

"She knows it wasn't you; she told *me*, remember?"

"Sometimes I think I should take out a full-page advert in *The Recorder* ... Jake Hampson is innocent," he said bitterly.

"What does it matter what people think?" Naomi said. "I know the truth your Dad knows the truth, Mum knows the truth and when I tell Holly the whole world will know it wasn't you. I'll let her in ... I'm coming," she called as she neared the front door and then she thought she should warn her mother about Jake. "Jake's here," she added as she opened the door and prepared a welcoming smile.

Jake joined her in the hall. "Who is it?" he said.

"No-one," she said.

"That's odd. It was the doorbell we heard, wasn't it?"

"I'm sure it was. Never mind," she said. She shut the door and lifted his arm around her neck, tucking her chin into his sleeve as if it were a feather boa. "It was probably kids messing about."

"Probably."

"Let's go and sit down again. You're not the only one with secrets, you know."

"Meaning …"

"I think I should tell you about Blanche."

"Your great-aunt?"

"Yes, and before you say anything, it has absolutely nothing to do with vampires."

CHAPTER 40

Helena relaxed into the soft leather of Guy's sofa knowing instinctively that their relationship would work. He was right, families were funny things, but it didn't stop her wanting to be part of his or wanting him to be part of hers.

They were just a family, each one leading their own life; each choosing to share but only up to a point. She reckoned it was healthy to have secrets from one another; small secrets, secrets that hurt no-one but enriched lives and made waking up a joy and a blessing. Blanche's secret was something else. It could have caused irreparable damage. For all she knew, it still might; she had no idea how Minty would take the news.

She knew she must allow Naomi her secrets, allow her to find her own road wherever that might lead; she was proud to think that the family was united in all the ways that really mattered. Not all families were so lucky. You only had to listen to the news. Feuding families made good headlines.

She was glad Guy's other relationships had foundered. If they had been more successful she would not be with him now. She knew the pitfalls that could bring down a marriage. If they ended up as husband and wife she would work hard to make sure they avoided them.

"Here we are," he said walking into the room with two mugs. "Coffee as ordered and then …"

"Come and sit down," she said patting the cushiony sofa invitingly; she had no more doubts, she loved everything about him. She was comfortable with him, she trusted him, there was no point not telling him about Blanche right here, right now. It would be wrong to keep it from him. The decision had been made. He smiled, his eyes full of expectation. She smiled back "And then, I've got something to tell you."

"That sounds interesting."

"You might be horrified."

"I doubt it," he said. "You'd be surprised at some of the things I hear. A solicitor's office is like a confessional."

"My name is Helena Henry and I have something to confess," she said primly.

"Go on, then," he said.

"I'm not who you think I am," she said.

"Intriguing," he said.

"I didn't know I wasn't who I am. I only found out recently."

"I haven't a clue where this is going."

"It's about Blanche," she said.

"Blanche? I can't believe there was anything suspect in her past. She was a very straightforward person. I've been dealing with the family for years."

"Well, you don't know everything about her."

"It's impossible to know everything about everyone but I refuse to think it's anything serious."

"You might not want to know me when you find out."

"I can't see that happening any time soon." He held her close and she melted into his embrace. "Do your worst, I can take it," he said.

She did not draw back. She liked their closeness. She loved him. He loved her. She felt loved. It was a heady sensation she had never experienced before, had never expected to experience. She certainly hadn't experienced it with Kevin Henry. With him she had mistaken infatuation for love. Theirs had been an epic mismatch. She wanted a new life with Guy, a life of togetherness and joy. It was not everyone who had a second chance. She felt lucky, so lucky. "Well, if you're sure," she said.

"I am," he said.

"What I'm about to tell you is bizarre and maybe even illegal. It might change your feelings for me," she said still a teeny bit anxious that her news would scare him away.

He dropped a kiss on her hair "Nothing can do that."

"You seem very sure."

"That's because I am. Look, for a long time after Emma died I didn't think I would ever fall in love again, that I *could* love again. I felt as if I had been hollowed out, as if my core had been removed and I had nothing left to give. I thought I'd feel like that for the rest of my life."

"You had other relationships," she said.

"I wanted to try again, I wanted a partner; I wanted Jake to have more than just me, but it didn't work out."

"I know exactly what you mean. Kevin was my biggest mistake. We were never right for each other. I don't think I even loved him. I want something better for Naomi. Do you think Jake is the one?"

"He certainly thinks so."

"It's so good to have someone to share these things with. Being a single parent can be lonely at times, especially where relationships are concerned but you must know that."

"Indeed, I do."

"I wish we'd got together before. What I feel for you is so different to what I felt for Kevin."

"I can't imagine my life without you now," he said.

"That's so sweet," she said. "Thank you."

"Why are you thanking me?"

"I suppose because you've made me feel special."

"You are special to me."

"Stop it, now I'm getting embarrassed. I need to tell you about Blanche and her children."

"Children? Blanche didn't have children. She wasn't married."

"You don't have to be married to have children."

"I know, but … fine … where are they now?"

"One of them is right here."

"You mean you, seriously?"

"Yes, me."

"I don't believe it."

"I know, it's hard to take in, but Blanche *was* my mother, biologically, at least."

"How do you know?"

"I'll explain in a minute. Aren't you going to ask me about the other one?"

"Go on then. No wait, I think I know. It's Minty, isn't it?"

"It is."

"Minty's her daughter, too," he said. "I don't believe it. I was only joking when I suggested it."

"It's no joke. Minty and I are both Blanche's daughters."

"Oh, my word, two daughters," he said. "I never had Alf down as a serial philanderer; he idolised his wife. She must have been a saint to take on the child of her husband's lover; let me get this clear, Blanche had a fling with Alf and then with your father."

"No, she did not. You make her sound like a scarlet woman. Blanche and Alf weren't lovers, either. It wasn't like that at all."

"I don't understand. What was it like?"

"They had what you might call an 'arrangement'. It was one of my grandfather's experiments; Blanche wanted us to know about it and so did Alf."

"Oh, I see, Alf's your father."

"He is."

"And I thought I'd heard it all. How did you find out?"

"He told me after the tea party."

"So that's why he wanted to see you. It must have come as a shock."

"To put it mildly. It took me a while to get my head around it. We discovered clues when we were looking for Mary Glebe, but we didn't realise the significance, then. The biggest clue was the wedding cake."

"Blanche had a wedding cake … very Miss Havisham."

"She didn't. It was Minty's wedding cake, although we didn't know that when we found it. They sent Blanche a piece and it was still in her desk after twenty years. She wasn't at all sentimental, so it must have been important to her."

"How do you feel about their um, *arrangement?*"

She gazed up at him. "I like the idea of being Blanche's gift to her sister. She must have really loved my mum to do it; I guess you could say I was her love child."

"They say love makes a family," he said smiling at her in a way that made her heart skip a beat.

"We're good, then."

"We are, good to go."

"What about Jake?" she said.

"What about him?"

"It's been just the two of you for such a long time."

"Same as you and Naomi. Look, they are both grown-ups. They have their own lives to lead. I'm sure they'll be happy for us."

"Will we be happy for them?"

"If it's what they want."

She settled herself more comfortably in his arms, safe in the knowledge that whatever happened he would not judge Jake or Naomi, Alf, Blanche, or even her grandfather. Safe in the knowledge that he loved her; so safe that she knew the answer to her next question before she asked it. "Have my iffy roots put you off?"

"Of course not."

"You know none of this, you and me, Naomi and Jake, could have happened without Blanche ... and she left me Barque House."

"She was your mother, your aunt and your fairy godmother rolled into one. Quite a lady."

"I couldn't possibly compete with that."

"Why would you want to?"

"I'm so ordinary. You might get bored with me."

He held her tighter. "Never ... to be in a relationship with a love child is every man's dream."

"Really?"

He laughed. "I don't know to be honest, but it's certainly mine."

Elisabeth Thompson was born in Crosby, Liverpool,
but is now resident in West Sussex.

She only found the time to write after a short career
at the Foreign Office in London followed by various
personal assistant posts in the north-west, after raising
her five children, years spent as a foster carer and as
a respite carer for children with special needs.

The common theme in all her books is the nature of
family relationships and the importance of close friends.
Her own core friends are of very long-standing and
important to her ... as is her husband and family.

Her favourite quote is from Jane Austen -
'Let other pens dwell on guilt and misery.'

Also available in this series

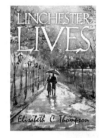  

Also available from Elisabeth Thompson